# Madison's Lost Cowboy

## by

## Sheryl Coumans

**Madison's Lost Cowboy**

Cover Art by *Debbie Taylor*

The Wild Rose Press, Inc.
PO Box 708
Adams Basin, NY 14410-0708
Visit us at www.thewildrosepress.com

Publishing History
First Edition, 2022
Trade Paperback ISBN 978-1-5092-4334-1
Digital ISBN 978-1-5092-4335-8

Published in the United States of America

Before she could move away, JC grabbed her arm, pulling her next to him.

"Why are you crying?" JC whispered.

"I'm not. It must be allergies," she hedged, trying to pull away, not wanting him to know how much his upcoming departure affected her.

"No, it's not allergies. Tell me what's really wrong." JC held onto her forearm.

She again tried pulling away, but he gripped her tighter, pulling her onto his lap.

"Nothing's wrong," she claimed.

"Nonsense, I insist you tell me," he commanded.

JC's authoritative voice pushed Madison's anger to the surface. "Don't you manhandle me, you-you Neanderthal!" Madison tried to get up, but JC wrapped his hands firmly around her waist. She bucked. The more she tried to get up, the more he held on.

"Sit still. I don't think it's a good idea to move about like that." His voice sounded like he was in pain.

"Let me go," Madison said through a grimace. Then she felt the cause of his discomfort underneath her. "Oh, Lord," she murmured, her tears temporarily forgotten.

"Please tell me why you are crying? Did I say something that hurt your feelings?"

She rubbed the back of her hand across her nose, swiping away the tears that marked her cheeks. It was just too darn much. Even being an inexperienced woman, she knew she'd just turned him on. "No, you didn't hurt my feelings. Sorry, I'm going to miss you," she admitted reluctantly.

"I will never forget you, Madison," he countered.

## Dedication

To my critique partners Alysia Ricks and Kathy Rochelle who helped me during the writing process, and to Sue Peterson, who gave me the final nudge to edit and get it sent in.

Prologue

Outside Reno, Nevada,1896

Lightning streaked across the distant sky, followed by an ominous drumroll of thunder. Blackened clouds rolled closer as if in a precise death march. Jonathan Christopher Berkley, known as JC, was conscious of the chilly late October morning and that this could be his last day on earth.

JC's heart raced—the noose dug into his throat—cutting off his air supply. As he fought to stay conscious, a vision of a small girl on her knees, praying for a cowboy to rescue her, was so vivid he opened his eyes. *Why is a child in my thoughts at a time like this? I don't even know any little girls.*

"Why'd ya do it?" Sheriff Willy Wilcox demanded. His gaze looked both angry and confused when he cinched the noose tighter around JC's neck.

"Willy, you know that I would never harm a child—for any reason," JC said, fighting to hold back the fear raging low in his gut. He'd managed to hold his head up with a small measure of pride after being accused. But pride wasn't going to save his neck. Only a miracle could deliver him from this grief-crazed man's actions.

Drawing in a deep breath, his mind scrambled for a way to reason with the sheriff. The tightly bound rope bit into his wrists as he struggled to free his hands. Shifting in the saddle, he froze as he slipped to one side. He tightened his knees on Zeus's belly, stabilizing his balance.

He didn't want to die. Especially for a crime he didn't commit.

The closed and determined look on the sheriff's face reinforced JC's resolve to continue reasoning with him to his last breath.

Henry Jacobs, his childhood adversary, gave him a satisfied smirk as he stood next to the sheriff. Henry's pistol was trained on JC as if he'd make sure there wasn't any attempt to escape. He knew Henry hated him and would love any excuse to shoot him dead.

The sheriff lifted his hand, preparing to smack Zeus's flank, but his hand tightened as he held it suspended. Willy's brows knit together suddenly as a moment of anguished uncertainty crossed his face.

JC, not one to ever give up, made another attempt to reason with the sheriff. "Willy, you know that Henry has carried a grudge against me and Nate since we were boys. I don't know what happened to your brother, but I promise, I'll help you find out."

"Don't listen to him. He's just trying to confuse you and wrangle out of paying for his crime. Besides, with all his money, you know he can buy his way out of going to jail. Do it, do it now," Henry demanded impatiently, moving his horse closer to the rope that Willy held in his fist. Henry reached over and tried to grab the rope from Willy's grasp. Thankfully, Willy eluded his attempt.

The sheriff's angry gaze shifted to Henry, and he shouted, "Back off, Jacobs. Let me think."

"What's there to think about? He killed Petey in cold blood. I saw him." Henry moved away from the rope but closer to JC. His cold gray eyes were determined, calculating, and ominous. His hatred, clearly visible as his eyes shifted to the rope and back to JC's face.

"Don't listen to him, Willy. You know darn well I'm innocent. Henry saw wrong or he's a liar!" JC emphasized each of the words. But no matter how much he'd protested his innocence, nothing he said seemed to get through to a man who was blinded by his grief over his twelve-year-old brother's death.

Willy was about to make a big mistake, hanging the wrong man.

JC ground his teeth together as he looked in the distance where he'd last seen his twin. His eyes scanned the hillside for every detail, hoping to see Nate coming to rescue him.

*Before it was too late.*

Where was Nate? His twin always seemed to sense whenever JC needed him. Why not now when he could use his help more than ever? He sent out another silent plea focusing on his current peril, urging his brother to hurry back.

Within seconds of his plea, he caught a glimpse of Nate. Thank God he'd finally picked up on his message of looming danger. JC watched as his brother came riding hell bent out from the overgrown scrub oak bushes. When Nate reached his side, he'd felt a glimmer of rising hope.

Before he could open his mouth to say anything, Henry viciously kicked Zeus while at the same time, a deafening boom of thunder and a blinding lightning flash came. As Zeus bolted, Nate dismounted and wrapped his arms around JC's legs. Just in the nick of time—saving him from dangling in midair. For the faintest second, he was aware of the tightening rope choking all the air from his lungs as Nate's arms held him up.

Too late, was his last thought as darkness threw him into oblivion.

Chapter One

*Outside Reno, Nevada – Present Day*

Madison Matthews glanced at her watch one more time before realizing she wasn't going to make it home to Reno from Lake Tahoe without making a pit stop. She'd drank way too much water after the morning's 5k run. It had been an annual fundraiser for the National Center for Missing & Exploited Children or NCMEC.

Taking the first exit off of I-580, she headed to a fast-food restaurant where she could use the ladies' restroom and grab a cold drink.

There was a lineup at the drive-thru window and only two other cars parked in the parking lot. She quickly got out of the car and moved past two scruffily dressed pre-teen kids that were walking their overweight beagle. A young couple sporting matching purple hair and nose rings were sitting under a pine tree on an outdoor picnic table, packing away their lunch between smooches.

Madison grinned, shaking her head at young love, before discreetly looking away. The young lovers were oblivious to everyone but themselves. A twinge of envy and a longing for someone of her own hit her in the gut.

Stepping inside the restaurant, her thoughts returned to the matter at hand, and she hurried to the ladies' room.

Afterward, she no longer wanted that soft drink and left the building. She noticed the two other parked cars were gone, and her car stood alone. Even the drive-thru was now empty.

Taking the same shortcut over the grass to her car, she saw a jean-clad leg with a cowboy boot attached. She froze when she caught sight of a man's prone body. He lay next to a juniper bush and the same picnic table the lovers had sat at only minutes before.

She knelt next to him. He looked dead, his face pale as a piece of marble. When he took a shallow breath, she let go of the breath she'd been holding. Although his breathing appeared labored, he was alive.

His sharp-cut features and hands were deeply tanned, like someone who spent a great deal of time in the sun. Long sandy-colored eyelashes rested on his cheeks. A riot of golden unruly curls framed his face along with a five o'clock shadow. Her gaze roamed down to his legs encased in jeans. A dusty gray Stetson hat lay upside down next to him.

She tried to rouse him by gently shaking his shoulder. His face glimmered with sweat, and his eyes scrunched together as he tried to open them.

"Nate?" he asked, blinking his eyes, and groaning.

Madison looked around before replying. "I don't see anyone around that might be Nate."

He closed his eyes again.

How he'd come to be here so quickly was certainly a mystery. His body lay in plain sight of her car, but surely the lovers would have noticed him if he'd been there earlier. There was no way she could have missed him either when she'd passed by. And she hadn't taken all that long in the ladies' room.

"Hey," she prodded, gently pushing back her anxiety. Reaching for her cell phone in her pocket, Madison remembered she'd left it in the car. She started to get up, but when he groaned again, she knelt back down.

"Where am I?" the man whispered. His sapphire blue eyes opened briefly before he snapped them shut again. It was obvious he was in pain. Plus, the clothing he wore was too warm for a hot June day. A woolen plaid shirt, denim pants with worn leather-scuffed brown boots. No wonder he felt hot to the touch.

Madison looked around again for help, hoping someone would appear so she wouldn't have to leave him. Darn, no one. She put her hand lightly on his forehead. He groaned out a raspy breath and flinched as if even the lightest touch hurt him.

"Sorry," she soothed. "I can't wait much longer, you need help." Madison rose unsteadily to her feet to get her cell phone. The cowboy opened his blue eyes again, mumbling something incomprehensible before his eyes rolled back, and he passed out again.

"You're going to be all right," she reassured him, before sprinting the short distance to her car.

It took less than thirty seconds to reach her vehicle and grab the phone from the side pocket of her purse. She called 911 while hurrying back to the injured man.

After telling the operator the situation and location, she was instructed to stay with him. Sheesh! Like she'd think of leaving him! The operator promised an ambulance would be there as soon as possible.

Madison knelt by his side. "Hey, are you awake?" she prompted, while gently touching his shoulder.

The operator told Madison to see if she could get a

response. Unbuttoning the top two buttons of his shirt hoping it would help, she winced at the purplish-red bruise that encircled his neck, as if someone had tried to strangle him with a cord. Placing two fingers against his skin, she breathed a bit better.

"He does have a pulse," she told the emergency operator.

The man seemed to hear her and opened his eyes. He blinked rapidly, coughing as he tried to sit up. Madison put her palms on his chest, trying to get him to lie back down.

"Help should be here soon. Just try to hold still," she advised, keeping her voice level and calm.

"Nate?" he scratched out hoarsely.

"Are you Nate?"

"No. My brother's name. I'm JC."

"Listen, you need to lie back and try to relax. I don't see anyone else around here. Maybe your brother went for help?" She thought it was unlikely since the restaurant would have been the most logical place to go for assistance.

He complied with her request and laid back, closing his eyes. She breathed a sigh of relief.

Looking at her watch, she noted it had only been minutes since she'd called for an ambulance, but it seemed like hours. She spoke into the phone and when the operator didn't reply, Madison realized she must have hit the disconnect button while dealing with the man. His eyes opened again, and he stared at her as if trying to focus. Deep dimples appeared in his cheeks, and he smiled.

The words were raspy, but she made out what he was trying to convey. "Are you an angel?"

Relieved that he was coming around, she answered, "No." Madison couldn't resist the chuckle that escaped her lips, now confident he'd be all right. "I'm not an angel."

\*\*\*\*

*Where am I?* JC wondered. He had the worst headache he'd ever experienced. Bringing up his hand, he touched the stinging pain around his neck, and also acknowledged the lightheadedness and disorientation plaguing him. Raising his head, he looked around him but didn't understand why everything seemed different.

The woman gently pushed his shoulders back to the ground. Where had this strange woman come from?

He blinked his eyes, trying to focus. The temperature was hot, like summertime. This couldn't be. The last thing he remembered was the biting cold of a wet fall day. It had been a chilly afternoon with thunder rumbling in the distance.

Nate. Where was his brother? He felt sure he'd been with him only moments before. He could tell by the position of the mountains and terrain that he was still in the same area. Yet everything looked different. Strange-looking buildings, groomed bushes, and wooden tables that hadn't been there earlier dotted the landscape.

Touching his head in dismay, he closed his eyes in agony as the action caused the pain of his pounding head to intensify. When he opened them again, JC recognized the obvious changes were still there. Even the air smelled different with the hint of a smoky smell and—*is that food cooking? This isn't possible.* There shouldn't be buildings here or pathways. What are those whooshing sounds and humming noises? He put his fingers in his ears, shaking them to clear out the sounds, but the noises were still there.

A gentle tug on his shoulder and the woman's voice brought his attention back to her. JC squinted his eyes in the blinding sunlight of midday. She reminded him of an angel.

He may be hurt, but he was still a man with a man's needs. She was beautiful with those vivid green eyes and long chestnut-brown hair with golden streaks throughout. Her face held a sprinkling of freckles across her petite nose and the most kissable pink lips that he'd seen in a long time. Her face flushed in an attractive manner as she appeared to notice his eyes fixed on her mouth.

When he realized what she was wearing, his eyes widened at the sight of her form-fitting shirt and short trousers that came down indecently to her thighs.

They were the strangest clothes he'd ever seen on a lady. Her scandalously blue shirt had words written on it that said, *Michigan Tech*.

He put a hand to his neck, feeling the raw skin where the sheriff's rope had burned him. Memories of his almost-hanging flooded back, hitting him squarely in the gut.

JC had come close to dying. Thankfully, Nate had reached him in time to prevent the hanging by holding him up.

"What's your name? I'm Madison Matthews. You need to stay still until the paramedics get here. Are you in much pain?" the woman asked in a soft-spoken tone. She smiled. "Listen, you've been hurt, and I've already called 9-1-1. They should be here soon."

Even more confused by her words, he wondered

why she'd call out numbers. What did nine-one-one have to do with him? Could it be he hadn't heard right? Her worried look brought him back to the fact he was still lying on the hard ground.

Clearing his throat again, he forced the words through parched lips. "I'm fine, ma'am." JC attempted to get up, and his head started spinning anew.

Gritting his teeth until the dizziness passed, he finally lifted himself from the grass. He staggered slightly on shaky knees before he steadied himself.

"Sorry. Give me a spell to get my bearings," he managed to add in a hoarse voice, while searching for his brother, horse, and his hat.

He wasn't surprised to see Zeus had been frightened away. The lightning bolt had been bright as day, and the thunder boomer deafening. He'd almost gotten killed. Now he was without means of transport. What else could go wrong?

At that moment, a buggy-like contraption, one he'd never seen before, sped past them on a slick black road. JC's mouth dropped open in shock. Something must be wrong with his brain.

He blinked a couple of times, but still the impossible image didn't fade. He stared at the contraption as it raced down the stretch of road. JC continued to watch as the same type of buggies going in both directions like he'd never witnessed before, raced off into the distance.

He'd seen a few and heard about the newfangled motor wagons or horseless carriages that were being developed, but this was unbelievable. Nothing could go that fast.

He stumbled from the impact the memory of his

impending death had on him. Slowly falling to his knees, he sat back on the ground. *Lord, what happened? Am I dead?*

Putting his hand to his forehead, he sat in stunned silence.

Taking in his surroundings, he knew that everything was too different. Something had to be wrong. What happened? He remembered the noose tightening around his neck, his brother's arms catching his legs, trying to hold him up just before the loud thunderclap, and then dizzying blackness. *If I'm not dead, where am I?*

"I wish the ambulance would hurry." He wasn't sure why an ambulance was coming or what it even was, but she sounded worried. Wrenching fear coursed its way down his spine, and panic bubbled to the surface when she started to get to her feet.

"Please! Don't go." JC knew his breathing was too fast and shallow. He concentrated on slowing down his racing heart before he passed out. Having just awakened from that state, he sure didn't want that to happen again. There had to be a logical explanation.

She smiled at him. "I'm not going to leave you."

JC knew he wasn't dead since he could feel his whole body aching. His pounding head reassured him he still lived. "I'm sorry, ma'am, but I'm not sure exactly where I am."

She scrutinized him as if taking his measure before she turned his hand up, then lightly touched his wrist with two fingers. She appeared to be concentrating on something. "Shh—be quiet now. You're hurt, with the likelihood of a concussion."

"I'll feel better once you've been seen by a doctor,

but your heart rate seems to be normal." She let go of his arm.

He shook his head. "No doctor, ma'am. I'm sure I'll be fine.

"Well, it's too late now, since I've already called, and the paramedics are on their way. And just call me Madison. I'm not a ma'am, at least not for a few more years," she said with a dubious laugh.

His tentative smile was replaced by open-mouthed disbelief when his eyes were drawn up to the sky where he saw a large flying object streaking a white trail of smoke behind it as it crossed the heavens. Then, back to the strange-looking road where he saw a line of those fast-moving horseless carriages passing by on both sides of the road. Unbelievable!

He looked back up following the streak of white from the flying machine until it vanished on the horizon.

What next? He saw the red brick building with large windows. From the smells coming from it, JC figured it was a food place. Something was wrong, terribly wrong.

Unfortunately, the sick feeling roiling in his stomach confirmed his suspicions. "Where am I?" His voice lowered to a whisper.

Madison's intense green eyes studied him as if she was looking right through him.

"Nevada. We're less than ten miles outside of Reno. Are you having problems with your memory?" she asked, rising to her feet, then shifting nervously from one foot to the other.

Not sure how to phrase the words, he decided to ask the question uppermost in his mind. "Can you tell me what today is?" JC picked himself up off the ground for the second time and brushed off the dust.

"Sure, it's Saturday," she stated with growing concern reflected in her eyes.

His gut twisted again, knowing he wouldn't like the answer, but he had to ask anyway. "Can you tell me the exact date?"

"June 1st 20—are you sure you don't want me to call your doctor? Otherwise, you'll see whoever is on call at the hospital." She dug something out of her pocket and showed him a silver box. When she touched the box, it lit up with a printed picture.

"No." He wanted to ask her about that box she had in her hand but held his counsel. JC clenched his fists to his side, and his head battled with the knowledge that he was somehow no longer in his century, but more than a hundred and twenty years in the future. He had to be careful what he said.

"Fine," she agreed, putting the box back in her pocket.

*This can't be possible. What am I going to do?* Panic surfaced, and his head spun with the impact. He'd been in sticky situations before and managed, but this was out of his understanding. For the time being, he had to keep calm and get through…whatever this was.

He drew in a deep breath and coughed. "I'll be fine in a moment. I must have hit my head. I was riding my horse." He picked up his hat, brushed off the dust, and plopped it on his head. The brim helped shield the sunlight, and he searched his surroundings again, hoping against hope to see his horse. It didn't look like Zeus had made the journey with him.

"Did you fall from your horse?"

"Yes, ma'am, I must have," he agreed, realizing that would explain his confusion.

Now what was he going to do?

When one of the horseless carriages coming toward the building pulled between two wide painted stripes, he watched in fascination as a large balding man with a pockmarked face and dark glasses squeezed out of the too-small vehicle.

The man wore a shirt like Madison's but with the word "*Hooters*" written on it and dark blue dungarees with a good portion of his rear hanging out. He watched as the man walked to the entrance, took another puff of his cigarette, and threw it in a container standing next to the door before going in.

JC's mind was quick. It didn't take him long to figure out that he needed help. He couldn't do this alone. Not only was he far from home, but more than a hundred years away from his time. His options were limited to finding someone to help him.

It looked like this woman was his best chance of survival. He knew he had to figure out a plausible explanation, at least temporarily, until he could return home. His previous excuse of hitting his head and losing his memory when he fell from his horse would suffice for now. He really didn't like the idea of lying.

If he told Miss Matthews or any other sane person the truth, that he came from 1896, they would think him crazy. What other choice did he have? All he knew was he'd have to find a way to survive until he could get back to his own time and life in Carson City. "Ma'am, I mean Madison, I'd be mighty appreciative of your help."

## Chapter Two

Madison carried her gardening tools and the colorful crate of purple and yellow pansies to the side of the yard. It was early morning. The sun brought a pleasant warmth to the top of her head and shoulders. She lifted her eyes to the heavens. The spun cotton-candy puffs of clouds drifted in the East as she searched for answers.

Normally a logical person, today she struggled with indecision. JC was intelligent and kind, not to mention being a hunk of a man, but he acted like he didn't know anything about electronics or other household appliances.

After he'd been checked over by the emergency room doctor and released, he'd been curious about the hospital. He acted like he'd never been to one before. She'd chalked it up to his memory loss. Either that, or he'd been living somewhere in the remote backwoods.

Madison decided it was time to dig for some answers. It'd been four days since she'd brought him home, and she still didn't know anything more about him, except he was a hard worker.

He'd managed to sidestep any personal conversation about himself during that time, leaving her to wonder what he could be hiding. Did he really not know where he was from? There was little doubt in her mind he was keeping something back.

After driving him over to the homeless shelter in Reno, she'd changed her mind and hadn't had the heart to leave him. Something prompted her to bring him home.

Thinking of her lost baby sister, she hoped that someone would have taken her in too. Luke, her brother, met them at her house and grilled JC. When he gave the final okay that he seemed safe, she'd given the stranger one of the guest rooms on the ground floor, farthest away from her own bedroom. If one of the cabins out back had been furnished and cleaned, she would have put him in one of those.

Digging precise holes in the dirt, she planted the purple and yellow pansies in a uniform line around the small holly berry bushes. She sat back on her heels and admired with satisfaction the neat flower beds that surrounded her well-loved new home.

The scent of dirt, fragrant flowers, and bushes had a calming effect. She swiped at the beads of sweat on her face and glanced over to the front where JC was working on the entryway. Today she would have to find out what he really knew about his past. Drawing in another deep breath, she put fresh bark on the newly planted flowers.

Feeling pride for her home, she studied the large redwood lodge. The welcoming design was emphasized by peaked wooden beams in the portico and a hand-cut flagstone entryway that gracefully swept to the circular driveway. The home had been built during the early 1970s as a getaway retreat for a reclusive movie star who'd been part of a well-known television show.

The rustic lodge was over ten thousand square feet and sported ten bedrooms, six bathrooms, a formal living room, a family-style entertainment room with a big movie screen, a TV, and plenty of room to entertain over fifty people at the same time.

It had an elegant courtyard patio with gray cut-stonework floors with a matching stone fireplace out back. It was ideal for socializing. She smiled, visualizing her guests sitting cozily on brightly-covered cushioned chairs, drinking wine or herbal tea under twinkling fairy rope lights.

The property had sat vacant for almost five years after its owner passed away, and the lodge and surrounding buildings all needed extensive repairs. It had five cabins and a separate guest house with three bedrooms where her brother Luke and his family lived.

She'd planned to open her bed and breakfast up to visitors in the fall, but with Luke and JC's help, she thought it could be opened by midsummer if not sooner. JC had already accomplished so many of the repairs she'd asked of him in four short days. He spent most of the evenings in his room watching the small television or reading. She'd allowed him to help himself to the books in her library. One night, she'd invited him to play cards with her. He'd managed to skirt any personal topics relating to his past and she had to admit, she'd enjoyed his company.

Madison looked over at her temporary guest who was scraping faded and peeling paint off the beams of the portico entrance. His muscular appearance attested to being a man who worked physically hard. With his somber blue eyes, golden curly hair, and twin dimples, he could be a male model. Not that she'd noticed. Yeah, right.

Thoughtful, she turned back to her task, moving on

to the next garden section. She pulled a purple pansy loose from the plastic cup and placed it in the hole she'd just dug. The knowledge JC was hiding something bugged her.

The sunny sky and pungent scent of dirt and cedar chips somehow calmed her like usual. Her gaze unintentionally strayed again to JC. Where could he have come from? His mannerisms and speech were so down to earth and old world.

Trying not to further speculate on JC, she shifted her focus to her own business. Soon she'd open her doors to the public, and she'd have a special cabin dedicated to families of missing children. Her brother and sister-in-law would help manage her lifelong dream of running a B&B.

Madison had been pleased when she'd received a call from her brother Luke a few months ago, asking if they could move closer to her in Nevada.

When she offered him the guest house, he jumped at the chance. Luke planned on expanding his photography business and promised to help her with maintenance around the B&B.

His wife, Paula, had volunteered to help cook and prepare some of the meals for the guests.

Glancing up from the garden bed she saw JC and her brother talking. She wondered if she'd ever outgrow the need to rescue lost souls. Goosebumps pebbled her bare arms. This was the first time she'd brought a man home.

Her common sense battled with her need to save the world. JC's doctor had said his amnesia most likely would be temporary from his head injury and there was no concussion

The recent rope burns around his neck had been puzzling, leading them to believe someone had tried to strangle him. They hadn't found a police record of any kind or a missing person report that matched JC's description.

What else could she do except take him in? He had asked for her help, she reasoned. She couldn't let him live on the streets until he found his way back home, besides he was earning his keep.

JC assured her that he'd never been married, of that, he was positive. All he'd had that distinguished him was a handful of old coins that were worth a lot of money. Most of them were still shiny gold coins and had been minted between 1890 through 1896. She concluded he must be a coin collector.

After all, she had plenty of room. It was good practice having a guest in her house. Taking him in had turned out to be equally beneficial to both of them. He'd been as good as his word, promising to help around the house and yard.

Chewing on the side of her lip, she smiled, remembering when she'd asked him to put the dinner dishes in the dishwasher after their first meal. He'd looked at her in total confusion. After she'd pointed out where it was located, he'd acted like he'd never seen one before. She patiently opened the door and showed him how to load and turn it on.

She flinched or jumped when Luke touched her. So lost in her thoughts she hadn't known he was there. Sheesh! Men!

"Hey, Maddy, JC was telling me you lost a buck-fifty to him playing penny poker last night." Luke laughed with twinkling green eyes. "You could do a lot worse than hooking up with someone like him."

"You're just mad because I always beat you at poker." Madison felt the heat blaze on her cheeks in embarrassment. She glanced at JC who happened to be within earshot, hoping he didn't hear. Luke was such a tease, and now it looked like he wanted to embarrass her with his matchmaking skills.

"I'll find my own boyfriends, thank you very much," she retorted, sticking out her tongue in sisterly fashion. Squinting her eyes, she placed dirty hands on her hips and gave him her best stink-eye look.

Luke laughed and saluted her. "Okay, I know when my company isn't appreciated. I need to go home to Paula anyway. I'll see you later, JC." Luke walked the short distance along the stone path that led to his place.

She watched affectionately as he turned, gave her a cockeyed grin, and waved before going into his house. He was getting way too chummy with JC. Paula complained that he spent too much time away from home.

Her brother's family had finished the process of settling into their new home. Paula and their son, Forrest, were getting ready to go to Northern Michigan for a short visit with her family to help celebrate Paula's parents' 25th anniversary while Luke stayed behind. He had lots to accomplish to establish his photography business and start bringing in an income to support his family.

She waved back, grinning. Her much-loved little brother was such a doofus, but she admitted to being grateful for Luke and Paula's company. She adored their son, eight-month-old Forrest. He was about the same age as Rachel had been when she'd last seen her baby sister before the kidnapping many years ago.

Blocking out that unhappy memory, she gazed proudly at her lodge, satisfied to see the repairs were coming along. Her home was fairly secluded on a winding road up a foothill with only a few neighbors that were spaced a good distance apart. They were located east of Reno. A small meandering river ran fairly close to her property where at times she'd spot deer and other wildlife.

Thinking of her brother's comment, so far since she'd been living in the Reno area, she hadn't met many single men. At least none she was interested in.

There was Vinnie, the blackjack dealer from the casino, who wasn't her type. Shuddering, she decided he reminded her of a stereotypical mobster character from a movie with his slicked back hair. He sported multiple gold chains around his thick neck and a Rolex watch. He gave her the creeps.

Then there was Bill, the truck driver. Bill was nice enough but also wasn't the kind of man she was interested in dating. He was a good twenty years older and had a couple of ex-wives with several children. Or Mike, the pretty boy who drove the cute little black BMW convertible. He was a hairdresser and was always looking in the mirror rearranging or combing his hair. There had been no connection with him as the conversation always centered on himself.

*What's wrong with being single? I'm young, happy, and financially stable. Not to mention making a contribution to society with my great job managing a small water reclamation company, opening a B&B, and volunteering for the Missing Children network. All three kept her busy.*

*Dang, if Luke thinks JC is potential husband material, he won't let up. JC is definitely attractive, and he would make a good husband for some lucky lady.*

"JC, just ignore Luke. He's working hard to push my buttons," Madison confided as she rinsed the dirt from her hands with the garden hose. She looked at the newly planted flowers with pride. Swiping the sweat dripping from her brow, she motioned her head toward the house. "Come on over to the patio so we can have a couple of sodas while we take a break."

Returning with two colas in hand, she gave one to JC. He watched her twist the top, and then he did the same. "I've certainly enjoyed your company the past four days, and I really appreciate all the extra hard work you've done. Have you remembered anything about your past yet?" She took a big gulp, waiting for him to say something.

"I appreciate your concern, ma'am. I've enjoyed being with you and your brother's family too. I'm positive that soon I'll be back where I belong," he said, taking a drink of his cola as he closed his eyes, seeming to relish the cold drink.

She noticed his evasiveness. "Maybe there's a clue we missed. Do you remember why you were carrying those old coins?"

When JC didn't speak, she added, "Why didn't you have any current money or credit cards or even identification with you?"

She studied him like she would a potential employee. "I find it rather peculiar that you give the impression that you know nothing about modern technology at all. I can't imagine living anywhere in the United States and not knowing about these everyday things." She took another swallow of her soda, giving him a moment to collect his thoughts while she gave him her undivided attention. He definitely looked uncomfortable all of a sudden.

****

Confessing the truth to Madison had to be the part of his story he'd been dreading the most. After spending time with her, he knew she could be trusted. Yet it did not make this challenge any easier.

He didn't know how much he should tell her. It wasn't fair not to tell her the truth. But, if he did tell her the real story, she might think he was totally crazy. Unfortunately, he couldn't wait any longer, and it was a chance he would have to take. He stared into her compassionate eyes and set the drink down.

Clearing his throat and closing his eyes, he squeezed his forehead between his fingers before looking at Madison trying to decide where to start his complicated explanation. Lord, she was so beautiful with her hair tied back in a ponytail and wearing her nicely fitting jeans and T-shirt. He trusted her. He really did.

"You've been a rock for me to hold on to. I really appreciate all you've done. What happened to me is so farfetched, so unbelievable, that I would commit myself to an asylum if someone told me what I'm about to tell you. Would you please wait until I finish my story before you decide I'm crazy?"

Her eyes narrowed as she looked him straight in the eye. Madison nodded her agreement while holding her drink with the grip of a vise. He realized she'd been prepared for the worst of whatever he was about to share.

"Whatever you tell me, I promise to keep an open mind. But if you're a criminal, then I will ask you to leave immediately and contact the authorities. Is that understood?"

"Yes. Don't worry, I am not a criminal. I can't ask for anything more. I do know where I am from. It's Carson City, only it's from the year 1896."

He watched her eyes widen in shock but continued on. "I know this sounds crazy, but the last thing I remember was…" JC proceeded to tell his story from the time he was wrongly accused of shooting a young boy by a man who'd always hated him and his family. The sheriff grieving over the loss of his younger brother, and then on to the part where his own brother, Nate, coming to rescue him from being unjustly hung for a murder he didn't commit.

"Henry Jacobs swatted my horse causing him to bolt. Nate grabbed my legs in time to hold me up to save me at the same moment a bolt of lightning hit. The next thing I remember, you were bending over me asking me if I was all right.

"It is crazy. I don't even believe things like this happen. Unfortunately, I have no other explanation for how I came to be here. More than anything, I want to go back home to prove my innocence. My mother has been through so much already. She will know I didn't do it, but she can't be left with another scandal such as her son being accused of killing a child."

****

Madison gasped and sat there stunned. Really! Why would he make up such a lame story? It couldn't be true. She stared at him trying to see if he was joking. He didn't crack a smile but continued to look her in the eye.

She exclaimed angrily, "Listen, if you can't tell me the truth, then don't tell me anything! You don't need to make up a story just to appease me. If you don't really know where you are from, then tell me." Madison couldn't hide the hurt and skepticism in her voice. "I thought we were friends."

He scratched his head, his lips thinning. "We are friends. Otherwise, I wouldn't have told you the truth. I know it's unbelievable. Remember the only money that I have is dated back during that time? Well, it's shiny and new for a reason, it is from my lifetime. I can't explain how I ended up in your century or why. All I know is, I am here. Whether I want to be or not. I have no idea how to get back home. End of story."

His sincerity and misery showed in his unwavering gaze. Is this man she'd brought into her home delusional? He seemed to really believe what he was saying. She assured herself that he was as sane as anyone. After four days of being around him, she would have known if he wasn't. Right? But his story had to be impossible. How could what he said be true? How many time-travel romances had she read over the years knowing it's pure fantasy? She shook her head in denial.

"I would prove it to you if I could. All I know is my family, the Berkleys, own the Double B Ranch in Carson City in 1896. We pay taxes and do our civic duty." JC's frustration clearly evident by the way he motioned his arms while talking.

"Even the Reno police department couldn't find anything about you in any of the databases. You're not listed as a missing person, a felon, or even have a driver's license. We couldn't find anything. It's as if you don't exist." She rubbed her head. The silence expanded as they both pondered his predicament.

"Please, I have no reason to lie about what happened," JC declared in a desperate tone.

An idea popped in her mind. If what he said was true, there would be something listed in the historical archives. She could do a search with Google. Madison shook her head, biting her lower lip, and stared off in the distance. At least if she didn't find anything, she could prove to JC he was wrong.

JC shifted nervously in his seat. "It's the strangest thing that has ever happened to me. I didn't know what to do when I woke up seeing cars and planes for the first time. My Lord, it was almost enough to make a man's heart stop. I need your help, Madison. Please." His blue eyes focused on her, his gaze silently pleading.

Her gut instinct screamed he was telling the truth, unbelievable as it was. "I don't blame you for not telling me the truth at first. I probably would have left you after the paramedics arrived and high-tailed it home. I'm sure there has to be a reason why you are here if it's true. Why did you end up in this century? We'll figure it out." She reached out and touched his arm to reassure him. "Together."

An electrical charge zapped through her fingers and throughout her whole body when she touched him, and she pulled back as if scorched. What's wrong with me? This can't be happening. She realized within the short few days he'd been with her, she not only liked him as a person, but unfortunately also found herself extremely attracted to him. Too attracted.

A relationship between them wasn't possible.

Especially if what he said was true and he'd be going back to his own time. She couldn't face that kind of emotional loss—not another one. She concentrated on hardening her heart against that possibility.

If it wasn't already too late! Her mind screamed.

She needed to remember JC as a friend and a lost soul that needed her help. They sat next to one another on the swing in silence.

Her mind churned trying to come up with a solution. If it was a normal question, she'd Google it online. Why not? The idea came to her with a wave of excitement as the perfect way to investigate the past came to her.

"Let's try the Internet Archives."

She smiled when she saw the blank look on his face. Of course, he didn't know anything about computers or the internet.

"I have an idea where I can start." She pushed up from the swing and jumped to her feet. "I'll see you later." Madison focused on how she'd research. She'd first find out if there could be anything written about JC's ranch or his family. If that didn't work, she could go to the public library to check out old newspaper archives.

Shaking her head in disbelief that she could accept a story like his with such calmness, she didn't wait for him to get up.

"You believe me?" JC asked.

"Let's just say that I'll keep an open mind, all right?" she said all business-like. He looked relieved, like a great burden had been lifted from his shoulders.

He'd fit in like a member of their family so quickly. Only she wasn't thinking sisterly thoughts of him. Luke had planted the notion that he would make good husband material. He would. Darn it. Only not for her.

The internet proved to have the information that he and his twin brother had disappeared during a lightning storm. JC and Nathaniel, and a man named Henry Jacobs had all disappeared. They were believed to have been incinerated by a lightning bolt. The sheriff had returned to town with three horses and no bodies.

Madison tucked her hair back behind her ears and looked at the picture of JC in wonder. It was one thing to say you believe in something like time travel, but quite another thing to see the evidence with your own eyes.

JC, his brother Nathaniel, and their mother had sat for a society page photograph that was dated July 4, 1895, in the Carson City newspaper. He looked exactly as he did now.

"Can I come in?" JC asked, appearing in the doorway.

She nodded her head, pointing to a chair. "Wow." She looked at the picture, then at JC. "Wow!"

JC looked confused. She turned the screen around so he could see the picture.

"Is that really me? Yes, as you said, wow! I thought I wouldn't be able to prove my story to you, even when I showed you the dates on the money in my pockets."

"Well, now it's proved to the point of certainty!" She cleared her throat. "Hmm. This is interesting. So, it looks like you were a big shot back then. Owner of the Double B Ranch."

\*\*\*\*

JC looked up from the computer screen. "Part owner. My brother and mother co-own our ranch. Willy, I mean Sheriff Wilcox and his younger brother, Petey, were extremely close, like father and son. But Willy has known us our entire lives and should have known I didn't kill Petey.

"I figure that Willy had been running on emotional steam from the lies Henry Jacobs fed him. Jacobs has always hated us. He isn't going to get away with his outright lies. I don't know who killed Petey, but when I get back, I plan to track Jacobs down, he has a lot to answer for." He read more of the article until she scrolled down to the next page.

"Hold on there! It said Nate! Can I see that article again?" She scrolled back to where the article started, and JC reread the story. His mouth dropped open. "It says my brother and Jacobs vanished too. What happened to my brother if he vanished too? Where could he be?" He sat back in the chair, staring off in the distance. Memories of his childhood flooded his mind.

They'd always had a mental connection with each other. He'd thought it was because of being a twin. It had amused their mother about all the unexplainable knowledge of each other's activities and feelings.

So why hadn't he even suspected that Nate had ended up in this time too? He knew with certainty that Nate had to be here, and he'd have to find him before he could go back.

Knowing Nate as well as he did, he figured his brother would have found his way back to their ranch. That's what he would have done if he hadn't met Madison. Hopefully their ranch still existed.

Chapter Three

"Please, God. Please help me. I'll be a good girl,"
she prayed with her hands fisted to her chin. In the
distance, she heard footsteps, and then a key turning in
the lock. She stood, prepared to leave the room.

"Mister, can I come out now?" She stepped over
the blanket that had been balled up to make a makeshift
pillow. The windowless room's overhead light always
stayed on.

"Yes. But no more messes. You got water on the
mirror last time," he complained.

Mister let her out to go potty but always made her
get back into the room. Maybe if she promised to be
really good, he'd let her go home. Mommy and Daddy
would be worried. She'd been locked in here a long
time.

"Hurry up, go to the bathroom." His voice, gruff
and impatient, frightened her. Seeing the kid's meal, he
carried and a bottle of water, her hopes were dashed
again.

She ran past him to the bathroom, where she shut
the door and tried to be quick. He would come in if she
didn't go fast, then he'd be angry. She didn't want him
to be angry at her ever again. When she finished, she
washed her hands like her mom had taught her, before
returning to the small room. "Please, Mister, I'll be
good, can I go home now?" The only answer was the

door shutting in her face and Mister turning the key in the lock.

Tears escaped down her face. She sank into the pile of blankets ignoring the food. Folding her hands together, she prayed again for that special cowboy to come rescue her.

**\*\*\*\***

JC observed the sights of Reno as they sped by the town in Madison's car. The city had grown and changed so much.

He closed his eyes, and a vision of the little girl he'd seen when the sheriff was getting ready to hang him formed in his mind. She was kneeling with her hands held in prayer. He heard her words, "Please, Mr. Cowboy, come save me. Mister is a bad man."

The illusion vanished, and an uneasy feeling lined the pit of his stomach. Why had he imagined this little girl?

Madison touched JC's shoulder. "Are you okay? You look like you've seen a ghost."

JC shook his head. "Yes, I'm fine." No way would he tell her about the crazy visions he was having.

Madison gave him a compassionate look. "If this is too much to take in, I can take you home."

JC smiled, trying to look reassuring. "No, I'm looking forward to seeing your place of employment." When she'd invited him to come with her to drop off some papers at her office, he'd jumped at the chance to keep her company.

"Okay, if you're sure. You asked so many questions this morning about my job, I thought it would be easier to show you."

"I'm glad you brought me. There's so much to see,

it's almost overwhelming," JC said, turning his head to stare out the car window. "I don't want to miss experiencing every aspect of this exciting century while I can. Especially seeing where you work."

****

When the door closed on the small elevator and they began moving upward, his stomach flipped over at the sensation of falling. He'd been in elevators in the past, but they felt nothing like this one.

She must have noticed his reaction because she put her hand on his forearm and smiled in reassurance. He was happy when the door reopened, and he walked out safely.

The reception area was painted with muted tones of beige and tan, and marble surfaces included black accent pieces. The central focal point in the room was the large desk.

A pretty young woman sat behind the desk that held a large arrangement of flowers. She glanced up with a look of surprise on her face when they approached.

"I'd like you to meet Missy Peters. She's a good friend of mine. Missy helps with the administrative side of our business, and she even manages to find time to help me volunteer with the Missing Children network." Madison made the introduction.

JC reached for the hand she held outstretched and gave it a shake. "Ma'am." Missy smiled and picked up the phone as it rang.

They moved on to Madison's office, where Madison pointed at double monitors. "This helps me to multi-task. I can work on one project and pull up other documents or information as needed on the other screen."

Madison had a lot of responsibility managing this company. Looking around at the modern office with the computers and fancy machines, JC thought it was unbelievable how much progress had been made between his century and hers. In a matter of seconds, a document could be copied, printed, and sent anywhere in the world.

He liked how her personality came through by the chosen nature prints and photos of her brother and his family on a bookshelf. There were framed awards outlining many accomplishments from academia to her personally achieved company goals.

Madison had started teaching him how to use the computer right after his time traveling confession. She'd told him while she was at work, he could do research when he finished his chores. Although he was still hunting and pecking at the keyboard, he was proud that he learned to use the computer.

If things had been different, he could have easily lived in this century. Everything about technology fascinated him. He'd excelled in his studies at the University of Nevada, graduating at the top of his class.

Society's advances had come far over the past one hundred years. Women's lives had now progressed to the point of being equal to men in family and work. His mother would approve of the changes.

It would be quite an experience to tell her about the future. Thinking about her reminded him of his task. There had to be a way back home so he could clear his name, but first he needed to find his brother Nate and that liar Jacobs. It was hard to feel sorry for Jacobs after what he'd caused the sheriff to do. Jacobs had grown up with an abusive father, but the bitterness he'd had toward Nate and him since grade school wasn't warranted.

He would love the opportunity to study all the different advances the world of today offered. Unfortunately, that would take time, time that he didn't have. He would have to be content with the knowledge that his grandchildren would live during this time and would have all the advantages he'd never dreamed of. Well, that all depended on if he cleared his name and found a woman willing to marry him.

When he visualized that woman, Madison's image was the only one who came to mind. She was everything he'd want in a woman, funny, smart, with ambition and integrity. Besides being beautiful, a sprinkling of freckles across the bridge of her nose, vivid green eyes, and the slightly crooked smile made her unique in his eyes. He pushed aside the image of Madison. It wasn't meant to be.

His attraction to her had to be stopped. At least to the best of his ability. He couldn't afford to be distracted.

If everything worked out, he'd be leaving and going back home. It wouldn't be fair to her or to him. And it could be that the feelings were only on his side. She seemed unaware of his attraction.

JC stood in the middle of her office and contemplated how to stay detached from Madison, his angel. He looked up as Madison walked in accompanied by a pale-faced, balding man who was tall and skinny. He kept looking at the floor and off to the distance. He wouldn't look JC in the eye. The man had the manner of someone hiding something.

The hairs rose on the back of his neck. His instincts told him this man was trouble, definitely not to be trusted.

"Daren Kushner, this is a friend of mine, Jonathan Berkley, who's staying with me for a while," Madison introduced the man.

JC held his hand out and accepted the limp handshake without surprise. When Kushner drew back, he noticed the knuckles were tattooed with letters that spelled out *love* on one hand and *hate* on the other. *What a strange place to have a tattoo.* When Daren noticed him staring at his hands, he quickly stuck them in his trouser pockets.

Nodding his head in greeting, JC studied the other man's face, positive he was right. *This man is definitely up to no good. What's going on here?* Daren nodded his head in return, looking past JC's shoulder. *Darn, I don't need anything else to worry about.*

He watched as Madison's employee walked silently from the room. Telling himself that Kushner wasn't his business, he returned his attention back to Madison.

"I've got the papers I need. Come on, let's go. We'll stop at the mall and get you some new things," Madison said as she locked up her desk.

They left the building and although JC wasn't sure what a mall meant, he looked forward to finding out. He was getting used to sitting in her car. The air conditioner made the ride truly comfortable. He could definitely get used to all these man-made wonders of science. Looking out the side window, he watched the casinos and buildings that slipped past so quickly. Holding back a grin, he eagerly hoped for a chance to get behind the wheel of her car and try it out.

At the mall he found himself fascinated by all the stores under the same roof. The smells from the food court made his mouth water. Madison showed him her favorite places to eat. Walking from restaurant to restaurant reading the menus, he'd finally decided on the steak sandwich place. They sat at the tables out in the open food court where he enjoyed every bite of his steak sub sandwich.

Madison had gotten Chinese food and given him a taste.

"I've never tasted Chinese food before," JC commented as he looked around seeing other patrons eating a variety of foods.

After they finished eating and dropped off their trays, a woman came up to Madison who didn't seem to be too happy to see the woman. "JC, this is Angie. Angie, my friend JC," she introduced them.

JC nodded his head in greeting while he noticed the woman's assessing gaze. The redhead was wearing clothes that left little to the imagination. Her leopard-printed top and shorts couldn't be much tighter or shorter. She had on a layer of face paint that made the color tone of her skin indistinguishable and that was a contrast to her pale unmade-up neck.

He'd knew the predatory look she'd given him from other women many times before and managed to keep his distance. They were after either sex or his family's money. When Madison looked away, the woman winked at him, slipped him a business card, and licked her red lips, before mouthing the words, "Call me."

He felt relief when they took their leave from the

too forward woman. He knew her gaze followed him as they made their way to the next store.

"Oh look!" Madison exclaimed, grabbing his elbow, pointing at the grand piano sitting in the middle of the mall. An elderly gentleman ran his fingers over the keys in a harmonious way before he resumed playing.

He felt the warmth from Madison's body radiate up his arm. It felt intoxicating to be so close to her, smelling her spring floral scent as they stood next to one another listening before they moved on.

*Knock it off, buster!* He balled his hands, trying to clear away the physical attraction he felt toward Madison. He put a small space between them.

She took him into a shoe store where he tried on canvas shoes. JC settled on a pair similar to Luke's and other men who were walking around the shopping area. She insisted on paying for his purchases with her credit card.

There had been too many choices to make, and he'd stood there looking confused. She'd laughed at his scowl of confusion, but indicated which jeans, belt, and T-shirts would suit him.

He'd tried on the clothing, coming out for her approval. When she held up a swimsuit, he crossed his arms over his chest with a scowl on his face. "No way am I going to wear those shorts." She only laughed, saying nothing. Her eyes twinkled with mirth as she handed over her card once again. His angel had a devilish streak.

"What did you tell me your worker, Kushner does?" JC asked as they walked out of the store.

"He's not my worker. He's part of the staff as our

senior environmental engineer. Why do you ask?" She glanced over at him as she pulled into traffic.

"There's something about him I don't like. Did you notice he wouldn't even look me in the eyes? And what's with that love hate tattoo on his hands?"

"No, I didn't notice he didn't look you in the eyes. Lots of people have tattoos these days," she added.

On the ride home, JC mulled over what he could say to convince her she needed to be careful around him.

Madison unbuckled her seatbelt, slid out of the driver's seat, and looked at him over the roof of the car. "Come on, JC. Today, people are different than during your time. The poor man probably has insecurity issues and isn't used to dealing with the alpha-male type." She grinned, giving him an appreciative look. Closing the door, she retrieved her package from the seat.

"Alpha-male? Is that supposed to mean me?" Gathering his purchases, he followed her to the kitchen door.

"You could be classed that way. You certainly aren't what they'd call a metro male. And your old-fashioned ideas cling to the outdated beliefs of the male-dominated society, henceforth the alpha-male terminology."

"What's a metro male?" he asked with a confused look.

Turning toward him, she smiled, "I don't think there's anything to worry about with Daren. He might be a techno geek, but he's totally harmless."

"Harmless?" Frustrated that she wouldn't take him seriously, JC searched for the right words. He decided to keep silent for now. She was too darn independent for her own good. He realized with irony that had been one of the qualities he'd admired only a short time ago.

Now that he wanted her to listen to him, that particular trait was an annoyance. He knew he was right, that she needed to be on guard because he couldn't protect her when he was gone. He'd speak to Luke. Maybe her brother could talk some sense into her.

Madison, unconcerned with his warning, walked over to set her bag on the kitchen counter as if the conversation with him was done.

He stood there with packages in hand, watching her as she wrote something down on her grocery list.

JC turned toward the room he'd been allotted thinking about what she'd told him while they were in the car.

He unpacked the items he'd picked up at the shopping center—a new shaver, deodorant, toothpaste, and a brush. Then he put his boots in the closet and the new T-shirts, jeans, socks, and night clothes in the dresser.

These purchases should last him until he could return home. The additional set of clothes were so Madison wouldn't have to do his laundry as often, not that he planned to stay long. He dressed like everyone else now. It amazed him how easily he'd fitted in so quickly while picking up this new way of life.

Rubbing the soft cotton of the T-shirt, he readily admitted to genuinely liking the feel and textures of the modern clothes. Most of all, he liked taking a hot shower and learning to use the computer.

\*\*\*\*

Madison looked suspiciously at JC, and then Luke.

They'd stopped over at Luke's place for a visit after running down to the hardware store for supplies. She'd stepped into the kitchen to grab a bottle of water. When she came back to the family room, they were having a serious conversation.

Luke glanced her way, giving her the impression that whatever was being said probably had something to do with her. Curious, she moved closer.

When she reached them, she noticed JC seemed satisfied with Luke's answer, and they switched the topic over to a discussion about fishing.

"Okay, you two, what's going on?" She looked suspiciously at them both.

Her brother and JC answered at the same time. "Nothing."

Madison didn't believe them. They were up to something. She just didn't know what. Her mind wandered over her dilemma of quitting her job when her B&B was up and running and hopefully making a profit.

Raised voices caught her attention, and she tuned in to hear the tail end of their argument about the best way to catch the most fish. JC certainly acted like part of their family.

He was a great handyman, and so driven. He worked hard accomplishing all the tasks around the place she'd asked him to finish.

Even though he was earning his keep by helping, he wasn't satisfied. He needed to find his brother, and then he would leave. Just thinking about him not being here made her sad. But if she was in his place, she'd want to get back to her family too.

She laughed when Luke and JC shook hands.

"Okay, the bet is on. Prepare to get your butt kicked!" Luke boasted with the confidence of a serious fisherman from Michigan. Not that he was serious!

"Madison, would you mind if I go fishing with Luke tomorrow morning? I should be back early enough to fix that gate in the back yard and paint the shed though." JC looked at her to make sure she was okay with that.

"No problem. I'm heading into work at eight in the morning anyway. I have a project I need to get started on. I will try to make it home by lunchtime, or after five. If you're home and I don't make it back in time, you can fix yourself a sandwich or microwave something."

She listened to them as they planned their fishing trip. "It's getting late, come on, JC, let's head for home." As soon as she said the word, she realized how intimate that sounded, but it was JC's temporary home.

Once back at her place, they stopped by the mailbox to retrieve her mail.

"You sure have a great brother," JC commented.

"Yeah, I'm pretty lucky," Madison replied with a hint of sadness.

"What's wrong?" JC stopped in his tracks and turned toward her. He'd picked up on her sadness.

Wistfully, she answered, "I was just thinking about my younger sister. How I wish she could be a part of our family too. You know, one of those *if only wishes*. I haven't given up hope on finding out what happened to Rachel, even though it's been over twenty-three years since she disappeared."

"What happened?" he asked.

They both sat on the porch swing in the cool

evening air. The full moon gave off enough light so that Madison could see his concern.

The crickets and other sounds of the night seemed to quiet down as she recounted the story as best as she could.

"It happened when I was only eight years old, and my sister was eight months old. Daddy took Rachel and me to the grocery store." She stared ahead. Remembering. The day in her mind's eye slid back to that time, so many years ago.

"Daddy, that man took Rachel," Madison shrieked as she tugged on her father's sleeve while tears ran down her face. Her father, in the process of reading a soup can label, shoved the can back on the shelf as his attention focused on his frantic daughter. Madison followed her father to the now empty cart where her baby sister had been sitting moments before. He grabbed Maddie's hand, pulling her behind him as he yelled for help finding his missing child. Only minutes later, the store manager and his other store clerks came running. They locked the doors, hoping the kidnapper couldn't escape. Everyone seemed to join in the search but soon discovered that it was too late. The camera captured a stocky man in a black jacket with his hood covering his face leaving with an infant.

The nightmare started.

"How could anyone kidnap a child?" JC's tone was empathetic, and his eyes were misty with emotion. "I'm sorry. I just can't imagine what your family went through."

"Thanks, it's been a long time ago. I'd like to believe that Rachel was raised by a family who cares for her. Dad never got over the guilt and left Mom a year after it happened. He stayed in contact with us only by mail and through his attorney.

"I believe he still loved us by sending us money and gifts for the holidays. It was sad for mom as she was expecting Luke when dad left, but she managed to hold the three of us together. Mom actively participated in the local Missing Children organization until she died."

Madison stood up. "Guess it's time to go in and get some work done." Opening the front door, she led them into the house. She quickly made her way up the stairs to her office where she could allow the tears to flow in private.

****

The chill of the early morning fishing expedition was barely noticed as they cast their lines into the Truckee River. Blue sky with a few clouds to mar the otherwise perfect day.

JC pulled out a decent-sized rainbow trout from the river and unhooked his catch before tossing it in the bucket with the rest of the fish. Luke shook his head in disgust. "How about our bet?"

JC smiled at Luke, who threw his hands up in the air.

"You win!" Luke reached in his pocket and pulled out a five-dollar bill, holding it out to JC. "Here, next time you'll be paying me."

JC took the money staring intently at his catch in the bucket.

"Are you okay?" Luke asked as he packed the rest of his fishing tackle away.

"Yes. I am just thinking about Madison. I'm sure her coworker is up to no good. I warned her yesterday, but she seems to think he is harmless."

Luke nodded, "A stubborn woman, just like our mom. She's normally a pretty good judge of character, but don't worry, I will keep an eye on her."

"I know Madison told you about my time-traveling experience."

Luke nodded his head. They walked over to Luke's car, stowing the bucket of fish and the fishing gear in the trunk, "I wasn't going to bring it up unless you did, in case it was a sensitive subject. She also mentioned how she found your picture on an old newspaper archive online. I never would have thought to do that," Luke admitted. "Of course, I wouldn't have believed your story either."

"She didn't believe me at first, and lucky for me she found that article."

They took their seats in Luke's car in silence. When they were settled in, Luke turned to JC. "I wish you could stay. I haven't seen Madison this content or happy in a long time. Not like she has been since you got here three weeks ago."

"I wish I could too. I care for her." JC fisted his hands. "If it was just about me, I wouldn't leave. But I have to get back home if I can." JC shared with Luke about their family's scandal and how important it was to clear his name.

"I understand, but I don't have to like you leaving. Leaving Madison is going to break her heart," Luke said as he started the car.

## Chapter Four

Madison reread the complaint letter, written by a disgruntled individual, about the company's water reclamation process. The letter requested her to put a stop to the company messing with their ecosystems.

She shook her head. Anyone who understood what they did would realize it had been the oil companies and mines who had contaminated their water and ecosystems—her company was trying to fix the problem. Besides, it was too late since the company had been here for the past couple of years cleaning up the toxins in the water to make it usable. Not likely to stop now.

Shoving the letter into a pile of similar correspondence, she turned on her computer and pulled up the project she was currently working on, shifting her focus to the job at hand.

Madison was sitting at her desk deep in thought when someone knocked on her door. She could see the visitor through the side window of the door. "Come on in, Missy."

"Am I disturbing you?" Missy asked as she entered, closed the door behind her, and parked herself into a chair. She slid off one red stiletto, grasped her foot in her hand, and rubbed the arch.

Madison looked up and smiled. "Nice shoes. No, you could never bother me. What's up?" She saved her work on the computer before turning her focus to her friend.

"Daren was supposed to have the James Company proposal finished so it could be given to a representative. Who, I might add, happens to be here now to pick up that report. Daren didn't show up this morning for work, and I have the James guy pacing impatiently in the reception area. I overheard him call his company a couple of times to complain about having to wait and getting shoddy service. All this while I'm trying to track down Daren." Missy put her heel back on. "What do you want to do about the James documents?"

Madison glanced at her budget analysis, one she needed to get to the Chief Financial Officer today.

"Thanks for bringing it to my attention. I'll go into his office to see if I can find the proposal." Madison, followed by Missy, went into Daren's office. The temperature was icy enough to cause Madison to shiver as she looked at the filing cabinet where he kept his files. It was locked, but as the manager of the company, Madison had keys to all the offices. It took a moment for her to retrieve the duplicate from her desk drawer.

When she returned, Missy was standing looking at the thermostat.

"He must have the air conditioning down to the fifties. Burr!" Madison said as she opened the cabinet.

"Yeah, it says fifty-eight degrees," Missy agreed while Madison opened the filing cabinet.

Madison flipped through the tabs until she found the folder marked James Company. One thing she'd give Daren credit for, his files were well organized. Thank goodness!

She looked around his office. Everything was neat and lined up perfectly. There were no personal items. No family pictures. Nothing that would give away any hint of his personality or his personal life. The room was so sterile, she shuddered, remembering JC's words of warning.

No, it was just cold in his office. Daren was the proverbial geek. He never caused problems. This was the first time he'd been a no show for work. She'd give him the benefit of the doubt. He would have a good explanation when he came in to work tomorrow. Shaking her head at her paranoia, Madison relocked the cabinet, turned off the light, and closed the door behind them.

"Please make a copy for me and give the James guy the original." Madison handed Missy the file before going back to her own office. Dismissing her earlier unease, she dug back into the budget she'd been working on.

By lunchtime, she'd forgotten about Daren and was sliding the spreadsheet into a folder. When the phone on her desk rang, she looked at the number display. It showed her home number. Since the only one who could be calling from there had to be JC, her heart raced a little faster, and she smiled as she picked it up.

"Hello. This is Madison," she answered, holding the phone back a bit from her ear. He tended to talk loudly in the mouthpiece, as he was still unaccustomed to using the phone. She waited as JC explained why he was calling.

"I found on the computer that our family ranch, the Double B, in Carson City still exists. I bet my brother is there. Would you mind taking me to the ranch?"

"No problem. I'll be home in a few minutes, and then we can go." She remembered how excited he'd been learning to use the computer over the past three weeks. He'd been a quick study. She grabbed her purse and turned off the lights. Stopping by Missy's desk, she gave her the budget report. "Could you give this to Smithers for me please?"

"Certainly, where are you headed? Lunch?"

"No, I'm taking the rest of the afternoon off for personal business. If you need to reach me for an emergency, call my cell." Madison walked briskly toward the door waving to Missy.

"Are you meeting a tall hunka-hunka cowboy? That cute guy you got stashed in your house?" Missy wiggled her eyebrows.

"Yes, I'm meeting him, but it's business." Madison stopped at the opened door and turned to search her friend's face. "And he's not *stashed there*, he's working for room and board as a handyman."

Missy tilted her forehead down to the right and gave her a knowing look. "Sure, it's only business, sweetie."

Madison gave her a fake stern look. "Don't forget to give the budget report to Smithers."

"Yes, ma'am!" Missy grinned mischievously showing a set of perfectly white but crooked front teeth. "Like I'd forget such an important duty!"

Her genuine smile was infectious, and Madison couldn't help the surge of laughter that bubbled up. Missy was a hoot and extremely efficient at her job, and since she was going back to school to get her business degree, Madison suspected it might be hard to replace her. During the time she'd known her, they had become close friends. She'd embraced Madison's passion of volunteering with the Missing Children Network and helping her numerous times posting banners and posters of missing children.

The phone rang. Missy wiggled her fingers at Madison and stepped through the open door to become the efficient office assistant once more.

Madison loved working in the ultra-modern building. During different times of the day, the shadows played on the angles creating a whole new look. The building was an architectural miracle.

She'd worked at a couple of other environmental companies out of college in Michigan and had attracted the attention of the president of her current company. When he'd offered her the opportunity to manage this company, she'd taken him up on the offer even though it involved moving from Northern Michigan to Nevada. The change had been welcome, and she'd found and bought her future home and B&B.

When Madison arrived home, JC met her at the door holding it open for her. The look of excitement on his face caused her stomach to clench. "You know we could call the ranch and ask if your brother is there."

"No, if it's all the same to you, I'd rather go in person. I would be able to see the ranch and if Nate is there at the same time."

What if he decided to stay at the ranch? What would she do without him? It had only been a few weeks since she'd brought him home, but she had become comfortable having him in her house. She liked waking up to find him in the kitchen and sharing a meal together.

When she walked into the kitchen, she smelled

burnt popcorn, and her nose twitched with the pungent smell. JC wore a sheepish look as he followed her in.

It was hard not to appreciate his cooking efforts. He still had a problem figuring out which setting to use while using the microwave. It was funny how he managed to be more adept with using the computer than the kitchen appliances.

"Come, see what I found," JC directed her toward the stairs and up to her office where the computer was still running. "See here? This is a picture of The Double B Ranch. Of course, it looked different during our time, but it's still the home I remember. The best part is it's still owned by a Berkley." His eyes twinkled. "That means either Nate or me survives and has children."

"That's great news. I guess that means you and your brother will be leaving soon." She tried to speak in an enthusiastic way. But the thought triggered a lump in the back of her throat.

"I hope so. First, I have to find Nate and Henry Jacobs. Then we will need to figure out how to get back home."

Madison went into her room and changed out of her business clothes. She put on jeans and a light-weight short sleeve top. She spoke up as she walked back into the kitchen, "We can leave anytime you're ready." Walking over to the window for a moment to compose her emotions, she fiddled with the wooden blind to let in more light.

He looked up. "I'm sorry about burning the popcorn again. It only took two tries to make a bag that was edible. You want some?"

"No problem. Thanks for the offer anyway. Are you ready to go now?" She went over to adjust the temperature of the air conditioning and flicked on the stove fan to disperse the burnt smell.

"I'm as ready as I'm going to get."

She noticed his earlier excitement was replaced with a worried gaze. He followed her silently out to the car.

"What's wrong, JC? Don't you think we'll find your brother there?" Madison asked as she pulled onto interstate 580 and peeked over at JC who sat with his fists clenched in his lap. He stared straight ahead. His mind was obviously on what he'd find. "No matter what happens, JC, I'll be there to support you."

"Thanks. I knew you would. Knowing my brother as I do, I'm pretty sure he'll be at the ranch, that's if he was brought to the same time as me. I'm wondering if he ended up in a different century."

"I hope for your sake, he's here."

"Me too. Now if we can figure out how to get back home. Nate can help me clear my name, since we were both in Sacramento at the time Petey was murdered."

The rest of the drive was done in silence. Every now and again, JC would comment on the changes of the passing scenery. It was the first time he'd been this way since he'd ended up in the future. She glanced over at him, seeing the tension reflected in his face.

When Madison pulled in the private drive taking them onto his ranch land, JC gasped. "It looks almost the same, except for the white fencing surrounding the entry on the property, and the exterior of the house is different. I can't believe it's still here after all this time. I remember when it was built, and Nate, Mother, Sadie, our housekeeper, and I all moved in. It was the start of a whole new life for all of us."

"Where did you live before?"

"Before that we lived in a cabin on the property, and before that our home in Berkshire, England. After our father died, we moved to America to start a new life. Mother had some money from her father's family to purchase the land and build the ranch." JC's head shook sadly. "My mother is a brave woman who took a chance."

"I'm happy it worked out so well for you. Sounds like all of you had to work awfully hard to make the ranch a success." A horse corral sat off to the side of the large barn where the double doors stood open. A silver horseshoe hung above the door. Everything seemed neat, clean, and well cared for.

As soon as the car stopped in the driveway, JC got out, went to Madison's side, and opened her door like the gentleman he was. He headed into the barn, walking in like he owned the place. Madison watched him warily while she stood next to the car for a few moments.

She didn't want JC to get in trouble for trespassing on someone's property, so she debated on whether she should announce they were here to the owner or not. She glanced nervously at the house, but when no one came out, she figured he would be okay. She hoped.

Concern for JC determined her decision, and she followed him into the barn. As she walked in, she heard a scuttle and grunting from a fist fight. Horrified, she watched as the two men fought. No words. JC intent on punching the man ignored her.

"Stop it, JC." Madison hurried over and began tugging on his sleeve to pull JC off the other man. "What are you doing? You're going to get us in trouble."

"It's fine ma'am, he's my brother." Like that explained everything. The man's voice was breathless, but he sounded almost like JC.

Madison stepped back, getting away from the two men, and let them continue to throw a few more punches, and then they were hugging one another and laughing. Watching them together, she noticed how much they resembled each other. If she didn't know what JC was wearing, she'd be unable to guess which brother was which.

"I see your brother found you," an unfamiliar voice said directly behind her. Madison turned and looked into the amused blue eyes of a man who resembled both of the brothers. She held her breath, uncertain of the reception they would receive. Then, JC pulled his brother toward Madison and the newcomer.

Both brothers started talking at once. "This is Nate. Nate, this is Madison," he introduced. Then he brought his arm up to swipe at the sweat glistening on his grinning face.

Nate nodded his head. "It's nice to meet you, ma'am." Then he turned toward the other man. "JC, this is Nathaniel Berkley, the third. He's my great-great-grandson." He grinned proudly.

"What a remarkable family resemblance." JC chuckled looking at his grandnephew.

"Call me Thaniel," he offered. "Why don't you all come in the house, and we can have some coffee and civilized conversation," he invited, glancing from brother to brother. "Should I call you Grandfather and Uncle JC?" Everyone laughed when JC gave a stunned look at the joke.

They followed Thaniel into the house and to the living room, which was furnished with cordovan red couches and lazy boy recliners. The theme was southwestern with warm tones of beige and assorted reds. Thaniel invited them to sit down. "My wife, Casey's not home now but I'm sure she'll be thrilled to meet you."

Displayed over a massive fireplace was a family picture of the current owner and his family. He had a set of twins, boys that looked to be about six, and an eight-year-old girl.

A woman introduced as Betsy brought their coffee in on a wheeled trolley. She'd included ginger cookies and finger sandwiches. Madison's stomach growled as she smelled the scent of warm cookies remembering she hadn't eaten since breakfast.

Thaniel was older than JC and Nate and had darker blue eyes and a dimpled chin. The rest of Thaniel's face looked like them. If she didn't know better, she'd think all three were brothers.

"...and when Nate showed up on my doorstep, we invited him to stay." Thaniel explained.

"Imagine my surprise to find myself in the future. I didn't know what had happened. One moment I was holding up your legs to save you from hanging, then I felt a shock when lightning struck, and I blacked out." Nate shook his head in wonder.

"When I first woke up, you were gone, and Henry Jacobs was standing next to me holding his gun. Before I could get up, Henry knocked me out with his revolver. Then, when I came to again, Henry had disappeared. All I could think of was to head for the ranch."

Madison watched as JC's eyes widened in stunned

disbelief. "Shoot. Henry's already causing problems."

"Thaniel and I have been trying to find you and Henry all this time. We suspect Henry has robbed at least one person. There was a report of an unidentified man who was brandishing an antique revolver from the 1800s."

"Coincidentally it happens that the person he was robbing was a dealer of antiquities," Thaniel added.

JC sat in one of the recliners with his hands gripped on the arms of the chair. When Madison looked over at Nate, his eyes looked haunted as he recounted the events. The good news was they could go home together—the bad news Henry Jacobs had to be found first. Henry had a lot to answer for.

JC was surprised that Thaniel seemed to be accepting of the time travel concept. "This has to be the strangest time of my life. Here I am sitting on our ranch in the twenty-first century with my brother and having a conversation with him and my many-time great-great grandnephew."

After Thaniel told them to help themselves to the trolley of food and drink, JC picked up a plate, putting a sandwich and a cookie on the stoneware before handing it to Madison. She shook her head, but he pushed the plate at her until she reluctantly did as he asked. He filled another plate before joining Madison. She turned and scowled at his overbearing effort to force food on her but took a bite anyway.

"I'd heard tales about the two of you and your mother while growing up. You were the founders of our family ranch," Thaniel said, smiling at the memories. "It was strange enough having Nate here, and now here you both are, sitting in my living room having coffee with me." He whistled. "Life doesn't get any odder than this."

"Thaniel, I'd have to say you are sure taking this unnatural situation fairly well," JC remarked, looking over at the man with amazement. "I'm especially grateful for you taking care of Nate."

"Well, Nate here showed up at my door and asked for a job. I could tell we were somehow related, but I figured he was a distant cousin. I hired him on the spot. No regrets, he's one hard worker.

"History shows that Nate here had three sons and one daughter. They, in turn, had eighteen kids, and their kids had quite a few. I, being the direct descendant of Nate's oldest son, inherited the ranch. So, it was reasonable for me to assume he was one of those cousins."

Thaniel shook his head and took a sip of his coffee. "When Nate resisted telling me which branch of the family he was from, well, I did a little research. I'd already put him to work in the stables with the horses.

"My cousin Sophie who's the family historian came over and helped me figure out Nate wasn't a descendant, but actually the original Nathaniel himself. Of course, that was after we cross examined Nate here." Crossing his arms over his chest in a satisfied way, he wore a smirk on his face.

"Sophie resembles our mother," Nate added. "I couldn't help staring at her. She knew our history. She told me anything I asked…"He stopped talking abruptly and looked guiltily at JC then at Thaniel.

JC knew his brother too well. That look spoke volumes. There was something Nate wasn't telling him. "What did she tell you that you're not telling me?"

Before Nate could reply, Thaniel jumped in. "We don't know for sure if the outcome of history can be changed by the actions we take," Thaniel warned. "Put it this way, the history as we know it today states Nate marries and has a family, but you are never heard from again back in your time.

"It was assumed that the lightning storm disintegrated your body. Your horse was found along with Nate's and Jacobs'. The sheriff returned the horses to the ranch. Nate was found days later."

JC winced. "Was my name cleared of the murder?"

"No. Nate told everyone why you couldn't have committed the murder because you were with him in Sacramento. But many people believed he said that only to protect you. Shortly after the hanging, the sheriff admitted he'd made a mistake." Thaniel shook his head. "We think by then he knew he'd planned to hang the wrong man."

Thaniel got up and held out the coffee pot toward Madison. She held her cup up and smiled as he refilled it with more coffee. He then went over to Nate and JC filling their cups. "JC, you are welcome to stay here for as long as you need to," he offered.

After a moment or two, he turned to Madison. "Thank you for the invitation, Thaniel. If it's acceptable with Madison, I'd like to stay at your place and earn my keep. That's if I'm not putting you out too much?"

Madison looked up, and her eyes met his. "Of course, you are welcome to stay."

JC nodded his head. "Well, that's settled then. Now, the next thing we need to do is find Henry. What are we going to do with Henry if we can't figure out a way back to our own time?"

"Let me make a few calls to some friends of mine who are on the police force, one does some private investigating that I've used in the past and to give them a heads up about the situation," Thaniel replied.

"How are you going to explain about him being from another time?" Madison pitched her question into the conversation.

"I'm not going to mention that part, it's enough to tell them there is someone out there that we suspect may be mentally unstable or dangerous. Especially since they are already aware of the man who has robbed someone with an antique gun."

After Thaniel's housekeeper appeared in the doorway to see if they needed more coffee, JC and Madison made their excuses that they needed to leave.

Before they left, they exchanged phone numbers, with promises to meet again soon for dinner. JC and Madison could meet Thaniel's wife, Casey, and their children, while they could meet Luke and his family.

JC remained silent for a bit, but then he broke the silence. "I think that went rather well. Don't you?"

Madison looked over at him quickly before returning to watch the road. "I guess," she replied stiffly.

"Is something wrong?"

"Yes, the meeting went smoothly with your brother and Thaniel. But I don't appreciate you trying to force me to eat, like I don't know my own mind."

JC looked taken aback by her intensity at his thoughtfulness. Normally it wouldn't bother Madison, but she'd rather he think she was upset by his manners than at the thought of him leaving.

"You're right, I should have minded my own

business." He offered an apology. She nodded but stayed quiet, and they finished the drive in an uneasy silence.

****

Briana squeezed her eyes shut harder. The pain from the spanking was temporarily forgotten, although she wore a purple bruise on her leg. It had been nothing compared to her fear of Mister.

Mister was mad.

She'd wet her pants again. The door stayed locked and by the time Mister had come to let her out, it had happened. He'd given her dry clothes and made her change. Then he took her bedding and left. He'd put a kid's meal on the floor, but she didn't want what Mister had brought.

She wanted her mommy—she wasn't hungry. As she'd been taught, she knelt and put her hands together in prayer. "Please God, I will be a good girl. Please let me go home. I don't like Mister. I'm still waiting for you to send me my cowboy. Thank you, God."

## Chapter Five

A few days after their meeting at the ranch with his brother, JC sat at the kitchen table finishing his lunch. When he closed his eyes, he saw the image of a little girl on her knees praying. This was the third time he'd had this hallucination. What did it mean?

Shaking the image off, he opened his eyes and noticed how animated Madison seemed to be. Her backside was slightly raised in the air as she'd bent over busily putting dishes in the dishwasher. She was unaware of his scrutiny. Knowing he should avert his eyes, he couldn't look away if he wanted to. She was humming an unfamiliar song under her breath. A warmth settled in his heart. It wasn't only her beauty that attracted him, but also her kind and giving spirit.

He'd observed how her eyes had sparkled when they had been at the ranch, and he'd asked her if he could stay with her a while longer.

Funny thing, she had acted like she really wanted him to stay. He'd felt a surge of blood flow to his head when she'd readily agreed.

Madison claimed that with his help she could accomplish her dream of opening the bed and breakfast sooner than planned. He owed it to her for rescuing him.

She'd even thanked him for helping to get the repairs done so quickly. It had made him feel like he was earning his keep. But, if he was honest with himself, he'd have to admit, he wanted to spend as much time as he could with this feisty woman before he left this time. Not smart. He was supposed to be emotionally detached.

He'd almost taken up Thaniel's offer to stay at the ranch, wanting to be close to his brother. The truth was, he liked the feeling that he played a part in helping Madison. Besides, she'd taught him to use the computer, and he wanted to keep using it at her place. He'd never have the chance again once he went back home. He watched as she stood up to reach for another dish, this time when she glanced his way, she noticed he was looking at her. JC felt their mutual attraction when their eyes met.

He wasn't a schoolboy, but a man with needs. Needs that had been neglected far too long. As soon as he got home and cleared himself of the murder charges, he was going to find a woman to settle down with. He thought about finding someone back home who had many of Madison's traits, but he couldn't come up with a single woman.

Today, society accepted a man and woman living together even though they weren't married. That idea was hard for him to accept. If he lived with a woman, he wanted to be married. He knew that coming to care for this extraordinary woman would be an error. Even in her time, she stood out by being self-sufficient, opening her own bed and breakfast, and managing a staff of men and women. Yet she managed to find time for her brother and his family and volunteer.

He shook his head. If they lived in the same century, he'd be down on one knee asking her for her hand. She was everything he wanted in a wife.

That was the crux of the matter. She was a modern woman, and he was old fashioned in her viewpoint. They didn't think alike. She wanted a career and a family. She wanted it all. But darn it, he wanted her for his wife. He cleared his throat, shoving back from the table that he leaned against. It was time for him to get busy.

Madison laughed. "What?"

"Sorry for staring. Guess my mind was on something else," JC lied, feeling his face become hotter. Heck, he was a man, and with legs like hers, well, his thoughts went to where any red-blooded man's thoughts would go.

Before she could reply, the phone rang. "Could you grab that?" she asked as she put in another dish. He found the telephone, picked it up and said hello. All the while his eyes strayed back to Madison's backside. He'd enjoy the view while he could. No woman of his time would dress like they did today—all the more shame.

He waited for the caller to identify themselves as Madison had previously instructed. When he heard Thaniel on the other end, he pulled the phone closer to his ear.

"Sure. Good to hear from you too," he still spoke a little louder on the phone. He looked up at Madison again. "Thaniel is putting Nate on," he told her as he waited.

"Hello. Yes, Thaniel told me. No, I don't think so. You are? Let me check with Madison."

JC held the phone away from his ear grinning like an overgrown boy who'd just performed a magic trick.

"Madison, Thaniel and Nate want to come over now. Nate just wants to know where I'm living and that I am really all right. Will that be acceptable to you?"

Madison fit the last dish in, then closed the dishwasher door, pushing a knob to start cleaning. "No problem, they can stop by anytime. I'll invite my brother over too, and we can try to put all our heads together," she offered.

Later, when Nate, Thaniel, JC, Luke, Paula, and Madison were sitting around the dining room table drinking hot beverages, the topic was organizing the research on returning back to their time and locating Henry.

"From all I've read on the internet about time travel, even though there have been claims that someone has time-traveled before, they were dismissed as hoaxes or their mental stability was called into question. The experts don't know how or if it can be safely done. There is no accepted method, and the experts say getting to a specific time is highly improbable. The speed of light, quantum theory, the law of relativity is all speculation. A few other scientists are conducting experiments, but unfortunately little is known at this time." JC took a sip of the tea, looking at his brother.

"You've really managed to fit into this time." Nate looked somewhat sheepish. "I struggle just to get used to things like riding in the fast-moving cars, TVs, and all the gadgets that are new to me."

JC laughed. "Yes, I really wish I had more time to learn about everything. I feel like a sponge soaking up liquid, and I want to absorb everything. The best part is when I learned to use the computer. It's incredible.

Come on, I'll show you." JC encouraged them to follow him to the office where he was doing his research.

JC proudly showed his brother how the system worked by turning on the computer and bringing up some of the old newspaper articles of them and their family history. When the picture of their mother and the two of them came up, he heard Nate whistling in astonishment.

"This is why we need to get back home and prove my innocence. Mother is a strong woman, but she already lives with our father's disgrace."

Nate nodded his head, his eyes softened, looking at the picture of their mother. "I remember when that photograph was taken. It seemed like only a few days ago. You and I were going to the spring barn dance with the Derby girls." He snickered, elbowing JC.

JC's eyes met Madison's, and he felt a moment of awkwardness. "They were our closest neighbors," he explained, hoping Madison understood it hadn't been serious. Even though there was no commitment between them, he didn't want her to think he'd been attached to another woman.

"Barn dance, huh? I wouldn't have thought of you as the dancing type." She laughed at his embarrassment.

JC shut off the computer and led them back into the kitchen.

"I'll see what I can find out about Henry," Thaniel promised. "Tomorrow I'm meeting with those friends on the police force I told you about. If he's to be found, Sam Prentiss will find him. Come over about six for dinner, and afterward we'll compare notes. My wife Casey is looking forward to meeting you."

\*\*\*\*

The days were getting longer, and summer was in full bloom. Madison looked out the window and saw JC on the roof of the shed where the lawnmower and tools were stored. Butterflies danced in her belly as her pulse raced. He'd been working on replacing a couple of shingles. The temperature was hot, and he'd taken off his shirt.

She leaned closer, angling her head to get a better view of him, admiring the rippled muscles of his arms and shoulders. Wow, he sure was built. The work he'd done previously had certainly kept him in good shape.

This was the first time she'd seen him not fully dressed. Normally, he wore a shirt even with the hot temperatures, a habit she guessed from his time.

She didn't think she could ever adapt to the past he'd lived in. Giggling at the visual image of her dressed in JC's day. Like she'd ever wear a long dress with a corset! She cringed at the thought.

Would she go back in time with him if she had the opportunity? Maybe. No. Her life belonged here. Besides, she needed to find out what happened to her baby sister and help other families struggling to find their missing children. Besides, what would she do? She enjoyed her time left managing The Reclamation Company until her B&B was open. Helping to clean up the environment would leave an impact on earth long after she was gone. It was an important cause to her.

Stirring the pot of homemade spaghetti sauce, she put down the long-handle spoon and dropped spaghetti noodles in a pot of boiling water. Determined to stop thinking about living in JC's time, she muttered under her breath, "knock it off."

Madison glanced again out the window as JC

wiped his face with the edge of his shirt sleeve, then he pulled the T-shirt back on over his tan broad shoulders.

He looked up in time to see her and waved. Her heart beat stronger as she returned his gesture. Embarrassed to be caught staring, she moved back to the stove. JC already meant far too much to her in such a short time, and she needed to keep it in mind that he'd be leaving. She'd never met a man who'd made her feel this way. Just the sight of his smile caused a feeling like a butterfly fluttering in the pit of her stomach.

Drawing in a breath she closed her eyes, imagining what his kiss would feel like. She was putting the garlic french bread in the oven when he came in. Their eyes met. Madison could feel her face flush and her heart pick up the pace. Knowing where her wayward thoughts of him had been, she looked away.

She stood, put the oven mitt on the counter, and then cleared her throat. "Give me another fifteen minutes, and dinner will be ready." She turned away, hoping he didn't notice her face.

"It sure smells mighty good in here. I'll go and wash up." JC turned and walked out of the room.

A few minutes later, they sat at the oak dining room table eating—like they'd been a couple forever, Madison thought. That thought was abruptly nixed when JC spoke.

"I want to finish up the repairs to the last two cabins before I leave," he said before taking another bite.

"Leave? But I thought you were going to stay here until you could find a way back to your time." Madison's voice cracked as she spoke.

He looked up. "That's what I meant. When I leave

this *time*. I planned to stay here until then—if that works for you. I want to have as much done as I can around the B&B to pay you back for taking me in."

"Oh." She cleared her throat and sighed in relief. "Of course. You certainly don't owe me for taking you in."

"It will make me feel better knowing I did my share here. Besides, keeping busy helps me to keep my mind off things I can't control."

"That makes sense, I'm the same way. Want more spaghetti?" she offered, changing the subject.

"I think I could eat some more. This spaghetti tastes wonderful. I'm sure my mother and Sadie would love this. You are an excellent cook. I've never seen spaghetti noodles sold in the mercantile back home. Not that I ever looked." He chuckled. "Is there a way to make them?" JC forked up another bite, the look of pure pleasure lighting his face.

Madison couldn't help the surge of contentment at his boyish enthusiasm while thoughts of his leaving were put temporarily aside.

"Yes, there's a recipe, but you'll need a pasta machine to make the thin noodles. I believe spaghetti and Italian foods were introduced after World War II to the United States. Many of the soldiers who were stationed in Italy during the war craved the food and brought home the recipes. Italian restaurants started up and became popular. This was my mother's recipe that she always made while we were growing up. I can give you the recipe if you want."

"Sadie enjoys trying new recipes on us. I'll have to tell her about spaghetti and some of the other dishes you've made for me." His eyes gleamed in appreciation.

"JC, what's it like during your time?" Madison sobered, wanting to understand what his life had been like. She realized, although they'd spent considerable time together, she still didn't know much about his life.

JC took the last bite of his toasted garlic bread, and then lined the silverware neatly on the side of the plate. He looked up thoughtfully, meeting Madison's eyes. "It's a different world. Different values, a harder way of life. We eat simple food. Meat or fish, potatoes, vegetables, breads and biscuits."

"Tell me a little about your mother and what you do on a daily basis." She pushed her plate away and leaned back in her chair.

JC crossed his arms over his chest, a faraway look in his eyes. "We really have been fortunate. Coming from a family of means, Nate and myself have never gone hungry or without any of our needs being taken care of."

Madison saw the pain of remembering reflected in his face. "If you don't want to talk about it, I understand," she offered, willing to allow him to change to a less sore subject. She was no stranger to a painful past.

JC shook his head. "No, it's fine. Our father rarely gambled. I heard he was provoked into making an unwise bet. Unfortunately, he lost our ancestral home in a game of cards and then killed himself. Our mother became the brunt of gossip and humiliation. She decided to take a chance and start over in America with Nate and me."

"That was really brave of her. How old were you when this happened?"

"Nate and I celebrated our tenth birthday when we found out why we were moving. Both of us had been in boarding school in London.

"My mother's father gave us the money to start over in America and to buy the ranch and pay for start-up costs. Hence, we ended up in our new country and way of life. There was a small cabin on the property. The previous owners had recently died from an outbreak of influenza. We lived there while we built our new home.

"It took a lot of work for us to build the Double B and to become one of the finest cattle ranches in Carson City. Mother hired a wonderful older man who helped us build up the ranch. Seth became like a grandfather to both Nate and me."

"I'm sorry about your father. But your mother sounds like an amazing woman. A strong woman, who took a big chance for her family. You must be extremely proud of her."

"Thanks. I am proud of her. I know she'd like you," JC added.

"The ranch keeps us busy. We put in a full day of labor on the ranch. Of course, we are active in the community too. There are barn dances, along with other social activities that we are obligated to attend.

"It isn't an easy life, though. There are hardships like watching someone die from childbirth, an accident or disease that takes the life of a friend. Now, knowing the future offers cures for many of those diseases, it will be even harder to watch."

Madison saw the look of wistfulness in his eyes. "I'm sure you are anxious to get back."

"Yes. I need to get back as soon as possible." JC's

mouth twisted. "I have easily become accustomed to this time. I'm going to miss cars, television, computers, and especially the food." His voice sounded sad. "I'm going to miss you and Luke too."

Madison pushed herself up from the table, her eyes blurry and the back of her throat clogged with a lump. Before she could move away, JC grabbed her arm, pulling her next to him.

"Why are you crying?" JC whispered.

"I'm not. It must be allergies," she hedged, trying to pull away not wanting him to know how much his upcoming departure affected her.

"No, it's not allergies. Tell me what's really wrong." JC held onto her forearm.

She again tried pulling away, but he gripped her tighter, pulling her onto his lap.

"Nothing's wrong," she claimed.

"Nonsense, I insist you tell me," he commanded. JC's authoritative voice pushed Madison's anger to the surface.

"Don't you manhandle me, you-you Neanderthal!" Madison tried to get up, but JC wrapped his hands firmly around her waist. She bucked. The more she tried to get up, the more he held on.

"Sit still. I don't think it's a good idea to move about like that." His voice sounded like he was in pain.

"Let me go." Madison said through a grimace. Then she felt the cause of his discomfort underneath her. "Oh, Lord," she murmured, her tears temporarily forgotten.

"Please tell me why you are crying? Did I say something that hurt your feelings?"

She rubbed the back of her hand across her nose,

swiping away the tears that marked her cheeks. It was just too darn much. Even being an inexperienced woman, she knew she'd just turned him on. "No, you didn't hurt my feelings. Sorry, I'm going to miss you," she admitted reluctantly.

"I will never forget you, Madison," he countered.

"Now that you have your brother back, it makes me wish I could find my sister, Rachel. I don't even know what she would have looked like now that she's an adult."

"I'm sorry that you haven't found your sister. Believe me, if I could, I would stay and help you find her." He loosened his grip around her waist allowing her to get up if she chose.

"You would?" Madison remained on his lap. "Don't say what you don't mean."

"I do mean it, but I don't have a choice. I can't let Henry Jacobs get away with his lies. More than anything, I wish I could stay. Stay and be with you." He took her face in his hands, looking deep into her eyes. "I have never met a woman before that I admired as much as I admire you."

"Oh." She started, then he pulled her mouth to his. He kissed her lightly on the lips.

Madison's heart raced as she fisted a handful of his curly hair, pulling him closer. His mouth moved over her lips feather-light at first. When his kiss deepened, she knew she had lost her heart to this lost cowboy.

He would be leaving, yet she wanted more. More of his kisses, more time with him. Their tongues met, and they explored each other—keeping their eyes wide open—assessing the other's feelings. Nothing outside their embrace existed. For a short few minutes, time stood still.

The tingling in her lower belly called out for something more primitive. A need so intense it almost hurt. Becoming aware of the growing hardness under her, she shifted. Sanity returned, and she recalled where and whom she was with, she reluctantly got up. Anger at herself pulsed through her. What the hell was she doing?

Forcing herself to move away from him, she acknowledged the searing pain in her heart. *Okay, girl, pull up your big girl pants. It's time to put up a fake front. He can't know how deep my feelings are for him.*

"Madison, I'm sorry." JC's look of remorse chilled her even further.

"I'm not here for your sexual pleasure. I'd appreciate it if you kept your hands to yourself," she stated bluntly. Then she turned away with her mouth tight and nose in the air and left the room. The message JC sent rang loud and clear,. He didn't feel the same longing as she did. She knew he was attracted to her, evidenced by his kiss. Or was it just gratitude for giving him a home? Ever since she'd found out about him being from another time, she'd known he would be here temporarily. She'd never meant to fall in love with him.

## Chapter Six

"Shoot." JC watched as Madison hurried away in a huff. He'd overstepped the bounds of being a guest in her home. He never should have kissed or held her like that. *What was I thinking?* She didn't deserve to be disrespected.

He'd only wanted to hold her, but it hadn't been enough. Those tempting lips and her soulful forest-green eyes had mesmerized him to the point he'd been drawn to her like a moth to firelight.

Lately, he'd been contemplating things he never would have thought of doing before, let alone actually doing them. He shook his head, trying to dispel away his discomfort. He knew when he got home, he'd behave with more propriety as he should.

It had to be the time he was living in, or more likely Madison's irresistible charms he was unable to resist.

He couldn't get enough of her. Let alone the modern way of life.

Even the grand opening of her bed and breakfast that was coming up excited him. He could see himself working alongside her. Yet JC knew where his responsibility lay, and it was back in 1896.

Sighing, he pushed away from the table scraping the tiled floor with his chair. Picking up the plates and silverware, he headed into the kitchen to rinse and stow away the dishes in the dishwasher. If he was still back in his own time, he would never have thought of doing the dishes. It was considered women's work, or in his case, the housekeeper's job. He grinned, imagining the horrified look on Sadie's face if she could see him now. She'd have driven him off to do manly things.

****

Madison peeked around the corner, seeing JC cleaning up after their meal. She'd finally regained control over her emotions when she decided she had better get the dishes done. It put a smile on her face at the sight of JC tackling the dishes. What a pleasant surprise to see him do this task unasked. She turned and headed back to her office, not quite ready to face JC yet.

Bringing up the bookmarked section on the internet of the old newspaper, she studied the pictures of JC, his twin, and their mother. He was so handsome. Nate, his twin, also handsome, but not as much as JC. In her opinion JC had a little extra something special in his features. She could visualize him on their ranch interacting with his mother and brother. He'd be the dominant one. Built as muscular as he was, he'd have to do some extensive physical labor to have the well-formed physique he had.

Her friend Missy would call him "eye candy". She decided that Missy would be right. What she felt for him went beyond his handsome exterior looks. Deep down inside, she knew JC was her soul mate.

The past few years, she'd been too busy with life. First with college, and then moving out west to Reno, a new home and job, and finally getting the bed and breakfast ready for business.

She was so close to meeting her goal of opening the B&B. Yet the thought of not sharing her success with JC made her sad. She'd have to buck up, accept the way things were between them. Knowing he would be better off with his family didn't make it any easier.

Love sucked. Whoever believed the phrase, "Tis better to have loved and lost, than never to have loved at all", didn't know what they were talking about. In her view, ignorance was bliss. She felt like throwing something. Why should she be so surprised? She'd lost her baby sister, her father, and then her mother. She'd dealt with those losses, and she'd deal with losing her heart to JC too.

Putting her concentration back on her computer, she closed out the pictures of JC and his family. The cabins had to be fully furnished, so she pulled up the website that had free delivery and looked at bedding and furniture to order.

****

JC's head moved back and forth like a windshield wiper as he observed the heated discussion a few days later.

"There's nothing wrong with bringing in a few sheep and llamas. Heck, they are kept separate from the cattle and horses." Thaniel defended his position on one of the changes he'd brought to the ranch.

"I don't know why you'd waste good money or space on such an outlandish venture. Horses and cattle were enough back in my time!" Nate twisted his lips in derision and folded his arms over his chest.

"It's not about the money, it's a sign of the times. Besides, people want to see llamas, sheep, and designer goats," Casey, Thaniel's wife, added as she gleefully joined in the argument.

Nate looked over helplessly at JC, seeming to convey his thoughts of frustration to his brother. "No disrespect, ma'am, but if this is a working ranch, shouldn't everything be about function?"

JC shrugged his shoulders. "I think it's up to Thaniel and his family to make that decision."

"Unca' Nate, we likes the llamas," Jordan mumbled through a full mouth of cookie.

His twin brother, Jonathan, concurred. "Yeah, and the miniature goats." His six-year-old face sported chocolate around his mouth, and he wasn't missing any teeth. "I like to pet them."

Their older sister Cathy nodded in agreement.

Nate rolled his eyes heavenward, chuckling with evident affection toward his descendants. "By all means if you like the llamas, I guess you should keep them."

JC laughed seeing Nate's look of adoration toward his progeny.

Casey patted her twins on the top of their heads. "You know, Nate, there's no arguing with these two. They have a good point."

"Yes, I can see that," Nate agreed as he reached over and rubbed his hands over the tops of their shoulders.

These kids are adorable, JC thought as they squirmed under their mother's attention. They had their own definite opinions on running the ranch. It was obvious that Nate was already enamored, just by watching his brother's interaction with them.

Thaniel and Casey seemed to be great parents. His assumption was reinforced by watching how well behaved the kids were and their combined parenting skills. He'd be proud to have such well-mannered children for his own.

Casey picked up the empty plates and cups. "You two need to go finish your reading assignments, and I will be up shortly," she told them, handing them the empty dishes. "Would you please drop these off in the kitchen first?"

When the kids were gone, Thaniel pulled out a printout sheet from a manila folder. "I found there have been a few small-time robberies where the suspect's description matches Henry Jacobs. Nate has seen the robber's picture, and he is sure it's Jacobs. Henry doesn't appear to be too bright. He boldly goes into a store without trying to hide his identity."

"Sounds like Henry. He never was much for using his brain. Even back when we were kids, Henry was known for not having much common sense." JC got up from the chair and paced the room.

"That's why it was so odd that the sheriff took Henry's word about the murder of his kid brother," Nate commented.

"I can't imagine how Henry convinced the sheriff of his lie." JC bristled remembering the false accusation. "I thought at first it was just a joke," he said solemnly.

"Something made me feel a sense of urgency to return to our camp that morning. When I found Willy had you hoisted up on your horse with a noose around your neck, ready to hang you, I thought you were playing a trick on me. Except Henry was there." Nate's hands moved as he spoke.

"Um, what does this Henry Jacobs look like?" Madison asked. She pointed out the window to a lone man who stood next to the barn off in the distance.

When JC looked out the window where Madison pointed, he saw Jacobs. "It's him!" he shouted, watching warily as Henry ran toward the house with his gun held in a menacing manner.

Nate hurried over to the window and looked out. "Let's get him!" JC and Nate said simultaneously, before they shot out of the room like a streak of lightning.

Thaniel moved just as quickly to a wall safe, where he swiftly unlocked it and pulled out a revolver. "Stay here," he tossed over his shoulder before he ran out the door after the brothers.

Madison and Casey watched as JC, Nate, and Thaniel emerged from the house into the yard. Jacobs spotted them, taking off in the direction of the road. He looked over his shoulder once before jumping the bordering white fence and kept running.

"I hope they catch him before he becomes more dangerous," Casey said, the alarm clearly visible on her face.

"Me too." Madison jumped when they heard a gunshot. "Do you think we ought to call the police?" Her voice was calm, but her heart was pounding.

The alarm on Casey's face grew. "Not yet. I've got to get to the kids to make sure they aren't scared. You keep watch. There's the phone if needed." She pointed it out before rushing from the room.

Madison glanced at the land-line phone. She held up her cell phone for Casey to see. She'd be ready to call 911 if necessary.

When the men came back without Henry Jacobs, she went to meet them in the entryway.

"We didn't catch him," Thaniel told her.

Madison gestured with her phone. "Should I call the police?"

"No, he's long gone. What can we say? A man from the 1800s was on our land? I believe we're safe for the moment. He knows we saw him, so he will be on guard not to be caught. Besides, I've contacted a couple of friends in law enforcement while I was on my way back in."

Thaniel went to the wall safe, punched in a code, and locked up his gun. After finishing, he punched in another code into the security system before his gaze scanned the room. "Where's Casey?"

"Upstairs checking on the kids."

"Good. We're safe now. I've turned on the alarm for the grounds and the house. I'm going to let Casey know." He took the stairs two at a time.

Nate and JC wore serious expressions. JC looked around the entryway, with his brows scrunched together. "At least we know for sure that Jacobs is around this area. It should help to locate him. I wonder where he's been staying?"

The brothers moved back into the living room, and the tension already building escalated.

JC stood by the window, staring out while Nate paced. Madison returned to the seat she'd been sitting in before, managing to stay calm.

"What are we going to do about Henry? It's not safe for our family." Nate's frustration clearly showed in his eyes. Stopping to cross his arms over his chest, he scowled. "He's the cause of this mess we're in. If he hadn't accused you of Petey's murder, then we wouldn't have been struck by the lightning and brought to this time."

JC turned from the window. "We really don't know that he's the cause of us coming here. It could have happened regardless of what was going on at the time. I'm just grateful that I lived to see another day."

"If the three of us are here in this time, do you think Willy is here too?" Nate speculated.

"No, I read in the on-line newspaper clipping, that he returned alone. I don't know if we can change history, but by all accounts, you are a part of that time period. You go on to marry and have children. It's me that's never heard from again. Heck, I need to get back. I have to."

Madison gripped her hands in her lap wanting desperately to comfort JC. When the doorbell rang, Thaniel returned and answered the door.

Casey came down the stairs and joined them in the living room.

"Are the kids, okay?" Madison asked Casey.

She nodded but wasn't able to hide the worried look. "It's scary knowing there's a criminal around who could endanger our kids."

Thaniel escorted the two men into the room. Casey went over to the coffee carafe and poured two cups of coffee for the newcomers.

"Sam, Parker, good to see you. Especially after our recent scare," Casey said.

"Madison, Nate, JC," Thaniel introduced, "These gentlemen are my good friends, Sam Prentiss, who's a detective with the Reno police force, and Parker Davis, a private investigator. They're longtime friends. Both are excellent in their fields," He took a seat, and the other men sat on the couch.

Sam and Parker took the offered cups of coffee Casey handed them. They seemed relaxed and clearly comfortable in the room as long-standing friends would.

Both men were tall, muscular, and in top form. Parker was handsome with blond hair, intense blue eyes, and Scandinavian looks radiated a natural charm. Sam, a handsome older man about fifty and native American, wore his black hair with strands of gray pulled back in a ponytail with a leather strip. His coffee-colored eyes were intense with curiosity as he studied Nate and JC. He wore a doeskin blazer with fringe and a pair of jeans sporting a silver oval belt buckle. Cowboy boots completed the look.

Sam took a sip of his coffee. "So, tell me about the trouble you had with a man brandishing a gun."

They explained about Henry, explained about time-travel, ending with him coming toward them until he saw Thaniel holding a gun before he turned and ran away.

After they finished, Sam leaned in before he spoke. "Now that I know your predicament I want to be involved. I believe I have the means of getting you back to your time. There's a cave in the foothills that has a time-travel portal. In my culture, I have learned that there are many factors that we as humans don't understand, one being the ability to time-travel. There are many stories of men from my tribe doing exactly what you've done, going back or forward."

Madison gasped. She couldn't believe that a police officer just admitted to such a farfetched idea as time-travel.

Sam's glance shifted to Madison. "I can guess what

you are thinking, and you'd be right. Logically, it shouldn't seem possible." He took another sip of his coffee.

"But you're a police officer." Madison stated the obvious and felt her face heat up.

Sam smiled, nodding his head in agreement. "I'm human too. I can think outside the box. Logic doesn't play a factor in this situation. The fact is sitting before me, these two men who are in our time now. This is something more than any of us can comprehend. Only a higher power, such as God, can truly know how or why this happens."

JC and Nate nodded their heads, and spoke in unison the same words, "If this hadn't happened to me, I'd never believe it myself." They looked at each other at the same time and laughed.

"Most of us wouldn't," Parker added, looking between the brothers. "Sam has more ideas and knowledge about this kind of thing than I do. It boggles my mind, and I admit to being somewhat skeptical." He grinned and looked over at Sam.

JC leaned over his knees and put his face in his hands as he studied the two newcomers. "So, you both believe what happened to us?"

Nate sat back, crossing his right leg over his left, then bracing his hands over his knee.

"I'd say what we believe is irrelevant. What we need to focus on is why you are here, and how we get you back to your time." Parker's no-nonsense approach had everyone in the room agreeing but Madison.

Madison's gut twisted at the thought. Sure, she wanted to know why they were here, but she didn't want JC to leave—ever. "What if they are forced to stay in our time? What will they do?" she asked.

Thaniel spoke up. "If Nate and JC remain here, they are welcome to stay on here and enjoy the hard work they put in to establish the ranch. I will help them get reestablished. They can do whatever they please. There is more than enough acreage that they can each have their own homes built. Berkleys have always taken care of their own kin."

JC ran a hand through his hair. "Thanks, Thaniel. I'm sure we can work something out. Right now, let's focus on what we can do. We need to make sure Henry Jacobs is caught. He's dangerous and probably mentally unstable."

Nate added, "He's always been a nuisance even when we were growing up. I think this leap in time could have put him over the edge."

Parker pulled out a notebook. "Can you describe him?"

JC's brows knitted together as he spoke. "Henry's almost thirty years old. Nate and I have known him since we were kids. He always had a chip on his shoulder and was prone to getting into mischief. He has black hair, brown eyes, is medium build, and about six-foot."

Parker wrote furiously as JC described him.

"How about anything that would distinguish him like a limp or mole on his face or scars?" Parker glanced up from his writing.

"Now that you mention it, he has a scar that curves from the top of his lip down to his chin in the shape of a hook," JC added.

And when they were finished with the face and body description, Sam asked about his background.

After getting all the facts written down, Parker closed his notepad.

"We'll find Jacobs." Parker's confidence was evident. He grinned, his dimples deepened, and his blue eyes sparkled. He rose from his chair, tucked the notepad into the pocket of his jacket. "We'll be back later."

Thaniel laughed, getting up to his feet, patting the man's shoulder. "I knew I could count on you two."

"Always," Parker responded.

Sam stood up, folding his arms over his chest. "I'm going to pick up Baxter and return today to try to get Jacob's scent while it's fresh."

When Sam seemed to notice the confusion on Madison's, JC's, and Nate's faces, he added, "Baxter is my bloodhound. He's found many missing people. Jacob is on foot, so that shouldn't be a problem tracking him." He rose and strode out the door without a backward glance, Parker following him.

Soon after Sam and Parker left, Madison and JC headed back home.

## Chapter Seven

JC scratched his chin trying to figure out why Madison was so silent on the way back to her house. Recalling how at the ranch she'd been more quiet than normal, he realized something hadn't been right.

He couldn't for the life of him figure out what had changed to incur the distance she'd put between them. He glanced at her, seeing her tightened lips and white-knuckle grip on the steering wheel.

"Are you angry?"

Madison looked sideways and shook her head. "I'm fine. Why do you ask?"

She didn't sound fine. Actually, she sounded annoyed. "You've been so quiet. I hope that I haven't offended you."

"No, you haven't offended me, I have a lot on my mind." She pumped the brakes, cursing at the car ahead that swerved in front of her. "Darn tourists."

"Do you want to play some penny poker tonight?" JC asked hopefully when they pulled into her driveway.

"No thanks, not tonight," she replied, not looking at him.

JC clenched his fists. His heart took a heavy dive into his stomach. Dang, whatever was going on with her, she'd closed off her feelings.

When they'd entered her house, she mumbled "excuse me," and had gone straight to her office. The door wasn't shut, but she'd pulled it partway closed, as if to reinforce a barrier. He'd pushed aside his need for understanding, deciding to respect her privacy by not disturbing her. For now.

It was still early enough in the evening that he wasn't ready for bed. The computer didn't interest him tonight. Restless, he went to the cabin he was working on. Drawing on the leather work gloves, he started scraping off the peeling wallpaper. In the distance an owl hooted, and trees rustled in the wind.

While he worked, memories of the sweet-scented apple smell in Madison's hair made him long for things that could never be.

A full-sized grin spread across his face as he thought about kissing her in the kitchen at lunch. He'd held her body close to his, making him wish she was his forever woman. I'm going to miss her, JC thought as a stab of pain struck his chest.

He put all his skill into removing the wallpaper. If luck held out, he'd have everything ready by the time he left for her to open her doors to her B&B. It was important to him to give her that much. He hoped when she looked at the improvements he'd made, she'd think of him.

It was getting dark when he packed it in for the night. He'd just walked in the back door when he heard the phone ring. As he passed the foot of the stairs, he heard her speaking with someone. He couldn't make out the words, but she was talkative. He even heard her laugh at whatever was being said on the other end of the line.

Perhaps she'd grown tired of him staying at her house. He thought she wanted him to stay here with her, at least to help with the repairs he was making. He heard her hang up the phone, and rose to his feet, ready to go in and ask what was wrong between them before he stopped himself. It really wasn't his business.

When Madison came into the great room, he was surprised.

"I'm…" She avoided looking him in the eye and turned to leave without finishing her sentence.

"Madison?" JC asked, feeling a sense of urgency. "Wait."

She stopped, turned to face him, and waited until he reached her. Her lips were clamped together. "Yes?"

"Tell me what's wrong."

Her vivid green eyes warily searched his. "Listen, I can't do this anymore, maybe you should go stay at the Double B until you can find your way back home."

JC didn't utter a word for a moment. He reached out wanting to pull her in his arms, before drawing back in retreat. "I'll go pack."

Searching her gaze for some inkling of what he had done wrong, they both stood there for what seemed like an eternity. JC saw her face pale even more. Her breathing sounded shallow and fast. He turned to go and when she didn't stop him, he walked away with his head held high.

Rejection hurt like hell. He wouldn't stay where he wasn't welcome.

If he'd followed his heart, he'd have wrapped her in his arms and kissed her. She would have tasted as sweet as strawberries and cream. The hunger he felt for this woman had him reeling with the intensity of his desire. It was time to live in the real world, not a fictitious world. She was his friend—only his friend.

The unwanted desire he felt for her hit him in the gut like a fist, and it took his breath away.

Friend indeed.

Lord, how he wanted Madison for his own. JC had never experienced deep feelings like this toward another woman. He wanted to make her his, in every sense of the word. He wanted her for his wife and to spend an eternity with her. Not just be her friend.

Fighting the urge to slam the door as he entered his room, he managed to gently ease it closed. "Marry me. Come back with me and be my wife." He tipped his head back against the closed door and whispered to the empty room.

*Yeah, like she would willingly leave her life here.*

Hopelessness settled in his heart. No one could ever fill his heart like Madison.

He couldn't grasp the thought of leaving her behind. Now that the idea of marrying her had taken root, it clung like a vine. If only it were that easy.

Unfortunately, he understood why she needed to stay. She had her life ahead of her.

The only thing he could offer was a good home and a life with him. Would it be enough? If she went back to 1896, she'd be giving up any hope of finding her little sister.

It wasn't fair of him to expect her to just up and leave all that she knew. Shaking his head in remorse, he realized she belonged here. Just like he belonged back in 1896 with his mother and brother.

Damn. At least he hadn't told her he loved her. He'd keep that secret.

He put the few things he'd accumulated in a duffle bag. Before he finished packing, he heard a soft knock on his door. When it opened, Madison stood in the door frame. When he looked at her again, his heart splintered when he saw the tears in her eyes.

"I'm sorry. I don't want you to go. Please stay." Her voice wobbled, and when she opened her arms, JC couldn't resist the appeal.

"Just hold me," she murmured in his chest, shivering with despair. "I don't want you to leave."

\*\*\*\*

"Hurry up," Mister demanded, as Briana scurried to the card table and chair near the bedroom window. He'd set another kid's meal with a small box of milk on the table, and then held out a garbage can. "Put the trash in here."

He jerked his head toward the wrappings of her last meal that sat on the closet floor. She picked up the bag and quickly did as he bid, not wanting him to get angry.

Briana had been so good lately and hadn't taken so long to go to the bathroom. She'd even fixed her bed to look neat. Mister liked things to be in order. He even commented on what a good job she'd done to pick up her room.

Maybe now he'd let her go home. She really missed her family.

She knew it had been a long time since Mister had taken her away. Mommy and Daddy no longer lived together. Had she done something wrong that Mommy didn't want her anymore?

Mister was getting ready to shut the door when he stopped and looked her in the eyes.

"What's your name?" he asked.

"Briana Collins."

"No, your name is Tara. Remember that next time I

ask," he said before closing and locking the door.

"I'm not Tara, I'm not. You can't make me be someone else," Briana said stubbornly to the closed door.

\*\*\*\*

Madison beat her pillow, then flopped to the side of the bed facing the window. The moon was full, and there were a million brilliant stars, but that wasn't the reason for her sleeplessness.

Even aromatherapy, the soothing scent of chamomile and lavender misted on her pillow didn't have the desired effect it normally did. Her turbulent thoughts were causing her unrest.

Had she really asked JC to leave because she was becoming too emotionally attached to him? Why couldn't she just accept the limited timeframe he was here and let him earn his keep by helping around the house until he found a way to return to his real home?

Falling in love with JC hadn't been a smart move. But how could she have prevented her growing feelings for him?

Clearly, having a relationship with him was impossible. She'd grown to care for him. Actually, if she was honest with herself, she knew that in the past weeks he'd been at her house, she'd fallen hopelessly in love with her lost cowboy.

JC was attracted to her. It was evident when he'd held her in his arms and kissed her. His kisses were like a lifeline to pure delight. She couldn't get enough of him. If he felt the same way she did, and what if he wasn't able to leave? A smile crept to her lips at that thought. Would it be possible to share a life together? Madison felt shame for selfishly wishing he couldn't go. He would be leaving, and she'd just have to remember that. All they had together amounted to too short a time.

Turning over in her bed again, trying to get more comfortable, she heard the creak of the hallway floor. She'd have to see if there was something she could do about that squeak before she started having people stay here.

Giving up on all pretense that she'd get to sleep in the near future, she rose from her bed. Finding her fluffy robe, she tugged it on as she walked to the kitchen. JC stood in front of the fridge. He gave her a guilty look when she entered.

"Couldn't sleep either?" Madison asked, going to the cupboard and pulling out two glasses.

"No. I hope you don't mind me going through the ice box, um I mean the refrigerator."

Madison sighed. "No, I was thinking about getting some milk and cookies myself." She grabbed the milk jug and glasses and poured them a glass. "Have a seat," she invited JC.

Her thoughts were on more than cookies, and she could feel her face flush. It was a good thing the lights were low. His fitted tee emphasized his muscular chest and arms in the dim lighting, and a flashback of that earlier kiss reminded her just how much she wanted him.

"Sounds good, thanks." He closed the door, standing in close proximity to Madison. She could smell his woodsy aftershave. It smelled wonderful. She drew in an unconscious breath of his scent and sighed. His warm breath caressed her cheek as he leaned in closer.

"The cookies are over the stove, second cupboard door to the left." She indicated, trying to slow down her pounding heart and lustful thoughts. Man, her mind sure was occupied by unwanted desire. He was a guest in her house, not her personal man-toy. She laughed nervously at where her thoughts directed her.

"What are you laughing about?" His voice seemed husky.

Sobering, she felt her face grow hotter. There was no way she was going to admit what she'd been thinking about. "Ah, nothing really," she assured him. Moving to the kitchen counter she pulled out a barstool.

He gave her a puzzled look, seeming to accept her words, and took a seat next to her.

Madison took the Oreo cookie and dipped it in her glass of milk. Moaning, she closed her eyes, trying to hide her embarrassment.

JC mimicked her, dunking his cookie in the milk. "This is wonderful." He dunked another one and put the whole cookie in his mouth.

"Why couldn't you sleep?" Too late, the words were out of her mouth before she knew it. But she had to know if she wanted to get back to sleep.

JC stopped chewing, then swallowed and seemed to consider her question for just a moment.

Madison felt as if the kitchen suddenly lit up with sunlight. She drew in a deep breath waiting for his reply.

"I'm sorry I kissed you. It happened before I could consider my actions. Please forgive me."

His words hit her in the stomach like a sucker punch. He didn't say what she'd hoped to hear. The breath she'd held rushed out. She knew he was attracted to her, but she'd wanted him to feel like she did. Hopelessly, she felt disappointed he'd regretted kissing her. She knew that when he left, he would take her heart with him.

JC turned his head, looking into her eyes. "We get along so well, I wish I could bring you home with me." He folded the napkin next to the empty milk glass and then pushed it away. "It won't happen again." He promised.

Madison rose and picked up the milk glasses taking them to the sink. "No, you're right. I have too much to do here. It would have been wonderful to meet your mother though, she sounds like a wonderful and special lady. Well, I guess I better get back to bed. Tomorrow is going to be here before we know it. I have an early morning meeting with my staff. If you don't mind fending for yourself, I'll do a drive through for breakfast on my way in."

"Of course, I can fix my own meal," he quickly agreed.

"Great," she mumbled, feeling the lump at the back of her throat. She rinsed the glasses, then put them in the dishwasher before tossing the napkins in the garbage. "Good night." Madison turned away, feeling the burn of tears that threatened to come. She didn't want him to see her cry.

JC followed Madison. "Good night."

"Night. See you when I get home tomorrow evening."

He waited until she closed the door before moving on and entering his own room. What a close call. JC had almost revealed that he loved her. From now on he would need to be more careful.

Madison deserved so much more than a temporary man like him. Tomorrow, he'd have to concentrate on finding Henry and figuring out how to get back to where they belonged. He hoped that Thaniel's friend Sam really did know of a way for him to return home.

****

The next morning, Madison had already left by the time he'd showered and shaved and readied himself to work on the guest cabin. The cabin would require his full attention. A needed distraction that he was glad for.

Deep in thought, JC didn't hear the door of the cabin open and was caught off guard when Luke slapped him on the back.

"Morning!" Luke snickered at JC.

"You know during my time a man could get himself killed coming up behind someone like you just did."

"Aw gee, I was just messing with you," Luke said kicking at an empty paint can.

JC glanced up at Luke. "Are you busy right now? It looks like I need to go to that big hardware store in town to get a new window." JC pulled out the broken pieces and measured around the wooden frame.

"Yeah, I can run you over there. I have the afternoon free before I have a photography session scheduled."

****

A while later, JC managed to order a replacement window and picked up a couple gallons of paint, along with more supplies in the same store with the credit card Madison had given him for expenses.

"This is the biggest hardware store I've ever seen." JC shook his head in amazement.

"Yep, and there's more like this one." Luke grinned and took him over to the tool section. "I'm more than happy to show you all the *neat* things." They laughed and joked about the electric drill. Luke's teasing made him feel right at home.

"You remind me of Nate. I think the two of you would get along. He's always playing jokes on me."

"I'm glad. I hope to get to know him better before you leave. I bet it was freaky to find out your brother and that bad guy were both here too?"

"Freaky?" JC repeated the word. "It was definitely quite a surprise to learn that they are both here in this century. Usually, I would have sensed Nate's presence. But I never suspected he could have come here too." JC climbed in the passenger door.

The Jeep's motor revved, and Luke pulled onto the road before he looked over at JC. "You know, Madison's going to have a broken heart when you leave."

"I've been trying to keep my distance. It's not going too well. I have deep feelings for her."

"Sorry, buddy. You're missing out on a terrific lady. My sister is one of the most caring and best friends anyone can have," Luke emphasized.

"You don't have to tell me. I already knew that. I couldn't help but fall in love with her."

"Then stay, damn it!" Luke pulled over to the side of the road and stomped on the brakes.

JC jerked forward, his chest slamming into the seatbelt. "I can't! It's not by choice."

Luke shook his head. "You do have a choice. You need to choose whichever is more important and go with your gut instinct."

"If only it were that simple."

\*\*\*\*

Madison listened to Daren explain why he'd missed work. They sat in the boardroom waiting for the others to join him. She'd gone in early to prepare for the meeting, and he'd followed her into the room.

"Like I said, it won't happen again," Daren promised. His glassy gray eyes never met Madison's. She had the feeling he was lying.

Or, she decided, she could have been influenced by JC's claim that there was something wrong with him. JC's warning words impacted her ability to think about Daren clearly. Not to mention the few hours of sleep she'd had the night before. After she'd left JC, she'd been too restless to sleep much.

"That's fine." She looked impatiently down at her notes, hoping he'd leave her alone. She felt a new dislike for him. She decided that she was *cranky* from lack of sleep. Feeling relieved when he finally left the room, the temperature seemed to go up a notch.

After spending the morning going over proposals, she developed a headache. Unfortunately, the last person she wanted to run into was Daren. She'd gone to lunch before making a quick stop at a department store to pick up a bottle of aspirin. He had a shopping cart with a frilly lavender dress and Beauty and the Beast pajamas.

"Hello, getting some shopping done too, I see," she commented, puzzled at his choices but trying to act friendly.

"Ugh, yeah. My niece's birthday is tomorrow," Daren mumbled looking down at his feet. His normally pale face seemed to be flushed with a guilty look.

"That's nice of you to shop for your niece. How old is she?" Madison asked politely.

Daren shifted from one foot to the other nervously. She'd never noticed him being so uncomfortable around her before. Most likely because she'd been short with him earlier and she'd never paid much attention to him.

"Six. I better get going. Don't want to be late back to work." Then he hurriedly pushed his cart away.

Perplexed, she watched him walk briskly to the checkout, turning to glance over his shoulder at her.

What an odd man, Madison thought. Shaking off the feeling of unease, she located the pharmacy section and picked up the pain reliever.

Chapter Eight

When she returned from lunch, she noticed, Missy held the phone to her ear. She looked up and smiled, then covered the mouthpiece and said, "Daren's on the phone and wants to speak to you."

"Give me a minute to get to my office." Madison strode into her office, pulled the blinds down to cover the midday sun, and picked up the phone. "Daren?"

"I've got a migraine and need to go home to lie down," Daren spoke in a low monotone voice. "Can I take half a day of unplanned time?"

Madison's head also still pounded so she could relate. "That would be fine, Daren. Hope you feel better tomorrow."

When she hung up, she wondered if her newfound dislike was why she'd felt uneasy around him earlier at the store. Shaking her head, she put any thoughts of Daren behind her and picked up the bottle of painkiller. She was swallowing the pills when she heard the knock on her door frame.

"Come on in, Missy. What's up?" She pushed a planter to one side on her desk then took her seat.

"How come Daren called?" Missy asked as she closed the door behind her and slipped into a chair.

"He said he has a migraine."

Missy had a file in her lap. "Oh, that's too bad." Her tone was less than sympathetic. "You don't look like you feel terribly well either." This time there was the usual genuine empathy in her voice.

Madison studied her friend over the desk. "I have a minor headache. You truly don't like Daren much, do you?"

"Is it that evident?"

"We've been friends for a while, and you're usually concerned about people. You seem less than empathetic about Daren."

"I don't like him, but I can't say why. I don't want anything bad to happen to him, but he gives me the willies." Missy raised her shoulders in an I don't know gesture.

Madison admitted to feeling some apprehension herself. Thinking about their conversation earlier in the conference room, and previously at the store, she couldn't explain her perplexed feelings either. "We can't like everyone, I guess. He hasn't done anything to you, has he?"

"No. There's just something about him that seems, ugh, I don't know, creepy-ugh maybe off?" Missy shrugged her shoulders. "Sometimes the look he gives me leaves me cold. I bet he doesn't like me either. But I try to be polite and helpful to him."

"I'm sure you're pleasant to everyone. I think he's just a techno-geek, and a bit socially awkward," Madison half-heartedly rationalized.

"Are you sure there's nothing else you want to tell me? If he has said something offensive, I hope as friends you'd let me know."

Missy chewed her lower lip, as if considering her words. "I'd tell you if he'd done or said something inappropriate. He uses few words and is always direct when he requests tasks from me. He makes a point to thank me politely when I complete the work he requests."

"That's good. I'm sure he just isn't a sociable person."

"Hmph, that's what you think." Missy snickered. "Now that the topic of Daren is out of the way, more importantly, how's your handsome house guest doing?"

Madison chewed her lip, trying to decide what to tell her friend. "Last night, I couldn't sleep so when I got up to have some milk and cookies, I found JC looking in the fridge. He said he couldn't sleep either, so I invited him to join me for a midnight snack." She paused.

"That seems innocent enough," Missy commented.

"It was, but what happened earlier wasn't so much, ugh, we kissed. That's not what concerned me, it's that when we were eating our snack, he apologized for kissing me earlier."

"Oh wow, so you're a couple now?" Missy replied, rubbing her hands together in glee.

Madison couldn't help the misery reflected on her face. "I thought the kiss meant something to him too. I know it did to me."

"I guess what you are saying is, it's not just about business anymore, especially when he happens to throw in a kiss or two?" Missy covered her mouth, choking on a laugh.

When Madison didn't smile, Missy added, "You're serious about him aren't you?"

Madison nodded. "Unfortunately. I knew he would only be here temporarily, yet I managed to let myself become attracted to him. He's smart, funny, fun to be with, and he's a perfect gentleman."

"He could decide to stay, right?" Missy cocked her head to the side.

"No, he has an obligation and commitments back home. He's been upfront about that from the beginning. He knows I'm attracted to him, and I'm positive he's attracted to me. The crux of the matter is, I've fallen in love with him," Madison admitted self-consciously. "I can't let him know. I don't want to sway his decision."

"Don't give up hope, my friend, sometimes things work themselves out. I'm here for you anytime you need me," Missy promised.

After Missy left, she felt as if a big weight had been lifted from her shoulders. She was grateful to have a friend she could confide her feelings to about JC.

Her cell phone rang, breaking up her thoughts. The carpenter's number she'd hired a month ago showed up on the display.

"Hello, this is Bill. I have your reception desk ready to install. Is this afternoon a good time?" He was gruff and all business.

Madison checked her calendar as he waited. "Sure, I'll meet you in an hour, if that works for you."

After hanging up, she thought about how great it would be to have the desk installed. And that made her think of JC, and their conversations about Daren. Add to Missy's distrust and unease, she needed to take a closer look at Daren. What was she missing? He'd seemed fine to her before.

She knew he'd been uncomfortable when she'd run into him in the department store. He'd been on his lunch break. So, was there anything to be uneasy about. What did she know about him? She knew he wasn't married. He must have at least one sibling. After all, he'd been shopping for his niece. She tried to shrug off the niggling sensation that something didn't seem right. He'd never talked about his life outside of work. She'd seen his resume. It showed his college credentials and minimal personal details such as his address, phone, and single status.

****

Madison was thrilled with her new reception desk, now installed in the entryway foyer. She was tilting her head sideways looking at different angles when JC walked in.

"What do we have here?" he asked as he came up beside her.

Madison felt a surge like a magnetic pull to move closer to him. Her cheeks burned as she remembered their kiss—hungering for more. She resisted that pull in favor of stepping back.

It took a second for her brain to catch up to his words. "Isn't it gorgeous? One step closer to opening up the B&B."

"That it is." JC ran his hand over the smooth wood surface.

Their eyes met and held. Something intense flared between them. Madison sucked in a deep breath. She wanted to tell him that she wasn't sorry for their kiss, and she'd welcome another one or as many as he wanted to give her.

Only before she could get the words out, the phone rang. The opportunity was lost as JC walked away.

She reached for the phone noting the caller's name, and quickly picked up. "Hello Sonia, what can I do for you tonight?" Her heart always sank when Sonia called—it usually meant someone had lost a child.

She turned off the new reception desk computer and grabbed a notepad. Sonia was one of her favorite liaisons who helped out families with missing children. Madison liked working with this woman who'd lost her child to a kidnapping. Only, in Sonia's case, they had found her child murdered. Now, Sonia was an advocate and a key player in organizing assistance and search parties.

"We have another missing girl, her name is Briana Collins," she stated in an unemotional tone, but Madison knew Sonia was anything but unsympathetic. With Sonia's history, a missing child always brought up the reminder of her loss and heartache.

"Oh my gosh, that's terrible," Madison said understanding because she felt the same way. She'd never forgotten about her missing sister, Rachel. But in her case, her sister had never been found, so there was still hope someday Rachel would be found alive as an adult.

"What needs to be done?" Madison wrote down the description of the little girl and pertinent details of the kidnapping. She concentrated on getting the facts down, pushing aside the emotions that bubbled up to the surface. Praying it would turn out well for the little girl.

"I will email you a picture of Briana." Sonia added, "Oh yeah, as usual, the media is having a field day." Sonia continued, after giving her time to write down the details. "It seems that the kidnapping is suspicious because the girl's father didn't report his daughter missing for almost a week. The mother who is divorced thought Briana was still with her father in Reno during a scheduled summer visitation.

"He's a member of that anti-government group out in Sparks. The dad claims he thought his ex-wife came to the compound and picked her up early. Briana was in daycare at the time. And apparently, there was a woman who picked her up saying she was picking up Briana for her mother. When Mrs. Collins went to collect her daughter yesterday, she discovered her child was missing."

"Oh, my word. So, this little girl has been missing for over a week now?" Madison repeated, shocked, and knowing that after the first twenty-four hours the chances of a safe recovery were dramatically reduced.

"The FBI is heading up the case as usual. The mother needs a safe place from the eyes of the press, and I was wondering if you could put her up in your bed and breakfast?"

"Of course. It's not open to the public yet, but I'll prepare a suite for her immediately. Send her on over." Madison swiped a tear away as she went to her office. The email from the forwarded document contained a picture of a happy-looking six-year-old. She was printing it out when JC came into the room.

"Is everything okay?" he asked, scanning her face.

Madison wiped away the moisture that had collected in her eyes. "Not really. I just had a call that there's a missing child." She looked down attempting to hide the tears as she held out the picture for JC to look at.

He took the printout and scanned the page. "Hmm, I know this sounds strange, but she looks familiar. Impossible, I know. Let's hope her family can get her back. Is there anything I can do to help you?" he asked, shaking off the image of the girl from his vision.

"JC, that's kind of you to offer, but you have enough going on with trying to find Henry Jacobs and get back home." She grabbed a tissue and wiped away her tears.

"I really would like to help. What can I do?" He met her eyes, handing the page back to her.

She took the sheet of paper from him. "I will be posting flyers around Reno tomorrow, and you could come with me, if you'd like."

"That sounds easy enough. I bet if I asked, Nate would help too if you needed any more help," he said. "Guess I should ask him first before offering his services. Can I use your phone?"

She handed him her cell phone that had Thaniel's number programmed in her contacts. JC called the number.

Madison watched him while he spoke to his brother, and her heart fluttered in her chest. She loved the fact he was willing to put his own problems aside to help her.

Looking from his boot-clad feet to the top of his curly mop of unruly hair, she admired his genuineness. What she felt for him was not mere infatuation, he was the person she wanted by her side for life.

*Okay, so he's not meant to be yours, but you can enjoy the time you do have left with him. Stop feeling sorry for yourself and put on your big girl pants. Focus on things you can do, like helping to find little Briana.*

With that pronouncement, she went to the closet where she'd stored the accoutrements meant to go in her new desk and started putting things away.

JC's call had been short and to the point. After explaining about the missing child and what help they needed and getting a satisfactory answer, he'd hung up grinning. "They will help. Thaniel offered to help too. He said to text him the place, and they will meet us there." He handed back her cell phone.

Madison gathered up clean sheets for the bedroom suite she'd designated to use as a sanctuary for missing kids' families. Only, she hadn't expected it to happen so soon.

****

The next morning, she walked out to her flower garden. Bees were buzzing around, and droplets from the sprinklers dotted the flowers' petals. The earth was pungent and moist.

The peaceful feeling of the garden rejuvenated her spirit, and she quickly gathered a bouquet of white daisies and Japanese irises to put in the special guest room. Madison hoped the flowers would make the woman feel welcome. She was sure that no matter how welcome she made the woman feel, nothing could surmount the pain and helpless feeling for her missing daughter. Madison hoped that they would be able to find Mindy's little girl. She was walking back in the French doors with the bouquet when she looked up and saw Luke standing in the foyer with JC.

"Morning." She greeted both of them, moving over to kiss Luke on the cheek. "Other than going to the hardware store, what trouble are you guys up to, hmm?"

Luke kissed her back on her forehead. He'd always told her how much he liked that she was a good six inches shorter than him and that made him feel more grown-up. His tall, lean frame towered over her, and he had to bend down for his kiss.

"Love you."

"Love you too, sis!"

JC saw her put the phone in her jean pocket. He was still amazed every time he spoke on this modern miracle. It was becoming almost ordinary. The ability of conversing with a person across town within seconds of dialing their number was no less than a wonder. Thinking about the cell phone that Madison never went anywhere without made him wish he could have one back home. It would be mighty handy.

Shaking his head, trying to clear the wishful thinking aside, he glanced over at Madison. Her eyes were scrolling up and down his body studying him. She seemed unaware that he observed her. He liked the thought that Madison felt comfortable enough to look him over like she approved of what she saw.

He'd been aware she'd fit perfectly in his embrace when he held her the other night. He liked the fact that, even in a T-shirt and hip-hugging blue jeans, she attracted him. She didn't need fancy clothes or embellishments on her face or hair. She radiated an inner beauty with her generous heart. Someday, she was going to make a great wife and mother. The pain hit him in the gut at that thought. He wanted her to be happy, only he didn't want her to be with another man. *Mine.* If only, but no, he couldn't wish for the impossible. He had to let her go.

When their eyes met, he smiled, attempting to hide his melancholy thoughts. He watched her face turn just a tiny bit red when she noticed he'd caught her staring.

Her eyes lit up to bright forest-green, and her freckles seemed to stand out. Her full lips puckered, seeming to invite his mouth to hers.

Darn, his eyes were drawn to those inviting lips calling to him to quench a powerful thirst. He felt mesmerized, like a moth attracted to a beacon light. He took a step forward, then stopped in mid-stride.

No, he shouldn't start something he wouldn't be able to finish. It wouldn't be fair to either of them. He changed his direction, moving toward the door. He'd already done enough damage by hugging and kissing her, which only made him want to do more hugging and kissing.

Madison blinked her eyes as if to clear her thoughts and swallowed.

"Luke's going to take me to a coin dealer tomorrow morning to cash in some of my coins, but afterward I will be free. If it would be all right with you, I can help you after doing my errand with Luke?"

"You don't have to cash in your coins. I've been thinking for the past month you've been working around here, I need to pay you. How does room and board and a hundred dollars a week sound?"

JC held up his hand. "Money isn't necessary. You've already been mighty generous. You paid for the new clothes and personal items I purchased the other day."

"Of course, if you want to cash in your coins, that would be fine. It is your money. Later will give me time to make a quick stop after work. I better get busy. I have a few things to do before the girl's mother arrives. The poor woman, I wish there was more I could do to help her while she waits for word about her daughter."

JC watched as she left. He knew this new missing child had to be hard on her. Something about the picture of the girl reminded him about the visions he'd been having. Could it be the same girl? And if so, why him?

Madison told him about her baby sister who'd been kidnapped, and he knew she was never far from her mind. She'd shared with him that she hoped someday to find her alive and well even after all this time.

JC felt comfortable with Nate being here with him in this time, even temporarily. He didn't know what he'd do if he'd lost his brother like Madison had her sister. At least Nate staying with Thaniel had turned out good for him. Until they could return to their rightful place in time, Nate staying at their family ranch was the best place he could be.

JC wasn't so sure he belonged back in 1896, His heart belonged here—here in this time with Madison.

\*\*\*\*

The next morning, JC finished his coffee rinsing the cup before he put it in the dishwasher. When he glanced up and saw Luke and Madison's easy show of affection he smiled. He'd never told his brother that he loved him. Of course, Nate never would have admitted how he felt either, even though they both felt that way. It just wasn't done. He shook his head at the thought. If he'd hugged Nate that way, his brother would have punched him.

He grinned at the thought, but just maybe he'd have to try it sometime.

His contemplation was interrupted when Luke told Madison, "Bye, sis. We're off to breakfast, then the coin dealer and bank." JC followed him out of Madison's home to Luke's Jeep getting in on the passenger side.

It had been almost a month since JC had found

himself in this time. He got a kick out of riding in automobiles. Especially Luke's red Jeep. Someday, he'd own an automobile in his own time. He looked at the pictures of the early cars on the internet around his lifetime. Not as dashing as the ones in this time, but they would do. That's if he managed to survive. With that, he shifted uneasily in his seat.

Breakfast at the café was an interesting affair. So many new choices to choose from. Luke told him what he was going to get, and he copied his friend's order.

They'd received their food and started eating when JC noticed Daren Kushner, Madison's employee come in. The man walked in alone and sat at a table for two. JC watched as he immediately adjusted and rearranged his silverware meticulously.

The waitress brought him coffee and when she left, he took out a white hankie and wiped the rim of the cup. He then proceeded to wipe the silverware as if to make sure it was clean.

The man carefully unfolded his newspaper, shaking free any specks of dust onto the floor. When he seemed satisfied, he put the section he wasn't reading across the table from him angling it to be perfectly aligned.

JC's eyebrows rose. He couldn't help watching in utter fascination. This wasn't normal behavior. Alarmed now even more than when he'd been introduced to him in Madison's office, he decided to point out the man to Luke.

"Luke, see that man over there to your left? He's the man I told you about that I met at Madison's workplace. There is something odd about him."

Luke glanced over his shoulder as they both sneaked a quick look at Daren. Kushner forked a bite, put it in his mouth, then set his fork back on the table while he chewed his food. He repeated the procedure until he finished what was on his plate. The waitress brought his bill, he paid it, and picked up his newspaper, and walked out of the restaurant.

"That's one weird dude! It looks like he has a serious case of OCD." Seeing JC's confusion, Luke clarified. "It means obsessive-compulsive disorder," Luke explained after Kushner walked out the door.

"That's doesn't sound good. I hope Madison will be extra careful around him, especially if he has some mental instability."

Chapter Nine

Madison's drive to work had taken longer than usual because of an accident. She arrived late, around the same time Daren was entering the building.

"Good morning!" she greeted him in the cheeriest voice she could manage. "Is your headache any better?"

Daren nodded his head before glancing down at the flyer of the missing girl she held in her hand. He paused, and his mouth turned down in a frown. He sputtered gruffly, "Morning. Yes, it is." He mumbled and hurried away to his office.

Sheesh! What was up with him? All she'd said was morning. Some people just woke up in a bad mood. Oh well, she had plenty to worry about without adding Daren's strange behavior to the mix.

She went by Missy's desk, giving her the copy of the flyer, briefly telling her friend specifics about the little girl, Briana. Missy studied the little girl's picture sadly while Madison told her about Mindy, the mother who would be staying with her.

"JC and his brother offered to help too," she added with a smile.

"I can give you a few hours tonight after work myself," Missy offered.

She'd helped Madison in the past with distributing flyers. "These situations always break my heart. I will never understand how anyone can be so cruel as to kidnap another person's child."

"I know." Madison hurried back to her office to deal with the essentials that needed to be done before she could leave for the day.

Soon after, Missy walked into her office. Her usual calm manner missing.

"Daren's acting weird. He just accused me of bullying him because I told him the mileage on the company vehicle he's using back and forth to the site doesn't match up, and I needed him to redo his report." She rolled her eyes. "It's not that big of a deal, and if it had been anyone else, I would tell them the same thing."

"I wonder why he thinks you're bullying him."

"Well, I might have also mentioned that he was wasting energy with his office air conditioner temperature set so low. He's an environmental engineer for Pete's sake. You'd think he'd be more careful about wasting valuable resources not to mention costs to the company." Missy tugged on a curl of hair next to her ear. "He is grouchy today."

Madison's lips quirked. "I noticed his mood when I came in. I doubt that a few extra degrees lowered in his office on the central air will make that much a difference to our electric bill. How much off was the gas milage?" Madison asked.

Missy sat back in the chair. "Over a hundred miles. You know Mara in accounting keeps a close eye on those figures, and she's liable to blame me for the expense report error."

Madison shook her head, closing her eyes. "Did you ask him why the numbers were so far off?"

"I didn't get a chance. As soon as I mentioned the

air conditioner setting, he got angry and asked what I was doing in his office anyway. I told him about collecting that report he was supposed to have ready for The James Company the day he didn't bother to show up for work."

"I better go talk to him. He does seem to be getting more and more careless about his punctuality and taking more last-minute personal time off lately." She rose to her feet. "Thanks for letting me know."

She dreaded talking to him. Daren had seemed to have an issue with her from the time she'd taken over managing the facility. She assumed it was because he'd been qualified and already working at the company and expected he'd get the supervising position. Or it could be he was uncomfortable working for a woman. Either way, she'd ignored his attitude, hoping he'd get over his angst.

"Missy told me there's an issue regarding your gas mileage report. And you accused her of bullying you." Madison stood just inside Daren's office. A chill went up her spine.

He was looking down at a document and didn't look up. "I may have gone up to Green's location in Tahoe a few extra times and forgot to write it down," he admitted as he continued to stare down at the document.

*Odd, that he wouldn't look at her.* Madison moved a few steps into his office looking around at the sparse generic space. Nothing to indicate the office was occupied. He finally looked up, directing his eyes beyond her, avoiding eye contact.

"So, what's going on Daren? You are normally on time and by not showing up when you were aware The James Company employee was due to come in, made our company look bad when he had to wait for me to find their documents. Missy overheard the James employee complaining to his supervisor about us." She crossed her arms and stared at him.

Daren shifted in his seat, looking uncomfortable, but he did look up at her. "I slept in because of being sick. I told Missy when she called. I've just needed extra personal time lately, that is all," he said in a low monotone.

"What's this nonsense about Missy bullying you?"

"It seemed like she was ganging up on me. My office being too cold, car mileage being off, and why was I late. You were late too, I saw you come in," he defended.

She dropped her arms and sighed. "Missy is responsible for the accuracy of those reports, timekeeping, and mileage. I was late because of an accident that stopped traffic, and I assumed you had the same problem."

"I may have overreacted," he admitted sheepishly.

"We all have off days once in a while."

"Is that all?" he asked bluntly.

"You know Missy is responsible for turning in both those reports accurately."

He didn't answer other than a single nod before returning his attention to his work.

"Yes, that's all and if there are any more problems, feel free to let me know," she offered as she left. A chill ran up her spine. Something wasn't right about him, but she couldn't put her finger on what bothered her.

Madison stopped at Missy's desk to let her know Daren admitted he'd overreacted and that there shouldn't be any more issues. She told her to go ahead and readjust the mileage to cover the extra miles.

By the time she finished her work for the day she was ready to go home to relax and forget all about her suspicions of Daren. She decided it was more than likely that JC had planted the idea he needed to be watched, and then Missy also said she felt uncomfortable around him.

****

JC felt a new level of independence since he'd arrived in this time. Feeling the bulge of the current money in his pant pocket reassured him that no matter what, he could take care of himself. He'd sold only three coins, and now had quite a bit of money that belonged to him. There were more of those coins for later if he needed them. Feeling like a satisfied kid who'd just found a prize-winning frog, he followed Luke from the coin dealer's store.

"So, is there anywhere else you want to go to?" Luke asked walking toward his Jeep.

JC thought a minute. Then an idea came to him. "Yes. I'd like to buy a gift for Madison. She's been mighty hospitable, the past weeks since I've been staying with her."

Luke started the engine. "What did you have in mind?"

"Well, don't all women like jewelry?" JC scratched his head and twisted his lips, deciding if Madison might like a ring or necklace. She wasn't the typical woman of his time. As far as he knew, the only jewelry she wore were the triangle-shaped diamond studs she wore in her ears. He'd wondered why they were shaped so odd having never seen that particular cut before. He decided he'd have to ask her.

"Maddie isn't much into jewelry. She'd prefer a good book or something for her B&B. But it never hurts to look. Let me take you to a jeweler I met recently from the photography club I belong to in Reno. I have to warn you, it's a bit pricey. My second anniversary is coming up in a few weeks, and I planned to pick up something special for Paula."

He turned the car onto the freeway, bypassing the slower neighborhoods. Within minutes, they pulled into a parking lot, parked, and entered the store. The proprietor, happy to see Luke again, talked about photography.

JC moved away giving them space to visit and scanned the shiny glass cases for just the right gift. His eyes skirted the wedding bands and diamond rings, then went back over the selection. There was a triangle-shaped diamond ring. It was perfect. "How much is this one?" He pointed to the ring that had caught his attention.

The salesperson chuckled. "Good choice, this trillion-diamond engagement ring is…"

JC didn't hear the price. All he'd heard was *engagement ring*. Lord, he couldn't give her an engagement ring. He was going to be leaving. The salesman pulled out the velvet tray and picked up the ring, rubbing at it with a cloth. Then he handed it to JC.

Just at that moment, Luke came back to see what JC had found. "What do you have there?"

Heat attacked his face at his faux pas. Embarrassed, he quickly handed the ring back to the clerk. "I was just looking. The shape of the stone caught my eye," he stammered.

"Madison loves the shape of a trillion stone. But

this is an engagement ring." He looked intently at JC. "I thought you wanted to give my sister a gift?" His confusion was evident.

JC cleared his throat. "I do. I mean, I was only looking at the cut of the stone."

Luke laughed. "Well, if you could find something that was cut in a trillion shape, she'd love the gift."

The clerk understanding the mistake put the ring back into the case. "I think I have the perfect item. He locked the case and indicated for them to follow him. He took them to a case filled with earrings, pendants, and necklaces. They found a pretty deep-blue Tanzanite trillion cut necklace on a delicate gold chain.

"What do you think?"

"Perfect. How much?" JC waited as the clerk took the payment, and then put Madison's present in a pretty velvet box. He was relieved that he now had an appropriate gift.

They were driving back to Madison's house when he asked Luke.

"Do you think you could teach me to drive a car?"

"You're a man, right?" Luke chuckled. "Men like to drive. I can teach you." He turned off at their exit. "How about right now?" he asked, seeming not to expect an answer when he pulled into a deserted parking lot.

Luke opened the door and slid out of the driver's seat, and JC did the same on his side of the car. "This is what they call an automatic transmission. It means the car adjusts to the speed on its own and you don't have to shift or anything. All you have to worry about is putting it in gear, the gas pedal, and the brakes. And turning the wheel the way you intend to go."

JC's sense of adventure had him reeling with delight at being able to drive the car. He'd watched Madison and Luke when they drove around, and it didn't seem all that difficult. He associated it with breaking in a wild stallion. He could do this.

"Now buckle up." Luke pointed to the seatbelt before he buckled himself into the passenger seat.

"Now what?" JC's heart raced with excitement, and his hands gripped the wheel as he waited for Luke to continue.

"Can you see out the mirror above, there and there?" He pointed and adjusted the interior mirror to fit. "Remember gas is on the right and brakes are on the left. Use only one foot. And start off slow. Turn the wheel in the direction you want to go or hold it steady if you want to go straight," Luke patiently explained. "Put it in drive. Lightly put your foot on the gas pedal."

JC did as instructed, and the vehicle slowly rolled forward.

"Now, press down a bit harder to give it more gas and turn the wheel to follow that white line."

JC could hardly contain his enthusiasm when the car seemed to respond to his touch. He followed the direction of the white line, going around the parking area.

"Now, gently put your foot on the other pedal until the car slows to a stop. Very good," Luke encouraged.

JC felt the car slow, then it stopped all together. "I did it!"

"Put the car in park, it's easy. You did great. Now one more time, let's head the other way," Luke walked him through all the possible scenarios of driving and even had him park the car.

"That was fantastic. I drove a car." He shook his head in wonder, with a huge smile on his lips. "Can we do it again sometime?" They traded places, and Luke drove them to Madison's house.

"You bet." Luke said giving him a fist bump that he'd taught him while fishing. Madison's car was already in the driveway even though it wasn't noon, she'd beaten them home.

With all the excitement of driving Luke's car, JC had almost forgotten his promise to help with the flyers. He walked into the house behind Luke, who called out a greeting.

She came out of the office and stared at both of them. "Any luck with the coin dealers?"

"You're not going to believe how much my coins were worth," JC began, pulling the wad of bills from his front pocket. He held them out for her to witness.

"Looks like quite a haul. How about if we put some of it in the bank?"

"Why?" JC was puzzled. He didn't think a bank was necessary. After all, he would spend what he needed, and leave the rest with Madison.

"I guess that doesn't make a lot of sense. We can't open an account for you because technically you don't exist. At least we can't prove you are who you say you are." Madison's gaze brightened. "I have a safe, if you'd like, you can store most of it in there?"

JC looked at the folded bills, then nodded. "I want to keep out a hundred dollars."

Madison took the remaining money. "We'll keep it in here, but if you need more, just let me know. It's your money. I wanted to give you some money for all your labor."

"It's really not necessary. You've already done so much for me. Fed, clothed, and gave me a roof over my head. I can never repay all you've done to help."

Madison turned away, going to the wall safe, dialing the code. "There's no need to repay me. You're my friend," she said almost choking on the words. He was more than a friend. She found an envelope, wrote his name on it, added another two hundred dollars to it, then tucked away his money in the safe and locked it again.

She felt another presence behind her, turned, and saw it was Luke. Luke's gaze caught and searched hers. When he moved to touch her shoulder, without words, she knew that he was aware of her deep feelings for JC.

Needing to lighten up some of the tension in the room, she sought a safer topic. "So, what other kind of trouble have the two of you have been up to?"

Luke smiled, "Trouble? Who, me?"

"Oh, brother, I know that look. What have you done?" Madison shook her head as she noticed the guilty glee on Luke's face.

"You haven't quite mastered the innocent look yet. Spill the beans."

"Did I mention that Paula is coming home day after tomorrow?" Luke rushed, his eyes going from her to JC.

"I'm pretty sure you mentioned that before." She put her hands on her hips, giving him the evil eye. She stood there like that, waiting.

Luke cleared his throat. "Well, you see, it seemed like a good idea at the time."

Madison watched her brother's discomfort. He shifted from foot to foot, while avoiding eye contact. "Um-hmm? And what seemed like a good idea?"

"Well, JC and I were on our way home, and I kind of let him drive my car." He smiled through gritted teeth.

Madison started to laugh at his guilty look, then looked at JC who stood there with a big, contented smile on his face. He didn't seem to be intimidated like her brother. "So, when you *kind of* let him drive your car, did it ever occur to you that if he was stopped by a police officer, he wouldn't have any way of proving who he was?"

"No. I'm sorry. I figured we'd be safe enough in that old, abandoned car dealer's parking lot." Luke spread his hands regretfully and shrugged. "Sorry."

JC jumped into the fray putting a hand on Madison's shoulder. "It was completely my idea. Luke was just accommodating my request."

At his touch, everything was forgotten. She wasn't aware of holding her breath until she gasped for air. JC pulled his hand back as if he'd been burned.

"Sorry, I didn't mean to startle you."

Luke started laughing. "That will be the day when Madison is startled. You should have seen JC drive. He was like a kid in a candy store." He continued laughing while wiping at his tears.

Neither JC nor Madison was laughing. They stood staring at one another. It seemed as if he was looking into her soul.

Collecting her thoughts Madison moved the short distance to her brother and slugged him in the arm. "Stop laughing. You could have caused us all a lot of trouble if you'd been stopped by the police."

"Ow! Hey, that was supposed to be a compliment. You are never caught off guard," Luke rubbed at his bicep.

"I hit you because you took a chance by breaking the law. We don't need any more problems. I have too much to do right now than to add more problems to my day."

Luke held his hands up in front of his face in contrition. "Sorry, sis. I guess I didn't think it through. Figured if I let him practice driving in that parking lot, we'd be okay."

"Don't be mad at your brother. I talked him into teaching me to drive. It's my fault. I didn't realize that it was against the law."

"Of course, you didn't know. You are supposed to take a driver's license test, then get in some practice behind the wheel. I don't mean to overreact. It's just that we don't need anything else to worry about right now." Madison saw the disappointment written on his face. He'd been adjusting so well. She hadn't realized he'd want to learn to drive.

She couldn't help herself and relented. "Let me call the driver's license bureau and see if it would be okay for you to practice in a parking lot." Her heart beat faster when she saw his face light up with an enthusiastic smile.

"Well, now that we have that settled, we'd better get those flyers posted around town." She hurried and turned before her brother saw the telling heat on her cheeks. Luke knew her pretty well, and he'd be a merciless tease.

Chapter Ten

Madison watched Missy enter the coffee shop shortly after they arrived. Her eyes lit up when she spotted Madison, JC, and Luke. "Hi!" Missy said with enthusiasm.

"Hi. Thanks for coming, Missy." Madison smiled, pulling a chair out for her at their table. "You remember JC, right? This is my brother Luke."

"Hello, Luke, good to finally meet you. Of course, I remember JC, and it's nice to see you again." Missy hung her purse on the back of her chair.

"Nice to see you too, Missy," JC returned scooching his chair a bit closer to Madison, making more room. The coffee shop was long and narrow with round tables that normally held four people or less located in the middle of the room. Next to the wall, tall bar stools were tucked in under the long butcher-block style table for more seating. Madison had him pull over two extra chairs for their group.

Thaniel and Nate entered the coffee shop shortly after Missy. Introductions were quickly made between Missy, Luke, Nate, and Thaniel. They all placed their drink orders and sat down.

Madison shared some of the facts she'd learned about the process of locating missing children.

"There are over 400,000 children reported missing every year according to FBI's National Crime

Information Center, also known as NCIC. Amber alerts began in 1996. There are different types of missing children, such as family abductions, non-family abductions, and 91 % are runaways.

"One out of six of the children that are runaways become victims of child sex trafficking. Federal law requires that a report of a missing child be entered into the database." Madison glanced around the table and felt relief when they all seemed interested. She knew she tended to expound on a subject that was important to her.

"The many volunteers like me do all sorts of jobs. I help by distributing the flyers hoping to help locate the children.

"There are many levels of professional volunteers and staff and members who offer their support and services for this worthy cause," Madison finished her spiel.

"Sorry, I tend to ramble on. Any questions?" When their questions were all answered, she finished her now cold mocha latte. "It will save me a lot of time with you all helping to distribute the flyers around the area, so thank you. Hopefully, someone will remember seeing Briana's whereabouts and call it in.

"JC and I will go to the University of Nevada and that general area. Missy, would you prefer going to Sparks or some of the businesses around the Riverwalk District?" Madison asked.

"The Riverwalk area would work best for me. It's on my way back toward my apartment," Missy answered and took the last sip of her drink.

"We can go to the Sparks area and distribute a few there if it's okay with you since it's on our way back to the ranch," Thaniel said, glancing at Nate for his agreement. "I can't wait to tell Casey about this volunteer opportunity. If she'd been available, I know she would have loved to help today. I suspect she will be interested in helping out in the future."

"I'm sure any help will be appreciated. I will give you the contact number of the woman who heads up the volunteers. Or you can call the Team HOPE Volunteer number if you want to get more specific information about helping."

JC watched how passionate Madison spoke as she explained about the NCMEC's network.

Breathing in the perfume scent she wore intoxicated him. The fruity, exotic smell was different than what she'd previously worn. He knew that whenever he smelled fruit and flowers, he would always have memories of her.

JC stared intently at Madison, knowing someday that she would make a wonderful mother. He shook his head, trying to remove the picture of her pregnant with their child. If only it could be true.

Nate cleared his throat bringing JC back to reality. And although he detected amusement on Thaniel's face, Nate wore an angry frown on his.

Having been caught staring at Madison, JC hastily turned his attention back to the conversation. It soon became evident Missy had experience volunteering on other occasions by vocalizing her pertinent questions. Madison told them about preparing a room for Mindy, the missing little girl's mother who was staying with her from back east.

JC couldn't ignore his brother's quiet mood. He knew Nate was angry about something. Generous by nature, his twin had always been willing to give a helping hand. The only thing that he could think of for Nate's anger had to be he'd picked up on JC's attraction to Madison.

It wasn't his choice to fall in love with this woman of the future, but it happened. Nate would have to get over his anger.

He'd be on guard from now on. He'd do what he set out to do, find Henry, and get himself and Nate back home to where they belonged.

****

Madison became aware of Nate's coolness toward her. She contemplated what made him so reserved all of a sudden. He gave the impression he disliked her. She wondered if he resented helping her instead of spending the time on finding a way home.

"You don't have to help," she stated, deciding he resented her for involving them in the search for the little girl.

"Yes, ma'am, we know that we don't have to, but since we're here, we might as well be helping out."

Madison had a hard time ignoring Nate's tense tone. But it wasn't up to her to figure out Nate's problem. Her job was to get the flyers posted.

"Thanks for taking the time to help," she returned with a forced smile before turning back to the others.

Thaniel finished his coffee, then got up from his chair. "Guess we better get started. You ready, Nate?" Wordlessly, Nate rose, nodded his head, and followed Thaniel out of the coffee shop.

Madison watched the two men leave. Putting aside her hurt feelings of Nate's attitude was easier said than done. She couldn't help but want JC's twin to like her.

Not coming up with any reason for his attitude, she turned her attention back to JC, Luke, and Missy. All three were standing and waiting for her. Madison pushed aside her empty coffee cup and followed them out the door.

JC and Madison managed to put up their posters throughout the college campus and the surrounding area. They'd formed an organized routine of taking turns to hang up the flyers. It went faster with the two of them working together.

After several hours they were done. Madison looked at her watch, realizing that Mindy Collins would be at her house within the hour, and she wanted to freshen up before meeting the missing girl's mother.

Madison struggled to put aside her concern about Nate's coolness. Once she parked in the garage, she started to get out. JC put his hand on her arm, stopping her.

"Wait, you've been so quiet since we left the others at the coffee shop. I'm sorry if I've upset you." He withdrew his hand from her arm.

"What?" She shook her head. "I'm not upset with you. Sorry if I gave you that impression. Guess I have a lot on my mind." She watched him cock his head to the side and cross his arms over his chest, waiting for her to tell him the real reason.

"All right, I couldn't help wondering why your brother dislikes me. I hardly said a word to him."

"What did Nate say to you to make you think he didn't like you?"

She shifted in her seat, putting her hands on the steering wheel. "Nate didn't say anything. His displeasure came across like he didn't want to be there with us at the coffee shop."

"I doubt he dislikes you. It's more about the circumstances of us being here and the situation. We are both worried about finding Jacobs and getting back to our home. If it would make you feel better, I can call and talk to him."

"No, that's not necessary. I'm sure you're right. It's fine. Besides, I have plenty to worry about with my guest, who should be arriving anytime now."

JC swung his legs out the open car door. "If you change your mind, I can talk to him."

"Not necessary. I'm a big girl. Besides, if I have issues with Nate, I'd take it up directly with him." She looked over the roof of the car at JC. "You're right. I probably misinterpreted it."

****

Madison liked the woman the instant she met her. She'd been expecting a woman out of her mind with worry and grief but was surprised by the calmness and optimism coming from Mindy Collins.

"Thank you so much for putting me up. Your place is lovely, so warm and inviting. I appreciate you opening your home for me while I wait for Briana's return." Mindy sat in one of the cushioned wicker chairs on the patio.

"I'm happy to have you here." She looked up when JC came out onto the patio. "Mindy, I'd like you to meet JC." He walked over to the woman and held out his hand. She got up and shook it.

"It's so nice to meet your husband," Mindy said, adjusting her skirt as she settled back in her chair.

Madison was taken by surprise by the misconception and hurried to correct her. "He's not my husband. We're just friends. JC is staying here for a bit to help me out while I get ready to open my bed and breakfast."

"Oh, I'm sorry. My mistake," she offered quickly.

"That's okay, and we are good friends." Madison realized how compromising that sounded, amended. "I mean, we...ugh." She couldn't think of a way to explain without coming across wrong.

Mindy seemed to understand what she meant and chuckled. "How fortunate to have such a good friend." She then adroitly changed the topic to her frustration at the media for hounding her. "Hopefully, the reporters won't find out I'm staying here. Be warned, it could happen."

Madison listened to Mindy talk. She was a petite blonde woman with pixie features. The woman exuded a calming effect as she spoke.

"I live in Manhattan. That's where I'm originally from. My daughter Briana is the best thing that came out of my relationship with Mike. He'd had a promising future as a corporate lawyer, but met an anti-government man who'd influenced him. Brainwashed is the better term. I've observed his mistrust with the government on previous occasions but thought with some time or counseling he'd get over his paranoia." She shook her head. "He refused the counseling."

"That's too bad. How did you find out that Briana was missing?" Madison crossed her legs.

Mindy took a sip of her tea. "He used to be such a wonderful father. So, when he asked to have visitation rights with her for the summer, I agreed. The divorce decree stated he got her every summer for a month and every other holiday if he wanted her. This was the first time he'd asked since we divorced two years ago, which left me little choice. I believed he had an apartment or condo. He came to New York to pick up Briana, so I never knew about his living accommodations."

Madison got up and brought the pitcher of tea to refill her glass. "How frightening to find her missing when you came out here to pick her up."

"Yes, it was a shock. Every time we talked on the phone, Briana seemed to be happy, even mentioning some new friends she'd made. Not only did I not expect to find Briana had vanished, but I never expected to find Mike living in that awful military-style compound and so entrenched in that way of life. It stunned me when he met me at the gate wearing a khaki uniform." Mindy's lips twisted.

"Mike was truly concerned when he found out that I didn't have her. In my heart, I know he'd never do anything to cause Briana any harm. He adored her." Mindy looked down at her fingers crossed in a prayer pose. "I believed him when he said he didn't know where she was."

Mindy wiped away a tear and cleared her throat. "I'm sorry. I feel like I've been side struck by a mac truck, not knowing whether Briana is all right or not."

"Don't even think about apologizing. You have every right to be upset." Madison handed her the box of tissues. She thought this woman was so brave. She prayed they'd find her daughter alive and well soon.

"This is my first time out west. Under different circumstances, I would have loved exploring this beautiful region." Mindy lowered her empty glass to the table.

"I wish it were under better circumstances too. I hope when you get Briana back safe, you'll come back for a visit. You will have a free room here," Madison offered. "Anytime."

"We will see," Missy replied.

JC got up and went into the house. He came back out to the patio. "The timer just went off. Would you like me to take the lasagna out of the oven?"

"That's ok. I'm heading in now, JC." She followed him in the kitchen and pulled out the entrée. She adjusted the temperature before putting the garlic bread in.

"Would you uncork the wine, please?" she asked as Mindy's words came back. JC did seem like a husband helping her with the meal. If only—

\*\*\*\*

Later after dinner, when they were alone, JC handed her a gift-wrapped package.

At first, she didn't understand why he'd given her a box. "What is this?" she asked, almost afraid to know.

A faint light twinkled in his cerulean blue eyes as he smiled. "A gift," he responded enthusiastically. "Open it up."

Madison hesitated before tearing off the paper carefully. When she opened the lid seeing the trillion-shaped pendant necklace, she drew in a deep breath. "It's beautiful. Why?"

"I wanted to give you something to remember me by. And a thank you for all you've done."

"JC, you didn't need to do this. All the help you've given around the B&B has been more than enough. Besides, how could I ever forget you?" She swallowed back the lump that suddenly formed in her throat.

"I know, but I wanted to give you something. I hope you like it."

"I love it. I will treasure this forever. Thank you." She reached out her arms, drawing him in, hugging him with all her might.

He returned the hug, laying his chin on the top of her head and stood there until Madison pulled back.

Chapter Eleven

A few days after distributing the posters JC and Madison received a call for an impromptu meeting at the ranch. Thaniel and Casey welcomed them. Nate even appeared to be excited to see him and Madison.

"I'm sorry I was rude the other day," Nate apologized to Madison as soon as they walked in the door. "I didn't mind helping to post flyers."

"No worries. We all have those days," Madison responded, taking the seat Casey indicated.

JC listened as Sam introduced the other man. "This is my friend Joe Brown. He's a very knowledgeable shaman." They shook hands.

"Not only is Joe a healer and spiritual man, but he also knows about supernatural elements in this world. There are things beyond our human understanding, including traveling back and forth through time," Sam told them.

It was apparent that Sam admired and respected the older man. Even though they came from the same culture, Sam displayed a more refined demeanor, while the other man had been raised off the land.

Sam wore creased Dockers with a buttoned-down blue Oxford shirt open at the neck and shiny leather cowboy boots. His ponytail, neat and discreetly pulled back. The older man wore his long graying hair down the middle of his back with thin braids of hair bound with leather strips near his weathered brown face.

A leather choker with colored stones of turquoise in animal shapes drew JC's attention. Joe had on well-worn boots of brown leather with thinning soles, jeans, and a colorful T-shirt. New hope for his situation arose in him.

"Joe is a highly-valued member of my tribe. He's experienced a trip to the past yet managed to return home. I shared with him how you ended up here, and he had some insight to offer that might be helpful for you to go back where you belong." Sam walked over to the window. Standing in the sunlight, he motioned for Joe to speak.

Joe began holding out his hands. "My family has maintained Penross cave that contains a mysterious time-travel portal near Lake Tahoe. The cave gives off an unnatural greenish shimmer, but not from a natural source." He smiled wryly as if in recollection of the sacred place.

JC's mind raced with questions, but he patiently waited for the man to continue.

If he could leave today, would he? No. He had to find Henry first. He almost laughed at himself. The truth of the matter, he wasn't ready to leave Madison or this time behind—yet.

"There's a cupboard of dishes that's been pushed against that wall, hiding the entrance to the portal." Joe's eyes lit up.

"The tunnel is marked with symbols on the wall from the ancients leading to a larger room with symbols on the walls. The cave is humid with an underground hot spring that has water bubbling from underneath and a waterfall inside. There is an opening like a small skylight window that allows light and fresh air in."

Madison got up from her seat, brushing against JC's leg. JC felt a full-charged shock run up the whole length of him and looked up to catch the mirrored surprise in her face. He wanted to pull her back next to him, keeping her near his side.

"What does this have to do with time-traveling?" she asked, moving away from him as she paced about the room restlessly.

Joe chuckled, "Patience, miss. You can't hurry a story along."

Madison returned to the chair next to JC, folding her hands primly in her lap. This time she sat far enough away that their legs didn't touch. JC was disappointed by the distance she seemed to prefer. He liked having her near him where he could feel the energy from her body next to his.

JC looked at Sam, whose eyes seemed to travel back and forth from him to Madison. A knowing look brightened the man's deep brown eyes.

"A bird flew in from the small window directly into the waterfall that ran from the ceiling to the pool. I watched, waiting for the bird to come back. When it didn't, I knew there must be an exit from behind the waterfall." Joe paused and looked at all of them.

"When I walked through the waterfall to the other side, I found myself in a different season. It was now summer and nighttime. I walked back through the waterfall, then back to the entrance where I came in originally, and it was day, spring, and sprinkling. I was confused how it could be so different. Then I wished myself back to my grandfather's time. I was able to speak to him about the mysteries of the cave and understand the obligation our family is under." There was a moment of stunned silence, and then it seemed everyone spoke at once. The room's atmosphere radiated noisy excitement.

JC saw Madison's face whiten, and her lips thinned into a half smile. But before he could question what her apprehension was, Nate spoke.

Nate's eyes shone with excitement. "Do you think that passage could take us back to our time?"

JC sat straighter in the chair. "Only problem with that is we still haven't found Henry. You know we can't leave without him," JC reasoned.

"I vote we leave him behind. The authorities will eventually catch him," Nate said as he turned his attention to JC.

"You just don't want to leave," he declared with disdain, and his voice level raised. The room quieted down, and everyone looked between the two brothers.

"That's not true. I'm just as anxious to get back as you are. Only, I feel obligated to bring Henry back with us. He's the one who accused me of killing Petey. You might not have a reason to worry about him, but I don't want to find my neck in a noose anytime soon."

Thaniel jumped in. "Nate, JC's right. If he wants to clear his name, then he needs to bring Henry back to confess."

Casey added with a sweet smile. "Haven't we treated you like family? You aren't that anxious to leave us now, are you, Nate?"

Nate's face flushed with embarrassment. "No, ma'am. You've been mighty hospitable to me. I've learned quite a bit from Thaniel about the ranch that I'm anxious to try out."

"Good, we've enjoyed you being here and hearing your stories about the ranch when it first started and how things were done in your day." Her voice soothed some of the tension.

"We don't belong here." Nate defended himself, then relented. "JC is right, as much as I hate to admit it. We do need to find Henry before we can return."

JC chuckled. He could hardly believe that his brother admitted he'd been right. Nate rarely admitted to being wrong to his twin.

Nate seemed to read his thoughts and added, "If I didn't know better, I'd say you were planning on staying here. You've managed to learn how to use all the modern equipment and gadgets and whatnots. And..." Nate paused, turning to look accusingly at Madison. "You've got it bad for Madison."

A hush filled the room, Madison choked on her drink. JC reached over patting her gently on the back, "I'm very obliged to Madison for taking me in and teaching me all the things she has. I don't have it *bad* for her as you so rudely implied. We're just friends. Right, Madison?"

"Ugh, yes of course," she agreed hesitantly.

Nate's eyes shifted toward Joe. "Is it a portal back to our time or not?" he asked bluntly.

"Yes, it will take you back. I found that I had to spend about half an hour preparing and visualizing before I walked through the tunnel to a time I wanted to be. First time I went through, I asked to go back to my grandfather's time.

"I remembered him when I was a child. He'd influenced my life to follow the direction of my heart. The second time, I went to my mother's village when she was a young woman. I spent time getting to know her. The last time, I went to the future to meet and spend time with my grandchildren. I wanted to see if our beliefs and traditions were still observed."

Nate looked happy at the news. "Then all I'd have to do is get back to that cave and go out the tunnel?"

"Yes," Joe admitted. "I will show you where it is." He swirled his hands around the room encompassing everyone in the room.

"How about if I go back home alone? Would you be able to find Henry and return without me?"

JC wasn't surprised by his brother's offer. He'd known that Nate was anxious to leave.

"That would be acceptable to me. I'm sure Mother must be worried sick by now. It's been over a month since we've been gone, but we don't know how long it's been for her."

Sam moved back to the others, standing with his arms crossed over his chest. "Joe, do you think it would make a difference if they both don't return at the same time?"

"I can't imagine it would. I believe Nate and JC all have a choice when and whether to return." He looked intently at JC with a questioning look.

Nate seemed to start with the realization. "That means I can choose the time I want to return. What if I go back to the next day after we traveled to the future? Mother wouldn't have had time to be worried about us then." He gave a sheepish grin toward Casey and Thaniel. "You both have been wonderful to me. I appreciate everything you've done, but I feel like I need to go."

JC saw the resolve on his brother's face. He

thought about it for a moment. "That would be a good solution. You make sure Mother knows the truth. I'd be willing to stay here until we get Henry and then when we get back, I can convince him to tell the truth."

"Thaniel, I appreciate you and Casey's hospitality, but I want to leave as soon as possible." Nate turned to look at Joe. "When can you take us to the cave?"

\*\*\*\*

Later, Madison left JC to his own devices. Feeling vulnerable and anxious with his impending departure, she was unprepared for this onslaught of emotions.

He'd be gone soon.

While they were at Thaniel's ranch, she'd struggled to be supportive and interested in Joe's solution for their return.

Shaking her head, she realized her heart felt like it was breaking. These feelings were not how she envisioned her life when she fell in love for the first time.

She had plenty to occupy her with helping Mindy to find her daughter, but her mind wouldn't cooperate by letting go thoughts of JC. There wasn't anything she could do to change what was, so she had to accept the fact that JC could leave at any time. Even that knowledge didn't prevent her heart from beating faster at the thought that JC lived under her roof, at least for now.

She'd make every moment count.

Spotting the stack of bedding to be laundered, Madison decided to take her frustration out on domestic pursuits. She was bent over, sorting laundry, when JC came up behind her.

"The telephone is for you, it's Luke," he told her as

he held out the phone for her to take.

Madison put the sheets into the washer, dumped in the soap, and then turned the buttons to start the load. When she reached for the phone, their fingers touched briefly, and it was all she could do not to jump from the physical contact. Their eyes met and held. Time stood motionless for a fraction of a second.

A physical desire for JC hit her to the very core of her being. Stifling those needs wouldn't be easy. Especially knowing he'd be gone soon. She'd spend the rest of her life wondering what it would have been like to hold him, touch him, to become one with him.

"Luke is waiting."

Her gaze followed JC hungrily as he handed her the phone and left the laundry room. She listened, distracted by the conversation, and when she hung up, she tried to recall what Luke had said. Something about picking Paula up at the airport. The phone rang again.

"This is Mindy. I'm on my way back to the B&B. I wanted to give you a heads up that my ex, Mike, is coming over. Apparently, he wanted to talk in person."

"Not a problem. Feel free to use the entertainment room or the patio for privacy," Madison offered as she finished loading the washer and dryer and started the next load. Her head down as she turned to leave, she almost ran into JC. He put his hands on her shoulders to catch her.

"I didn't mean to startle you." Desire flared across his features. "I just wanted to make sure everything was okay."

She made the mistake of looking into his eyes, and her heart melted into a quivering mass. "Everything is fine. Mindy's ex-husband is coming to talk to her about their daughter."

"Let me know if there is anything I can do."

*Sure, kiss me and never let me go.* "I will." She nodded, turning away to hide her thoughts.

## Chapter Twelve

Briana closed her eyes. It was getting harder to be patient, waiting for Mister to let her go home. She wanted her momma. The Cowboy hero still hadn't come for her. Her daddy's friends had scared her, but Mister frightened her even more. She was lonely all by herself. Maybe if she prayed harder, God would hear her and send the Cowboy. She dropped her head, "Dear Lord..."

**\*\*\*\***

Daren climbed the steps slowly. He held the bag of items he'd bought her—a new set of clothes and a doll. Girls played with dolls and toys. The next time he went shopping, he'd get her a set of child's porcelain dishes and maybe a book for her to read. He didn't know much about little girls, but he hoped eventually she would come to believe she belonged to him.

It had been awkward when he'd run into his boss at the store. He'd had to come up with a story about a niece in a hurry. He could tell she'd been curious, but luckily, she hadn't asked for any particular details. He didn't like anyone to know his business.

At the top of the steps, he heard the girl speaking. His heart raced with fear. Had she gotten a cell phone? Not possible. The bedroom door remained locked every time he left. There were shuttered windows almost to the top where no one could have given her one.

Tiptoeing to the door, he put his ear next to it.

He felt a guilty relief when he realized she was only praying. If only she knew that he wouldn't hurt her. He planned to raise her as his own. When the time was right, they would marry. She'd be protected from all the evils of society, and she would make him the perfect wife.

When he heard her finish her prayer, he stomped out in the hall, making his presence known before he unlocked and opened the door. Briana knew the drill, bathroom first, then she would get her meal. After she came back from the bathroom, he decided to make an effort to be friendly.

"Hello. How are you doing today?" Not waiting for her reply, he added, "I brought you dinner and some other things I hope you will enjoy."

Briana's lip quivered, and her eyes were reddened from a recent cry. He held out the plastic bag until she took it from him.

"Go ahead and see what I got you." He waited for her to see the doll. It would please her, he was sure. "Do you like it?"

"I'm sure it's very nice." He was disappointed when she didn't take it out of the bag as he'd expected.

He grabbed the bag and removed the doll and pushed it to her. Then he pulled out the clothing he'd picked out for her. *I hope I got the right size this time.* He fixed a forced smile on his face.

"Thank you, Mister."

Daren searched for something else to say. He had no experience with girls. Or women, for that matter. "What is your favorite toy at home?" He cringed at the word home. He didn't want her to remember that.

"Cowboy hero," Briana said simply.

"I don't know what a Cowboy hero is," Daren replied. He couldn't visualize that kind of toy and decided to admit his confusion, hoping she'd explain.

"Cowboy hero is a doll. He's a character from a movie I like about toys. Haven't you watched those movies?" She tilted her head and looked up at him.

"No, I don't usually go to the movies." He admitted he was at a loss for more words. He picked up the takeout food and handed it to her. "Your food is getting cold."

\*\*\*\*

Joe led JC, Nate, and Madison to the cave that would take them back home was located.

The early morning temperature remained brisk as the group hiked up foothills on the trail near the eastern shore part of Lake Tahoe. The narrow dirt trail was like any other hiking trail. Everything seemed so ordinary JC wondered how a time portal could be in such a place?

They had been walking off the main path for half an hour when they reached their destination. The spectacular view of the lake surrounded by the forest offered a peaceful setting. A bald eagle circled above. The natural scent of pine and the vast forest filled the air.

JC had tried to talk his brother into waiting until they could all go back together. But Nate had stood firm on his decision to leave. He promised to clear JC's name and return if possible. Joe offered to remain at the cave site for three days in case Nate returned. Joe had brought a backpack full of supplies with him.

"The portal's in here," Joe said as he removed a

key and unlocked the wooden door to an old mining tunnel. A *danger keep out sign* was posted on the door. Joe went in through the entrance first, beckoning the rest of them to follow him.

JC's curiosity prompted him to study the room. The room was warm, with a slightly musty and smokey smell. It had a high carved rock ceiling with roughhewn walls and modern lanterns scattered around.

The room was furnished just as Joe had described it would be. A small cot with a handmade green and brown-colored Army quilt rested next to one wall with a woven rug under the bed. On the opposite side of the room, there was a small kitchen area with a table, two chairs, and a dish cupboard.

Joe moved the cupboard aside with little effort as it was on small wheels. The cupboard hid the doorway to the tunnel, like a sentry protecting its treasure.

Joe advanced inside the hidden access and was gone for only a moment before returning. "Follow me."

Nate wore a grim but determined look. He turned to look at JC, his voice stiff, "I will do what I can and if it's possible, I plan to come back."

JC patted his twin on the shoulder. "I know you will. Tell Mother I love her. If I don't make it back home, good luck." JC pulled his brother into him and gave him a bear hug.

Nate seemed startled at first, then his eyes misted before he blinked. He returned the hug. Then he turned toward the others gritting his teeth and waved before following Joe into the tunnel.

JC hoped his brother would make it safely back home. Even knowing it was for the best, he immediately felt the loss. Anxiously he waited as Joe came back into the room alone.

"He's made his choice. He's gone," Joe confirmed, gesturing off in the distance with his hand.

"Should we wait around to see if he returns right away?" Madison asked, her words breathed against his neck as she spoke, and JC felt a measure of solace that she'd moved closer to him and put her hand around his back offering comfort.

"No. He won't be coming back today," Joe answered. "After I take you back to your car, I will stay here for the next few days."

Nate was where he belonged, back at their ranch. JC reached around pulling Madison even closer to his side and put his arm around her shoulders. His heart swelled with the knowledge that he had more time with Madison. It felt right that he belonged here.

Knowing wishes and logic warred within his heart, he knew there could only be one outcome. When he sighed, she turned to look at him, her eyes filled with her concern.

"I'm going to miss Nate. It was comforting knowing he was alive and well living on the ranch with family. I know he will do what he promised. Now, let's go home." Conscious he'd used the term home to describe Madison's house, JC knew he'd never felt so much at home as he did here with this woman. The trek down the side of the Sierra Nevada foothills to the car was somber.

**** 

Not long after they got home from the cave, Casey called to see how JC was handling his brother's return home. Madison and Casey had immediately become friends.

Casey was amazingly observant, or maybe Madison wore her heart on her sleeve, because she commented. "You're in love with him, aren't ya?"

Madison choked, "I don't know what you mean." When silence on the other end of the phone lengthened, she asked, "Is it really that evident?"

Casey laughed. "I can tell you love him. It has to be hard to know he will leave you behind when he follows his brother."

"It is, but I understand and want what's best for him. I've never been in love before. Now that I've found him, it is hard to know I will lose him. I know I can't hold him back, it wouldn't be right."

"It'll work out. It's not going to be easy. I hope we can be friends, no matter what happens," Casey said.

"Yes. I'd love to stay friends." Madison's lips curved in a half-smile, realizing how much this new friendship meant to her, especially after JC was gone.

As she hung up the phone, she thought about what Mindy Collins was going through, putting her problem in proper perspective.

She found Mindy pacing the floor, wringing her hands together, clearly agitated after Mike had left. Yet, she'd been insistent that she was fine. Madison brought her a cup of steaming chamomile tea. "Here, this always helps me settle down a bit. If you prefer, I have some wine. Want to talk about it?"

"Thanks, I better stick with tea. There's no news. I spoke with my ex. He's claiming that the government may have kidnapped Briana." She rolled her eyes. "My God, I can't believe I was ever married to that man. He's crazy as a loon!"

"I'm sorry," Madison offered. "I'm sure his

conspiracy theory doesn't make it any easier at a time like this."

"People change. Sometimes mental illness causes strange behaviors. He's not normal. I know that." Mindy continued to pace. "He told me the FBI went out to the compound to see him, and that didn't help with his suspicions.

"But I can't help thinking that there was something more I could have done. After all, I was married to the man for seven years. I saw him retreat into himself, closing off from our family and me. He was a good man, and I still love him." Mindy shook her head with a sad smile. "Sorry, I try not to look back on the past. I know I need to focus on Briana, what's important right now." She brought her hands up to cover her face and wept.

Madison watched the woman's shoulders shake. This was the first time she'd observed the usually controlled woman break down and lose her composure. Madison's heart ached for her, so she did what came naturally and wrapped Mindy in a motherly hug. She felt her small body stiffen at first, then she relaxed and put her arms around Madison. They stood like that for only a minute before Mindy seemed to gather her strength back.

"Thank you. I miss Briana so much, and I don't know what I'll do if she doesn't come home with me. No, I haven't given up hope. In my heart, I believe my little girl is out there somewhere." She wiped away her tears. "I'm going to go see Mike again and see if I can get more details out of him."

Madison saw her determination now that she had formed a plan of action. "Do you want me to drive or come with you?"

"Thanks, if you don't mind. I'll let you know when I'm going." Mindy managed to smile.

"Let me know if there's anything else I can do." Madison's eyes transferred to JC when he came out on the patio. He was followed by Luke and Paula holding their baby Forrest. Forrest saw Madison, and he reached for her, speaking in his baby language.

"Come on, Buster," Madison's mood lightened up considerably at the sight of her nephew. She'd missed him. She held her arms out to the child, and when he was positioned on her hip, she turned to introduce Mindy. "This little guy is Forrest, my nephew, and his mother, Paula."

"Nice to meet you." Paula shook her hand.

"I'm sorry about your daughter. Luke told me about her. My prayers are with you both."

"Thank you. We can use all the prayers we can get." Mindy touched Forrest's chubby arm. "Hello, Forrest," she said to him. "He looks like both of you." Forrest gave Mindy a toothless grin and chortled. "What a cutie," she added.

Paula walked over to the settee. "Yes, he's a cutie, but he can be a little demon when he doesn't get his way."

Luke nodded his head in agreement. "Just like his old dad."

"It's not something to brag about, dear," Paula said slugging him in the shoulder.

Madison listened to the interchange between the women as she bounced around her nephew. They shared stories about their children. It seemed to comfort Mindy to talk about her daughter.

She walked around the planters filled with flowers and foliage that were scattered on the patio, pulling a dead bloom from the mix. The flowers gave off a pleasant scent, and the baby reached for the colorful blooms. She laughed, pulling back. "No, sweetie, you just want to undo all Auntie Madison's hard work."

JC moved closer to the group. She'd noticed how quiet he'd been. They hadn't yet had a chance to talk about what he'd learned since they'd left his brother at the cave. He'd needed space and time alone with his thoughts. What was he thinking, she wondered? Was he feeling left behind now that his brother had returned to their time?

She wasn't ready for JC to go. Not yet. Not ever. Shifting Forrest to the other hip she looked away uncomfortably from the others. Lord, how could she be so self-centered? Disgusted with her thoughts, she felt gratitude for Forrest's distraction when he leaned toward a flower. She relented and gave him one of the blooms.

Of course, JC would be missing his family and everything he knew back in his time. Why would he want to stay here any longer than he had to? He managed a ranch. Here he was little more than a handyman. Her handyman.

Not that he couldn't do more, and he'd proved it by mastering the computer and by all the other technology he'd learned how to operate. He was bright and could easily succeed in this time. If she didn't know better, she'd swear he belonged here in this century.

Although, he'd probably be better off at his ranch with Thaniel.

When he'd chosen to stay with her after they'd

found his brother, she'd realized he'd stayed because he felt something for her. She knew he felt gratitude for rescuing him, but there was a mutual emotional connection between them.

Pacing around the patio, she walked along the perimeter. Forrest seemed to pick up on her distraction and held his arms out to his father. She brought him to Luke. He took his restless son, giving her a sympathetic squeeze on the arm.

JC watched Luke and Paula pass their son back and forth. They appeared so content to be together. He'd been impressed with how much the two of them were with their child. He saw the love and friendship between them. They seemed to have a wonderful life together.

He wanted that kind of relationship too. Unfortunately, the one he wanted to have that life with was out of his reach. He looked over at Madison.

His heart ached, and he felt a powerful sense of misery. Madison belonged here, and he belonged back in 1896. The only thing he'd have would be his memories of her. That was all there was to it.

"Hey JC, why are you scowling?" Luke directed his remark to him, breaking his glum thoughts.

"Sorry, I was daydreaming." JC smiled and put his morose thoughts aside. "Bet you are glad to get that beautiful wife of yours home. Not to mention this adorable little guy."

"Yeah, I am. Next time Paula goes back home, I'm going with her." He tossed Forrest in the air, then hugged him when he came back down. Forrest recognized this method of play and was laughing.

"Do you still have family back there in Michigan?"

JC asked, moving over to sit in one of the chairs next to Paula and Luke.

"Nope. Except for Paula's family, Madison is all the blood family I have left. Mom died a few years back, and we lost touch with our dad years ago. But we still have lots of friends back there." He held his arms out to give Forrest to Paula. The child seemed content to be passed around.

JC noticed how natural Madison was with the baby. She'd be a terrific mother. He had to stop wishing for the moon. It wasn't going to happen. They needed to find Henry so the two of them could go back soon. Otherwise, it would be more challenging than it already was going to be to leave Madison.

He looked away into the dusky star-filled night. The moon was starting to peek over the mountains. Crickets chirped, and the night sounds seemed to intensify. The air was cooling down, but still warm from the day's sun.

Nate should be back home with their mother by now. He wondered what his brother would tell her about their time in the future. Nate always had a good way with words. He wouldn't need to convince his mother of JC's innocence. She'd know neither of her sons was capable of killing an innocent person.

Madison and Mindy walked into the house talking. They were so different. Yet there seemed to be a common bond. They both had experienced a missing child. Mindy had a quiet and reserved demeanor, whereas Madison had a more outgoing personality.

She was perfectly proportioned to fit his frame. Shaking his head at where his thoughts led him, he looked over at Luke, who was giving him a knowing look. He hoped the yearning for Luke's sister didn't show and shifted uncomfortably in his seat.

"Hang in there, my friend," Luke mumbled as he rose from the settee and pulled Paula and their sleeping child with him. "Guess I better get my family back home. After traveling almost two thousand miles, it's been a long day for Paula and the kiddo."

JC followed the two to the door after they bid Madison good night. He watched them meander down the stone pathway that led to their little house. A trip like Paula's would take weeks. If he'd told someone back home that someday people would fly two thousand miles in a day, they would laugh at him. Yep, he was going to have to watch himself with all the knowledge he'd picked up while here.

Chapter Thirteen

Briana waited as she heard Mister come up the stairs. She'd been a good girl and straightened the bedcovers, neatly putting the doll he'd brought to her earlier by her pillow. Mister liked it when she had everything neat and tidy.

When the lock turned, she was waiting with a smile. She'd decided to be extra polite and friendly like her mommy had told her.

"Hello, Mister. Thank you for coming to take care of me."

Mister looked surprised for a moment, and then he pointed to the bathroom. "Hurry. I don't have much time to wait."

He held another bagged kid's meal. His eyes scanned the small room, and then he nodded his head approvingly. "You did a good job on cleaning up the room." For the briefest of moments, Briana saw him smile, then his scowl returned. "Hurry up."

Briana hurried to the bathroom where she pottied, then carefully washed her hands and face before returning to the bedroom. Mister didn't say anything more. He closed the door and silently left.

Briana was surprised when he returned a short time later. He usually stayed away for a longer period. This time, he brought a TV with a DVD player with some kid movies. The movie she loved was among the collection. He put it on a wooden stool and plugged it in. After he got the TV going, he showed her how to operate it. "Do this and this and turn off the TV before you go to sleep," he warned in a gruff voice.

Briana watched him warily as he left. He wasn't all that bad, she decided as she turned on the first movie to watch. Mister reminded her of the school bus driver. Mr. Pope acted grumpy and pretended he didn't like any of the kids, but when someone got hurt, Mr. Pope became very upset.

She was hungry and looked in the kid's meal bag. There were yogurt and apples to go with her hamburger. She grinned. The last time he'd brought her food, she'd told him burgers and fries weren't healthy for little girls. Mommy told her that. Then the grin faded when she remembered. If only he would let her go home. She missed Mommy.

****

Madison was deeply engrossed in her work the following day when Missy walked into the room carrying two mocha lattes.

"Here, I thought we could both use a treat." After handing Madison a large cup, she plunked down in the visitor's chair across from Madison.

"There's another one of those threatening letters telling us to stop destroying the environment from one of those left-wing anti-establishment groups. I think it said something like *put a stop to it or else. Yada, yada, yada. You know the spiel.*" Missy shook her head.

"Thanks." She took a cautious sip of the chocolate-laced coffee and sighed in pure contentment. "Anything else I need to be aware of?" She searched her friend's face with concern when Missy's lips twisted in scorn.

"Daren called in again that he was going to be late. Said something about having a doctor's appointment. Humph! Don't you think it's odd that he's suddenly started calling in and taking a lot of time off lately? I think something's going on."

Madison looked out the open door into the outer office and lowered her voice. "What do you mean something's going on?" She got up to close her office door.

"He's been fanatically punctual during the time he's worked here, but now and the past week, he's calling in, not returning after lunch or not showing up at all. I bet he's doing drugs."

"Come off it, Missy. He doesn't seem like the type to do drugs. Daren's different." When Madison saw her eyebrows rise, she admitted, "He's weird. My guess is he wouldn't do drugs or abuse alcohol because he has control issues. He's definitely obsessive-compulsive. But drugs, I'd have to say you are way off the mark." She shook her head.

"Ever notice the love-hate tattoo on his knuckles?" Missy frowned. "In my abnormal psych class, we learned about people who get tattoos like his. They get them in prison or jail."

"So, you're saying he's been in jail?"

"It's a good possibility. I asked myself why he'd be in jail? Since I couldn't come up with anything, I did an internet search, but I didn't find him listed. So, I have to admit if he was in jail, I couldn't find his name or why. Maybe he changed his last name."

"Missy!" Madison shook her head in dismay. "You are just looking for something against him."

"The other strange thing, you know that letter I told

you about that came today from the radical group? Well, they have a unique logo on the envelope, and I've seen that same logo on a letter that came from Daren."

"What letter?" Madison sat up straighter.

Madison thought about Daren. He was quiet, and not much of a socializer from what she could tell. He was a very private person. She hadn't known about any of his family, especially a niece until she ran into him shopping.

He was such a quiet man. But picturing him doing jail time seemed out of character to her, unless it had been when he'd been a juvenile. He'd always appeared to be a by-the-rules kind of man. At first, she'd thought JC's suspicions were unwarranted, that he just didn't understand the computer nerd type of today's male.

"Could I see this logo on the envelope that came in the mail?" She waited patiently as Missy went to retrieve it.

When she came back, Missy held out the envelope addressed to her company and the one that was addressed to a Senator in Washington, DC for her inspection. "It's a match. Odd that Daren would leave this lying around. What do you think he is doing with this logo stamp?"

"I'm sure it's not a good thing. I better put this back in case he shows up."

Madison rubbed her head when it started to pound. *Now what?* There was enough to worry about without adding Daren to the mix. If he was part of this leftist group, he could be potentially dangerous. As the manager of the company, it was her job to ensure everyone's safety.

\*\*\*\*

When Madison arrived home that evening, she'd felt the heavy weight on her shoulders. It was raining and windy, so she ran into the house after picking up the mail.

Walking into the foyer, she began looking through the stack of bills, when she came across a letter addressed to her from Michigan. Curious, she flipped the envelope over, seeing the stamped return address with the name of Penny Smithfield. Not recognizing the name, she started to rip open the letter when she looked up seeing JC standing there.

JC wore a grim look. Madison promptly walked over to the vestibule table and put her purse and the stack of mail down. "What's wrong?"

"I received a call from Sam," he said as he paused. His eyes had a look of purpose, as if he was waiting to see her reaction.

"And?" Madison prompted, feeling her stomach flutter in dread. She knew all too well news from Sam meant it had to be something that would affect them.

He drew in a deep breath. "He's caught Henry Jacobs, and I can go home anytime now."

"Oh," Madison managed to say, looking at the floor. She wasn't able to bring herself to ask when he was going to leave. She'd expected or hoped to have him here with her for at least a few more days or longer.

They stood staring at each other in awkward silence, waiting. JC was the first to speak. "You will probably be glad to get rid of me and have your house back to yourself."

"Why would you say that?" Confused, she tried to remember if she'd given him the impression she wanted him gone.

"I've been here for over a month. You have been so generous to put me up and help locate my brother. I don't know what I would have done without you." His eyes betrayed his misery.

"The time you've been here has been more to my advantage. Without you, it would be months more before I would have been able to open up my B&B." Her voice was raspy with raw emotion. "You are welcome to stay here for as long as you want or need to."

"I don't want you to think that I stayed at your place only because I'm grateful. It is because I wanted to be near you. For as long as fate would allow."

Madison's vision clouded with tears. Darn. She swiped away the droplets with her fisted hands. Just the thought of losing the man she'd come to care for so deeply hurt.

As if he'd read her thoughts, he pulled her into his arms, kissing her forehead. "I will be sad leaving you behind." She could feel both of their hearts beating fast as if in harmony.

When she attempted to speak, he put his finger to her lips. "No, let me finish."

Blindly, she nodded her head, allowing the tears to drip unchecked down her cheeks.

"I care for you. More than any man in my position should care for a woman. If things had been different, there isn't a thing in the world that would have kept me from you. I love you."

"I love you too." Madison's heart soared as if on wings and then crashed just as swiftly as if dashed to the ground. "I thought it was just me. That I was the only one who felt this way."

The smile he wore was bittersweet. Shaking his head, he admitted, "I've felt off-balance since the moment I met you. When I awoke to find you bending over me, I thought you were an angel. Since the third day I was here, I realized what I felt for you was more than a mild attraction. Knowing I would be leaving, it didn't seem fair to pursue a relationship with you. I fought to keep my feelings under control. My intention didn't work. I still fell in love with you."

Madison palmed the tears from her cheeks. "Really?" When he nodded his head, she threw her arms around him. Her breath came in a long drawn-out sigh of contentment.

It took a few seconds for the low-toned voice that came from behind them to register with Madison. She looked over and saw Mindy but didn't pull back.

"Ah, excuse me." Mindy was blushing in embarrassment. "I'll just grab my sweater from the chair and be out of your way."

"You are fine. We were just having a discussion," Madison said, realizing how lame her words sounded. It was pretty evident to anyone they were having more than a discussion.

Shifting nervously from one foot to the other, she watched Mindy make her way out the French doors to get her sweater, then retreat the way she'd come.

"Come on. Let's go into the living room so we can talk." Taking JC's hand, she led him into the other room closing the door behind them.

"Back to the part about love," Madison said as soon as the door closed, she moved closer to his chest. "I believe we agree that we love each other.

Unfortunately, there is no solution. I can't come with you. You can't stay here."

"In my heart, I feel as if I belong here. More so than my own time. I know it sounds crazy."

"Not to me, it doesn't. Please hold me, JC," Madison requested as she lifted her face to receive his kiss.

JC answered her plea eagerly. At first, the kiss was light and gentle. Slowly and seductively, it turned into something more demanding, more intense. Madison felt her heart quiver in her chest as the kiss took its toll on her equilibrium. The floor seemed to sway under her feet, and when she felt the sharpness of the wooden coffee table behind her legs, she looked in surprise at JC. They'd moved to the other side of the room without her knowledge.

She beamed with satisfied delight. His deep blue eyes were open. The pupils dilated with passion. There was a sense of accepting hopelessness between them as they held onto one another.

At this moment, all barriers were gone between them. There were no tomorrows, only today. Madison would extract every second of joy while she could. When he brought his mouth to hers again, this time his tongue gently touched her lips before he deepened the kiss.

His eyes gazed into hers as he watched her reaction. Madison held her breath as her heart met his in a slow dance. She couldn't get enough of him. His hand explored her back, slowly stroking from her shoulders to just the top of her behind, then back up again. The feeling was sensual and intoxicating. All her senses were charged with tingles that ran up her spine, and when she trembled, JC stopped.

"This feels so right. I want you desperately." He groaned, shaking his head as he pulled away from her. "We have to stop this before it's too late."

"I think it's already too late. I want you too," she whispered in a raspy voice. "I've never slept with a man before. But I need you." Her voice carried a plea, and she held her hands out to him.

JC shook his head, "No. I can't do this to you. You've saved yourself for your future husband. I would feel like a thief if we made love."

"There will be no husband. If we aren't meant to be, I will have no other man," she stated with certainty.

"I wouldn't be able to live with myself if I dishonored you. There is someone special out there for you. You weren't meant to be alone. You love children, someday you will have your own." He moved away to the door turning the knob.

"I have decided to leave tomorrow. Sam will pick me up and take me to the cave with Henry." Then he was gone.

Madison's heart shattered into a million pieces. She'd offered herself to him, and he'd refused. But she now knew that he loved her, and it mattered. They were star-crossed lovers. He belonged back in 1896, and she belonged here. They both had a mission. She would always need to help other families find their missing children. Pulling that bit of knowledge into her, she promised herself to be strong—tomorrow. Tonight, she could grieve losing JC.

Chapter Fourteen

The following day dawned, and the dismal gray clouds reflected his mood. Today, JC would leave. Today, his life would feel empty. The house was quiet yet, as it was only 5:00 in the morning.

JC looked around the room. He'd put all the shaving things, toiletries, and toothbrush, away in a plastic bag to be thrown out.

Then he'd taken all his neatly folded clothes from the little dresser and the closet and set them aside. There was too much to take back with him. He would leave all the things he'd purchased behind. She could give them away. He caressed the blanket. It had been a handmade jean quilt that Madison had told him she'd made. He'd liked sleeping under it, knowing she'd spent time putting it together. He'd like to take the quilt with him as a memento.

The room was ready for a new guest. It was almost time to leave. He felt satisfied with all the repairs and improvements he'd made while he was here. It would make it easier for Madison.

When he walked into the kitchen for coffee, Madison sat at the table, cradling her face in her hands, and her shoulders were slumped. He felt the intense grief of losing her. If only it would have worked out for them.

"Morning," he said, moving to the stand of coffee

mugs, chose the one he'd used every morning for the past month, and poured his coffee.

Madison straightened up in her chair. "Morning." Her voice held a false ring. "What would you like for breakfast? How about my special sour cream chocolate chip muffins?" She moved to rise.

"I don't have much of an appetite today. Coffee and a piece of toast will suffice."

"Let me put it in the toaster for you," she offered, again starting to rise, but JC waved his hand for her to stay.

"Thanks, I think I can handle the task." He put the slice of bread into the toaster and pushed the lever down. He reached into the cupboard for a plate. When it popped up, he buttered and put jam on it. He brought it to the table and sat next to Madison. Taking a sip of his coffee, JC searched for words to dispel the tension.

"Sam will be here at eight. I left my belongings in the room. I know you'll need to get rid of them, but they are out of sight." He took a bite of the cardboard-tasting bread and chewed.

She looked up at the kitchen clock above the sink. "Almost three hours."

"I thought I'd finish hanging the decorative lights on the patio before I go."

"You don't have to," Madison replied, her back ramrod stiff.

"Yes, I know. It will keep me busy while I wait for Sam." When he saw her lift her brows and open her mouth to argue, he added, "Let me do this, please. Waiting around with nothing to do but think will make it harder. We both know how miserable we feel." He watched her nod her head, then turn to leave.

While JC was hanging the fairy lights on the patio, he looked around the outdoor living area. It had been the place of many happy gatherings in the short time he'd been here. He liked how the natural stone flooring and the planters, filled with flowers, scattered around gave off a sense of homey warmth. Maybe his mother would like him to make her a similar place to relax. He'd tell her about it.

Out of the corner of his eye, he saw Madison talking to Mindy. They seemed unaware of him. It was harder than he thought it would be saying goodbye to Madison. Should he kiss her again? No, he would shake her hand. No. He would hug her. Or maybe kiss her on the cheek. Guess that would be an acceptable way to leave.

Shaking his head, he laughed at his indecision. This was crazy thinking. But when a man would say his last goodbye to the woman he loved, the process required some thought. It would have to be the last kiss—one he could store in his memories of her. He finished hanging the lights and was putting away the ladder when the doorbell rang.

It was Sam.

Time to go.

He stowed the ladder, then took one last long look around the area, trying to memorize all the details for when he was gone. When his eyes fixed on Madison standing in the foyer, her loveliness stole his breath.

More significantly, her inner beauty stole his soul. He couldn't stop the sharp intake of breath. He'd hoped it would be easier. *Come on, JC, you knew from the start she wasn't meant for you. You let down your guard. Now both of you will suffer the consequences.*

Luke followed Sam in the room. "Morning, JC. I saw Sam pull into the drive and thought I'd better come over and say goodbye to my fishing buddy. Madison told me you were leaving today." He'd put his hands in his jean pockets and leaned against the door frame.

"I planned to stop by after I got the lights put up to say goodbye," JC offered as he walked over to Luke and held out his hand.

After shaking JC's hand, Luke grinned, then gave him a bear hug. "You have to know by now. This family gives hugs."

"Yes. I know." He noticed that Sam stood by the door with his arms crossed over his chest with an amused look on his face. "I have one more person to say goodbye to, and then I'm ready to go." He faced Madison, who stood next to her brother.

"I wish things could have been different." He moved in to kiss her cheek, but his mouth moved of its own volition to her lips. Disregarding the others in the room, he kissed her thoroughly.

When he finally pulled back, her face was flushed, and her eyes were sad. It hurt him more knowing she was suffering than his pain. "I've got to go." Then he turned to Luke and touched his head, flicking his hand in a quick wave goodbye. "I'm ready, Sam." Stoically, he turned and strode out the door to meet his destiny.

Henry Jacobs sat in the back seat of Sam's sedan shackled with handcuffs. His chin was raised in rebellion. "Henry," JC acknowledged as he slid into the front seat before turning to look at him. "I believe you owe me an explanation for accusing me of murdering Petey."

"I don't owe you anything or have anything to say

to you." Henry spat the words out, and his eyes glared with hatred and anger.

"I don't know how you can live with yourself. You falsely accused me of murder when you darn well know it wasn't me. So, as I said earlier, you owe me a reason why you'd lie to Sheriff Wilcox?" JC's anger was forced back as he spoke.

"We had a little conversation, and I wrote up Jacob's confession." Sam nodded in satisfaction as he maneuvered the car out of Madison's driveway. "We have our ways of getting to the truth." He winked at JC.

JC turned back to get one last look at the house. He spotted Madison standing on the front porch with Luke. Her brother's arm draped over her shoulders. She'd be okay—she had her family for comfort, he decided. She waved when she saw him look at her. Right now, the anger he felt to the core of his being with Henry sustained him from the pain of losing her.

When the car turned onto the main road, and Madison was no longer in sight, he realized what Sam had said. "What?" he enquired over at the driver.

"I figured this rascal was going to give you trouble, so I took steps to ensure his cooperation," Sam repeated.

"How'd you get him to confess?" JC asked, sitting back in the leather seat, amazed it had been so easy.

Sam turned his turn signal on and then made a right-hand turn onto the highway. "I have my ways," he admitted without going into detail. JC understood he'd dealt with Henry the way he'd had to.

Sam reached over to the middle of the seats and pulled out a manila folder, flipped open the cover, and withdrew a piece of paper. "Here, put this in your pocket."

JC's eyes widened in shock when he read the letter stating Donald Sorrel had paid Henry to implicate JC. Donald had been trying to get them to sell their ranch to him for years. He'd even made a play for his mother. "Is this true, Henry?" JC turned to look the man in his eyes.

"Yeah, but I'm gonna claim that letter's a lie." Henry ground out the words resentfully.

The rest of the short trip to the cave was made in silence. JC's thoughts were on the woman he'd left behind and the bleakness of the future without her. Sam seemed to understand his need for silence and remained quiet. Henry sat in the back seat, sulking.

When they reached the trailhead, Sam got out and opened the back door, unlocking the handcuffs from the steel bar by the seat. JC watched warily as Henry, still handcuffed to a tether, followed Sam. Even though the day was sunny with blue skies and fragrant with the crispness of pine and the mountain air, JC couldn't take pleasure in the day. He felt like a man walking to his death.

Loneliness stretched out before him. They'd made the short trip to the cave in record time. When they entered the cavern, it was like it had been before, tidy. Joe sat at a small table with a cup of coffee. He nodded a greeting before rising. Sam explained what they were going to do.

Joe moved to the cupboard, swiftly moving it out of the way. He told Henry how they would walk through the tunnel to the waterfall and then to the other side. Henry would go first, and JC holding the tether would follow.

JC watched as Sam unlocked the handcuffs and handed JC the tether. Then they walked into the tunnel. The roaring waterfall looked clear but thick. They stepped into the pool, and Henry walked through the waterfall passage to the other side, tugging on the tether.

"Thanks for all you've done," JC said as he gave him a last look, then went into the waterfall. The tether went slack. JC met a wall of rock. No Henry. Pushing and twisting around trying to find the entrance, he held his breath for as long as he could. Dang! Henry was gone.

It was no use. JC was stuck. He turned around and went back to the other side where he'd entered. Joe and Sam remained standing there. "There's a barrier I couldn't get through, and the tether broke," JC sputtered through a mouthful of water. He was drenched completely head to toe.

Sam motioned for him to follow him back through the entrance. When they got back into the room, Joe shook his head. "It's not time for you to leave, son. You haven't finished your quest here."

"Quest? How do you know that?" JC asked, puzzled. "What about Henry? He had no problem going through the opening of the time-travel portal."

Joe shifted in his seat at the table, seeming to contemplate his words. "Yup, Henry and Nate were a mistake. You were the one who was meant to come forward. Otherwise, you would have been able to go through the portal too.

"You came forward because the spirits have a task for you to perform. You must do this undertaking before you can return. I've heard about others who have tried to travel to another time who were denied entrance. When they finished their mission, only then were they able to leave without any trouble."

"I don't know what I'm here to do." JC, frustrated, gnashed his teeth. Henry was probably hightailing it out of town by now. He wouldn't hesitate to up and leave. They'd be forced to hunt him down.

Joe gripped his chin in deep thought. "Could it be something to do with that pretty young woman you've been staying with since you got here? Why do you think she was the one to find you?"

\*\*\*\*

Madison dragged herself into the house after putting in a full day at work. She kicked off her heels, picking them up in one hand, then rubbed at her throbbing temple. It had taken everything she'd had to focus. Her mind tended to drift to her memories of the time spent with JC. She hoped he'd made it back to his home and had been cleared of the murder charge by now. He'd been gone more than eight hours.

Her heart ached, already missing him. Things wouldn't be the same around here without her lost cowboy. Laying the mail on the foyer table, she heard a noise in the kitchen that sounded like someone opening a cupboard. Puzzled, she went to investigate. Mindy was gone, and her brother took Paula shopping. No one should be here.

She couldn't imagine a burglar raiding her kitchen cupboards. A heavy frying pan sat on the counter next to the sink. She made the distance in three steps picking up the pan. Not panicking, she grabbed her cell phone, ready to call 911 as she looked over her makeshift weapon. However, if he had a gun, she'd be wiser to leave and get help.

She could run, but her fear simmered and went to anger within seconds. One bonk on the head should be enough.

The jean-clad behind was kneeling under the sink, and when she exhaled the breath she'd been holding, his head flew up, hitting the cabinet with a loud bang. The wood shook on impact.

"Ow!" someone groaned.

"What—" The words stuck in her throat as she recognized JC.

After he managed to extricate himself from under the lower cupboard, he stood there like a lost puppy. His blue eyes were as intense as the ocean on a sunny day. "I was fixing the pipe that you told me was leaking."

The man looked incredible. He stood there with a wrench in one hand while rubbing his wounded head with the other. She'd never felt so happy to see someone as she did JC.

"Sorry, I didn't mean to scare you. I thought you were a burglar. Are you hurt?" She watched JC wince as he touched the tender spot on his head.

"You did say I could stay as long as I wanted. Unfortunately, Henry had no problems going through the portal, but a barrier prevented me from following. So, here I am, I came back."

Madison's heart skipped a beat with pure joy that he was still here. She'd dreaded coming home to an empty house all day, knowing he'd be gone.

"Of course, you're welcome to stay. I was just surprised to see you. I thought you were robbing me of my—ugh, mixing bowls?" After she realized how ridiculous that sounded, she burst into laughter.

A wide lopsided grin spread on JC's face too, and he joined in the laughter. They managed to laugh for a long time before Madison's laughter turned into tears.

"What's wrong?" JC asked with a bewildered look on his face, then pulled her into his arms to comfort her.

They stood there in silence while Madison regained her composure. "I thought you were gone for good." She skimmed her fingertips up and down his back, more to soothe herself than him. His body was hard from all the physical labor he did. Darn, he smelled wonderful. Salty from physical labor and musky from the lingering scent of the aftershave he routinely wore.

"Are you all right?" JC asked, continuing to hold her, his chin rubbing against the top of her head.

"Better than all right. I never expected you to come back." She wiped her happy tears away with the back of her hand. "But I'll take every precious moment I can get with you."

Madison could feel his lips against her hair, and shivers of desire cascaded down her spine. Being surrounded and safe in his arms seemed as if she'd found a slice of heaven.

"I'm so glad you feel that way because, unless I can find out what the fates or Joe calls the spirits have sent me here to do, I can't leave. It wouldn't be so bad if it weren't for my damaged reputation."

Madison pulled back. "As much as I hate the thought of you leaving, I'll try to help you figure it out so you can go home." Madison looked down and saw water flooding the floor from the cupboard he'd just come out from under. "Oh no!"

JC looked down where her eyes had gone. "Darn, I

thought I had turned off the water valve. Luke showed me how. He quickly moved away, going to the sink, and then he reached in and managed to turn off the gushing water. "There."

"I'll go get a towel and sop it up." Madison hurried to the linen closet and picked out her oldest towels, returning in record time.

They got on their knees and were soaking up the water when their heads bashed into one another.

Madison sat back on the soles of her feet. JC remained on all fours holding a wet towel between them. They stared into each other's eyes. Then, JC reached over and put his lips to hers.

Madison was lost to everything around her but JC until she heard Mindy clear her throat and comment.

"Gosh, it seems like I'm always interrupting something between you two. No, don't bother getting up." Mindy chuckled.

"I just wanted to let you know I have an early appointment tomorrow at eight with the district attorney's office. I may have to put off meeting with Mike, my ex, a day or so. I'll let you two get back to what you were doing before I so rudely interrupted." Her shoes clattered on the hard floors as she left.

They finished mopping up the water silently in harmony. "Where were we?" JC asked after he gave Madison the wet towels. She tossed them in the sink.

"I think we were in the process of kissing. Let's go out onto the patio since Mindy has returned to her room so we can continue where we left off." Madison peeked around the corner into the hallway and then out to the patio, making sure it was empty. She could hardly wait to have JC back in her arms. "Come on."

He looked down at the opened cupboard which held the water pipe waiting for the repair. "Guess I can finish up later." His eyes twinkled with satisfaction.

"Guess you can. We've got more important things to tend to." She gave him a saucy grin.

"Yep, that we do," he agreed easily.

****

JC lay in bed later that night, trying to calm his mind. The welcome he'd received from Madison when she'd found him in her kitchen had been more than he could have hoped for.

They celebrated with takeout Chinese food and opened a bottle of wine. Mindy had joined them for dinner before retreating to her room once more. She'd laughingly promised not to interrupt them again.

JC wondered what this task that he was supposed to perform could be. If Henry were smart, he'd head as far away from Carson City as he could. When he caught up with him, there was going to be hell to pay. He'd almost died because of his lies. The signed confession remained with him. If they were unable to find Henry, at least he held the proof of his innocence. A lot of good that did if he couldn't make it back.

He could hear the crickets outside his window and the tree branches swaying in the wind. It would be July 4th the next day. He'd been here over a month, but not long enough, in his opinion. At dinner, they'd discussed attending the festivities to celebrate Independence Day.

He'd have more days and evenings with Madison until he managed to do the task that fate had brought him to do. Every day he remained in this century he'd cherish.

They'd spend the day with Luke, his wife Paula,

and Forrest. Thaniel, Casey, and their kids would meet them for a picnic and barbeque on Madison's patio, and then they would head to the park, where they would watch the fireworks later that evening. Mindy would join them too.

JC crossed and then uncrossed his feet, staring sightlessly at the ceiling. The realization hit him— Madison had included his blood relatives, his relatives, along with hers. It was as if he was part of a family here.

When he thought about it, he realized he wasn't alone.

Still, the fact remained, he'd come to this time for a purpose. He just needed to figure out what that purpose was. Closing his eyes, he thought about his life on the ranch. He had to admit that he'd been feeling a bit of discontent before he'd come to this time. There had been the sense of something missing, something important.

True, his life had been privileged even though he worked hard. His days were filled with routine issues concerning the ranch and family. The Berkley family held a position in the local society and were well respected. He'd had plenty of opportunities to meet the available young ladies from the area. None of whom appealed to him. There was no one quite like Madison. She was exactly what he was looking for in a wife.

His mother would love her.

Maybe the reason he'd been brought to this century meant he needed to meet Madison. What he felt for her was more than pure attraction. In his heart, he believed she was his soul mate.

He couldn't stay here.

Madison couldn't leave. She was needed here, not only for her job but to be part of helping to locate missing children and reunite them with their parents.

Switching his thoughts back to his purpose for being here, he tried to find some logical reason. Nate could manage their ranch just fine without his help. Madison had needed help for repairs, but he didn't think that was a strong enough reason for him to end up in this century. He thought about all the other people he'd come in contact with, but no one came to mind except for an image of the missing girl, Briana.

He bolted up in bed. Suddenly, he knew.

That was it. He felt chills from the revelation. He had to be here because of the little girl. Not sure why, but somehow JC felt that was his purpose. He got up and paced the room.

Why else would he have visions of her even before he'd come here? The first time the image had appeared, he'd been strung up to hang. If he was here because of the child, then what was he supposed to do? Rescue her as she'd asked in the vision.

Unthinking, his body turned to the door, and he crossed the long hallway to Madison's room and knocked on her door.

"Is everything okay?" Madison asked when she opened the door and saw him. A nightgown covered her body to her knees. Her hair was mussed, and she squinted at him in alarm.

"I think I figured out why I'm here and what I'm supposed to do," JC whispered.

Madison gestured for him to come in. She indicated a settee in the corner with a reading lamp. "Have a seat. Now, tell me," she invited calmly.

JC watched intently as she adjusted her nightgown around her legs as she sat on the edge of the chair. The thought of where he currently was filled him with unwanted feelings.

Lord, she was so beautiful. Even in her modest coverup, she looked highly desirable. Her sleepy eyes, filled with concern, tugged at his heart. He shook his head, trying to dispel the shameful lust that came to him. Knowing he should have waited until morning, he stood up to leave.

"It can wait. I shouldn't have come to your bedroom."

Madison held her hand up to stop him. "I don't know why not. If you have something to say, say it, please. Sit." She encouraged him with a smile.

JC sat back down, aware of the sensual tension between them. He shifted in his seat, trying to hide his obvious attraction.

Struggling with his awareness to focus on what he came for, he tried to ignore her sexy bare legs or the womanly shape he could barely make out under her nightwear. His eyes wandered back to her legs—legs that seemed to go on forever. When he realized he was staring, he quickly averted his gaze around the room.

Madison seemed to be unaware of his discomfort. "You said you thought you knew the reason why you were brought here to this time?" she prompted gently.

His gaze met hers. He hoped that she had no idea what he was thinking about her. "Yes. Thinking about how we met, I believe I was brought here to help you with your hunt to find the missing child, Briana."

Madison sat up straighter. "Really? How so?"

JC had to force his thoughts back to the issue.

Every time he looked at her, he wanted her. "Well, I thought about my life and couldn't come up with any reason personally, but when I thought about you helping to find the missing girl, I felt like I was going in the right direction. It came to me how you'd taught me to use the computer and the internet to locate information that would help me get back to my time. I think that's the key to finding Briana."

Madison stood, rocked back and forth on the heels and balls of her feet with her hands drawn to her chin as she pondered the thought. "I'm sure the detectives already have searched the internet for clues. What can we do that would be different?"

"I don't know. But I would like to try."

****

JC couldn't get to sleep after he left Madison's room. Finally, after tossing and turning, he gave up. Since he had permission to use Madison's computer, he made his way to the office. He pulled up websites on missing children. He sat there reading the details of the children and their families and details of their anguish. Shaking his head in frustration, he pleaded for guidance. If he were here to do this task, there had to be a way.

Hours later, he went into the kitchen and put on a pot of coffee. While the coffee brewed, he was conscious that he was no farther ahead than when he'd started. Thinking back to when he found the information he'd needed about himself, he realized it had been about asking the right questions.

He hadn't been asking the right questions. Instead of reading about other missing children, he needed to figure out why they were missing. Many had been kidnapped by a family member or friend of the family. Others were kidnapped by men who had psychological issues or were child predators.

JC decided to focus on Briana's father, Mike Collins since he was local. She'd been kidnapped while in his custody. He looked up the man's name on the internet.

Surprisingly, it had quite a few articles about him being a high honor graduate from Harvard. He'd been touted as a brilliant up-and-coming lawyer in New York. He'd also received high praise in the newspaper on his masterful handling of a high-profile corporate litigation case.

None of that seemed to lead to a clue. Then, he thought about where he was now and added Reno, Nevada, to his name. A picture of an unkempt man in ripped jeans and a flannel shirt and hair that looked like he'd just gotten up stood next to a gate with a shotgun pointing downward. He looked thin and ragged. No longer dressed in the fancy dress of a corporate lawyer. The internet article showed a picture that said, "Compound leaders threaten to shoot trespassers."

Since the girl was kidnapped from the compound, would Collins have known the person? He pondered that question for a long time.

JC knew what he needed to do finally. When Madison came into the room, he told her his plan.

Chapter Fifteen

It was early, but Mike Collins agreed to let them come and speak with him. Madison drove them to the compound that was half an hour away. Mindy arranged for Madison and JC to ride with her. Mike wasn't friendly, but he cooperated. It was apparent he cared about his daughter.

"Mike, could you tell us about the day that Briana was lost?" JC watched the man as he ran his hands through his thinning hair before he answered.

"Bree was playing on the swing set in the back. I watched her play with the daycare kids. I didn't think she needed me, so I went inside to work on the research that I'm doing for my book." Mike paused and looked from JC to Mindy. "I was pretty involved in my research, Mindy, and you know how focused I can be?"

"Yes, I know," she stated dryly. "Please tell us about that day."

"You know I would never let anything or anyone harm our little girl." Mindy nodded her head and looked at Madison and then at JC.

Mike continued. "Well, Bree and I had breakfast in the community dining hall, and then we walked out to the playground. We talked, and she told me about you, school, and her friends. Some of the kids asked her if she wanted to play ball. I encouraged her to go. I sat on the bench and watched for about an hour. Afterward, I went back to work. My research took longer than I'd planned. The next thing I knew, it was dinner time. I couldn't find her. She didn't come in for dinner. Then someone said they saw her leave with a woman." He shook his head in self-condemnation.

"Did they know this woman?" Madison asked.

"No, that's why I thought it was Mindy." He looked guilt-ridden when he glanced at his ex-wife.

JC bet his last dollar the man was telling the truth. His gut instinct was that they were missing something vital. "Could you tell me if you had any visitors during the time your daughter was here?"

Mike Collins paced around the sparsely furnished room. His eyes were downcast.

"There were about five visitors that week. The delivery service we use for supplies. Terry Paul, brother to one of the men here. John Jasper, a tradesman who is helping to build a chicken coop. Daren Kushner, who consults for us, and Sy Williamson from a neighboring farm."

Madison's posture stiffened, and her mouth opened.

"Did you say, Daren Kushner?" she asked intently.

"Yes. Do you know him?"

"If he's the same person, then he works with me." She shook her head as if to clear the confusion he knew she had to feel. "This man, does he have a slightly balding head, tall, thin, and about fortyish?"

Mike rubbed his chin. "Yes. Kushner's a brilliant fellow. He has an engineering degree."

"Why would Daren come here?" Madison queried.

JC saw Madison's discomfort at this revelation and additional confusion written in her eyes.

"He's been coming out here for a year or so. I heard he was a friend of a friend and started hanging out here, learning more about our way of life. He offered a few suggestions, and now whenever there are any technical problems with computers, Daren's our IT fix-it man. But he never embraced the concept of living on the compound."

JC's ears perked up at this information. He knew he hadn't liked Daren when he'd met him at Madison's office. Although not sure why he'd had a strange feeling. It could have been jealousy, as the man seemed too familiar with Madison. "What do you know about him?"

"Why? Do you think he knows anything about Bree?" Mike demanded. His intense look of pain supported the fact that Mike hadn't had anything to do with his own daughter's kidnapping.

"I don't know, but we are trying to talk to all the people who may have come in contact with your daughter." JC promised to do everything in his power to help find their little girl. If it were his daughter, he'd hope for all the help he could get.

Mike nodded his head in acceptance, his shuttered eyes shifting toward his ex-wife briefly. Pain and guilt were written on his face. JC felt sorry for the man as it was clear he still loved his wife and child. He'd lost his family all for a cause JC couldn't understand. In his mind, JC decided his family would always come first.

Why would Daren spend time with the anti-government group? After a year and six months of working with him, Madison had admitted that she knew very little about the man outside of the office. There was something very wrong with her co-worker, and he suspected it had some tie to the missing little girl.

\*\*\*\*

The Fourth of July holiday allowed JC to spend some time with Thaniel and his family while giving Madison some of his time in a relaxed setting. The thought of them as one big happy family caught and fired a sense of peace in her soul. The news Daren had been at the compound had honestly shocked her. Surely, he had nothing to do with Briana's kidnapping, but maybe he'd seen the woman who took her?

Mindy planned to share what they learned from her husband with the FBI agent in charge.

Madison watched JC play with Thaniel's children, Jonathan and Jordan, on the lawn in the backyard. They were tossing a well-worn leather football back and forth while laughing. Cathy sat quietly next to Casey, playing games on her cell phone. JC's carefree and contented look made her stomach flutter like a million butterflies. Even Mindy seemed relaxed and happy.

Although generations apart, the boys had a strong family resemblance to JC and Nate, and Cathy took after Casey's side of the family. They were handsome children—with the same blue eyes and dimples in their cheeks that their father, JC, and Nate all had.

Madison thought the Fourth of July BBQ get-together couldn't have been a better diversion for everyone looking around at the contented faces.

The weather was perfect, sunny but not too hot. There was a slight breeze where she sat with Mindy and Casey in the shade, enjoying an icy glass of lemonade.

Mindy shared a few memories of past years about her daughter, and she hadn't lost her faith that Briana would be found. She'd glance at Cathy, who was only a few years older than Briana, and a yearning would cross her features.

Madison was amazed at Mindy's positive outlook and strength of character.

She thought about the painful trials that her mother and father suffered when her baby sister, Rachel, had been kidnapped. As a child, watching their marriage fall apart within the first year after the kidnapping, she'd been affected.

Her mother blamed her father for the kidnapping, and it had destroyed their family unity. Her father never denied the accusation.

He told Madison he'd never been able to forgive himself for his mistake of leaving them alone for a moment at the grocery store.

Madison still felt guilty for not stopping the man from taking her baby sister. His bronzed skin and rippling muscles stood out in her memory. He'd barely glanced at her before he'd snatched Rachel from the grocery cart and ran out of the store. The police never found a trace.

All these years later, she'd never forgotten the kidnapper's face. That awful event entrenched in her memory as clearly as the day it happened.

Someday, in her heart, she knew she'd find Rachel and what had happened to her all those years ago. She would never give up hope.

Shaking her head, trying to dispel the ghosts of her past, she looked at JC. Her smile faded. He was going to leave her too—as her father had left. Not for the same reason, but he was leaving. Her heart ached with the knowledge she had such a limited amount of time with JC.

*Get over it!* Her mind reasoned, and she didn't have a choice.

It seemed cruel of Fate to snatch away JC at any time. It was only a miracle that he'd come back to her when the time portal wouldn't allow him to pass through. She had to focus on the moment and enjoy this brief interlude while he was here. This time had to be enough.

Madison's disturbing thoughts were interrupted when the football JC, Thaniel, and the children were throwing hit her in the shoulder.

"Are you all right?" JC hurried to her side. His eyes scanned her for injury, and then his intense blue eyes met hers. He looked alarmed.

"I'm fine. I was just wool-gathering," Madison assured him, feeling the heat rise to her face. Hoping JC didn't detect her self-pity, she forced a smile, then waved at the kids who were looking her way in concern. "Go play and have fun," Madison encouraged JC before turning back to the women's conversation.

She didn't need to look to know when JC left. It felt as if the sun had gone behind a cloud. Focusing on the conversation between the other women, she offered her opinion on the current state of affairs.

They'd temporarily steered clear of the topic of finding Briana. But it was on all their minds.

Madison wasn't sure how she made it through the rest of the day as her mind was filled with all the future possibilities with JC that would never happen. Finding it best to keep herself busy, she'd bustled about getting food prepared.

She bumped into JC while carrying the condiments to the table. A lump formed at the back of her throat.

Her eyes burned with unshed tears. She wanted to scream.

His eyes narrowed, and then his gaze slipped to her mouth.

Nervously, she licked her lips. When she noticed his frown turn into a grin, Madison knew that his thoughts were in the same vein as hers. Unfortunately, they had people waiting for them. "How are the hot dogs and hamburgers coming along?" Her voice came out in a squeak. She cleared her throat.

"We're getting ready to grill them. Luke sent me to find out if you had another oven mitt I could use."

"Third drawer from the left of the stove," she advised, hurrying away to hide her embarrassment. She'd been hoping for him to kiss her, and if the truth were known, she wanted a whole lot more than to be kissed. Yearning after JC was a no-no.

A slogan she'd heard years ago came to mind. *Time to get off the pity pot. It's starting to stink!*

JC was given the honor of grilling the hamburgers and hot dogs along with Thaniel and Luke. "How long do I have to cook these?" he asked.

Thaniel looked over JC's shoulder. "You might want to turn down the burner like this." He reached over and demonstrated the process.

JC concentrated on his task. He'd never grilled meat before, except over an open campfire. There were so many firsts with him, and it was like a child learning about the world.

Luke sidled up to her. "Hey, sis, if you don't watch it, with all the hot and bothered stares you're giving JC, everyone is going to think you're going to want us to leave right away, so you guys can have some private time."

"I am not giving JC hot and bothered stares. I'm just watching him, um, you know, cook our dinner." She put her fisted hands on her hips and scowled at her brother.

"Yeah, right." Paula came to his side with Forrest positioned on her hip. She whispered something in Luke's ear, and he sobered. Luke burst out laughing, not in the least intimidated. He looked down at the floor, then back at his wife.

Curious as to what transpired between them, Madison suspected Paula told him to quit his teasing. She looked up as JC moved next to her, then over to her brother and his wife. They stood there and watched.

JC smelled of wood smoke and a bit musky from the grill. There was a mustard stain that ran down the front of his T-shirt. He had a big grin on his face, and he was holding out a fully loaded hot dog for Madison.

"For you." Their eyes met and held. She felt as if she was sinking in a blue sea. All the other people no longer existed.

She took the frankfurter and slowly took a bite savoring the bite. "Yum."

His eyes widened, and his pupils dilated as he watched her chew. "Good, huh?"

"Yes. Compliments to the chef. It's perfect." She licked her lips after she swallowed, watching his reaction. Lord, this man wanted her. Just the thought gave her chill bumps.

JC watched Madison eat. He'd never get tired of watching his woman no matter what she did. She was so darn appealing.

He looked over at his noisy, great-many-times

removed niece and twin nephews bickering in a good-natured way. The kids already called him uncle. Thaniel and Casey had made him feel part of their family, offering again to let him live and work on the ranch if he wasn't able to return to his own time.

He'd promised to consider their proposition. If he couldn't return, he had a good feeling that Madison would welcome his offer of marriage. Only time and fate would determine what would happen to him.

In the meanwhile, he'd show his honor by not acting on those lustful thoughts with Madison. If he did return to his time, then she could accept another man's proposal without worrying about having made love with him.

She'd be fine without him. A lump settled in his throat, but would he?

****

Later that evening, they went to Idlewild Park to watch the fireworks. Everyone except Mindy, who'd pleaded a headache and stayed behind for an early night. When Madison offered to stay with her, she'd shooed her away, stating she was going to bed.

JC leaned over in his lawn chair next to Madison. "Thank you for thinking of bringing me to see the fireworks tonight," he said as another explosion of lights glittered in the dark sky.

"You're welcome. This is the first time we've come here to watch the fireworks ourselves. I'm glad we made it a family affair." She reached over and put her hand on top of his.

JC turned his hand up to enfold her hand in his. "I am too. Having Luke's family and Thaniel's family all together to celebrate Independence Day has been great.

All around an extraordinary celebration."

"It might have to be our new family tradition," Madison whispered with a catch in her voice.

JC enjoyed the warm evening sky and the people in the background, making excited oohs and aah sounds. In JC's opinion, the fireworks concluded too fast. But there was still the moon and evening stars shining bright.

Thaniel's family said their goodbyes as the crowd resumed their noisy chatter while picking up lawn chairs, blankets, and moving toward their cars. The children's faces still held the enchantment of the fireworks. It was good to see, but he knew that so many boys and girls would not be in the same safe environment as those whose parents held their hands.

JC recalled the first time he'd visualized a little girl praying for a cowboy to rescue her during their drive home. The memory made him even more sure that he was meant to help find Briana. Since then, he'd seen flashes of the girl asking for help several times. His gut instinct knew Kushner was somehow involved or responsible.

It couldn't be a coincidence that Kushner was affiliated with the anti-government compound. He'd been there the day she went missing. If this were the reason he'd been brought to this time to do, he would gladly take up the challenge and do what it took to find her.

Something niggled in his mind. The woman who'd taken Briana, could she be connected to Kushner?

What was he missing?

After they'd put away the lawn chairs and unloaded the remaining food and drinks from the cooler, JC felt a growing sense of urgency to find the missing Briana. It was late, but he was restless.

He'd read the informational packets that Madison had lying around her house for missing children. The longer they were gone, their chances of being found alive significantly diminished.

Every time he thought about Briana, an image of Daren Kushner came to mind. He was sure the man was up to no good. But what could the connection between a little girl and Kushner be? He acknowledged his dislike from the first moment he'd met him. He knew his dislike didn't justify him to suspect him of taking Briana. Regrettably, all he had was his gut instinct.

He stood out on the patio, looking up toward the star-filled night sky for answers. He'd stepped outside for a breath of air to clear his obsessive thoughts while Madison finished loading up the dishwasher.

He could hear the noise of firecrackers going off from neighboring houses.

JC knew he'd have the opportunity to leave once he accomplished what he'd been sent here to do. His feelings were torn between wanting to stay and going home. What if he chose to stay? His mother had Nate. Nate and his mother were more than capable of running the ranch. He shook his head at his predicament.

JC heard the front door open and close. Luke appeared behind Madison with Forrest in his arms. Luke said something to Madison, and she pulled the child into a hug. She was an affectionate woman yet strong and driven, and he liked that about her. Many of Madison's traits were similar to his mother.

His heart stopped for a moment. That picture of Madison holding a child close to her was a beautiful sight. He wanted her to have his child, no, their child.

JC knew his wants weren't just about him. It was about honor. Could he be honorable and not fulfill his duty to his family? Would he allow his mother to live with his disgrace? If he stayed here, his family would have to bear his shame.

No. He would have to go back. If he could prove his innocence, only then would he be able to come back to Madison.

The seed of an idea came to him. Joe had told them that he'd managed to travel to different times in the past and future and yet be able to make it back to his own time. There was no reason he couldn't do the same thing. He decided not to tell Madison his plan—just in case it didn't work out.

Chapter Sixteen

The next morning JC kept Madison company at the kitchen table while she ate breakfast and drank her coffee. She'd been distracted as she'd told him about her schedule for the day. There had been a problem at work with a filtration system that treated wastewater, and she had to meet with the engineers over the project to discuss options. He didn't understand much about the process, except it was helpful to their water and environment. He liked that she shared her concerns with him, just like she would a husband.

JC waited until she left before going to the office. He'd searched Google for Daren Kushner's name. He scanned each site, finally bringing up a professional social website, academic accomplishments. He was puzzled why this should be an important part of his research and decided to search Daren's mother's information. He'd been an only child, according to the article.

JC sat up straighter in his chair. Rereading the article, he knew this was somehow important. Daren's mother, Mabel, had a child abuse record filed against her. Daren had been taken away from his mother after they had found cigarette burns all over his body.

The article had delved into the mental health of children who'd been put through this type of physical and mental abuse. He pulled up more newspaper archives, finding more disturbing documents about the overdose death of Daren's mother. If he hadn't been looking into his own family's archives, he never would have thought to look at Daren's family.

He felt sorry for Daren, the child, for the life he'd endured. Yet, something was mentally wrong with the man. Picking up the phone, he called Madison at work. The urgency to talk to Daren was even greater.

Missy answered the phone. "Oh, hello, JC. Madison's unavailable. Do you want to leave a message?"

"No, I wanted to talk to Daren Kushner." His mind looked for an excuse to speak with him.

"He didn't come in today. He called from his house earlier. Didn't know you were friends." Missy's tone of voice seemed to convey her curiosity.

"No, we are not friends, Missy. I know this is going to sound odd, but I have a gut feeling about him. I don't know why, but I need to talk to him. He was at that compound the day Briana came up missing. Maybe he saw the woman who took her."

He took a chance and confided in Madison's friend about Kushner's abusive childhood and how he'd felt something wasn't right when he met him.

"I've been telling Madison that from the beginning. Daren gives me the creeps," Missy whispered into the phone. "Do you want his phone number or his home address?"

"You've got his address? Maybe if I go to his house, I can catch him off guard."

"I'm not supposed to do this, but—" Missy gave him the address and phone number before he disconnected.

He called Luke, and within minutes Luke picked him up in his Jeep. There was no time to think about what he was doing. He knew it had to be done. During the short drive over to Daren's, JC told Luke about his vision and his hunch.

It looked like no one was home. The Victorian-style gray house was shuttered. The garage door was raised slightly, and a yellow tabby cat peered at them from under the door.

A damp newspaper lay in the driveway, seeming out of character with the recently watered yard that was clipped and manicured to the point of excess. The downstairs windows were covered by curtains, and the upper window had what looked to be wooden boards almost to the top of the window. He thought that was strange.

Luke pulled his car alongside the curb, edging slightly past the driveway. JC unbuckled his seatbelt, but before he could open the door, Luke held up his hand to stop him.

"Hold on. Let me park farther up. Before you go in, I want to let you know I don't think you should be going in there without backup. Since you insist on going anyway, I'll wait in the car and have my cell phone ready just in case." Luke wore a grim look. "Besides, this might be breaking the law."

"What? Do you think I'm afraid of a man like Daren?" JC asked, puzzled by Luke's caution. "I can handle him."

"In a normal setting, yes. But he's in his environment, and we don't know if has a gun or if he's dangerous. Just remember he's been hanging out with that anti-government group. They are known to be a bit on the defensive side if you know what I mean?" Luke turned off the engine and rolled down his window.

"What kind of explanation do you have for him as to why you're suddenly showing up on his doorstep?"

"I was going to ask if he'd seen the woman who'd picked up Briana since we were told he'd been at the compound the day she went missing."

JC shrugged his shoulders. "All right, you have a point. Maybe I can come up with a better reason than that." He scratched his head, his gaze scanning the house and the yard.

"How about if I tell Kushner I'm a handyman looking for work? I could say that Missy, from the office gave me a list of people who may be looking for workers. He knows I'm staying with Madison. Probably even that I'm helping her with repairs around her place."

Luke nodded his head. "Yeah, that's kinda plausible. I'm going to pull up to the house across the street. Hopefully, there's no funny business going on. I'll give you ten minutes," he warned.

"I'm going to try to take a look out back of the house to see if there's anything unusual before I go to the front door." As soon as the car was parked, JC got out, and pulled his baseball cap down low over his eyes, and adjusted the sunglasses Luke handed him.

Studying Daren's house, he looked about him before going in the backyard. It was as neat as the front yard. So perfect, it seemed sterile. There wasn't anyone visible outside in the neighboring houses.

Since no one was around, he walked close to the patio window and looked inside where he could see a laundry room that looked tidy. He turned the doorknob, but it didn't open. Locked. Of course, anyone so meticulous about their house and yard wouldn't leave a door unlocked.

On the way back to the front entrance, he noticed the garbage bin. He again scanned the vicinity, seeing no one, and opened the lid. The bin was halfway full of black trash bags and a couple of kid's take-out boxes on top.

He knew that children liked those special meals created for them because he'd seen advertisements on TV showing children enjoying them.

Did Daren have family staying with him? That seemed like a lot of garbage for one person. Hearing a neighboring dog start to bark seemed to be his prompt to go out to the front of the house. He saw Luke leaning against a tree down the block, and then Luke gave him a mock salute.

JC knocked on the door and waited, but no one answered. He couldn't get a look inside the house because the curtains were shut on the windows. He knocked a couple more times, but when again met with silence, he tried to listen through the door. Although, he twisted the knob, it remained firmly locked. He looked back and saw Luke shaking his head and chopping his hands to warn JC. He reluctantly gave up and walked back the way he'd come.

"Well, what did you see?" Luke asked as soon as he joined him, in an anxious tone as they walked back to the car.

"Looks like he's an extremely neat person. Everything's in perfect order." JC's gait matched Luke's.

"No crime against order, except he probably

doesn't need a handyman," Luke commented as he unlocked the car doors and they got in. "Remember when we saw him in the restaurant, and he was doing his OCD thing with wiping down and lining everything up? That explains why his house and yard would be perfectly groomed."

He turned the car around in a driveway, and they drove in the direction of Daren's house. Just as they got in front, another car pulled into the driveway.

Luke pulled over. They both watched as a blonde woman got out of the car. Luke handed JC a set of binoculars from his glovebox.

JC adjusted the unfamiliar device as Luke instructed him to focus on the woman. He watched as she picked up a bag of groceries from the back seat and made her way to the front door. Her hand wrapped around the grocery sack showing a hate tattooed the same as on Daren's hand. That seemed odd. Was it a family tradition to have those words tattooed on their hands? He didn't really understand why people of today insisted on wearing tattoos all over their bodies.

They watched as the woman inserted a key in the lock and went in closing the door behind her. She returned seconds later and grabbed two more grocery bags before going back in.

"Do you want me to pull over so you can go back and talk to that woman?" Luke asked turning his head to look at JC.

"I don't know what we can do if you do find the girl. Maybe you should call that cop Sam. I think we're in over our heads, here. If you believe that he's a kidnapper, he could be dangerous."

"That might be a good idea. And although I don't

like leaving without talking to him or someone that may help us find the missing girl, it would be a good time to call Thaniel's friend. He can advise us."

Luke pulled out his cell phone and handed it to JC. After calling Thaniel, he dialed the number he was given. When it was picked up by Sam, he explained where he was.

Sam listened to JC's theory about Daren. "I don't want you to approach the house. Let me see what I can find out about him. He could be dangerous or panic if he does have the girl. Can you get me the license plate number of the woman you saw enter the house and I'll run it through our system?" Sam asked. "I appreciate you not taking the law into your own hands," Sam finished up, and his words were a bit abrupt.

"Yes, I clearly remember a time not too long ago when the sheriff took the law into his own hands, and I almost got hung because of him not hearing my side," JC admitted remembering. It still pained him to think that he'd been falsely accused and not believed by the sheriff.

"Don't stick around his house and tip off the man that we're investigating him," Sam cautioned.

After he'd promised not to go back to Daren's house and hung up, they headed back to the B&B. "I don't like leaving without any answers," he grumbled to Luke.

"I know, but it's for the best to do as Sam advised for now. Besides, if anything happens to you, my sis will murder me," Luke said as he pulled into the driveway then stopped the car gripping the steering wheel. "You know Madison's in love with you, don't you?"

JC, speechless at first, sat there reflecting on Luke's words.

"I know. I'm in love with her too. If things had been different…" he began and then cleared his throat that had suddenly become clogged with emotion. "I can't stay here."

"Why not? Your brother went back. Can't he take care of whatever business you have?"

"If it was only as simple as that. Nate will do whatever he has to, to clear my name, but unless Henry Jacobs confesses he lied, which I doubt he'll do, I'll remain guilty in many of the townspeople's minds. I can't put my mother through that kind of disgrace again."

"Again?" Luke's confusion was indicated by his frown.

"I haven't always lived in Nevada. Until I was ten, we lived in England, where my father got drunk and agreed to wager our home. During the card game, he was accused of cheating, lost our ancestral home, and then supposedly committed suicide. Mother never believed it was true." JC's words were factual yet bitter.

"Our mother survived the scandal by leaving the country and starting over in America." He paused, not being able to stop the sad smile. "We did well with our land by bringing in cattle and horses. Mother was able to hold her head up again with pride. Father's mistake almost destroyed her. I can't be the one who causes her that kind of grief again."

Luke cleared his throat but remained quiet, waiting for JC to continue.

"Nate and I saw how deeply it affected our mother. We both vowed we would never give her cause to feel shame."

Luke wiped at a strand of hair that had fallen into his eyes. "I'm sorry. This tragedy had to have been a heavy burden for your family."

"Yes, it was. I will not allow my family to be disgraced again," JC vowed, his lips firm with resolution. "I have no choice. My honor demands that I return."

"Hey, I can see where you're coming from, man. As much as I feel for you, I feel for Madison too. She's never been in love with anyone before. My sister's always been so focused on finding our sister, Rachel, her career, and all the other things she does. I love my sister and don't want her to get hurt." Luke moved to open the car door. "She's going to be devastated when you're gone."

"Believe me, if I had the choice, I would marry her and stay here. I love this century. There is a slight chance I may be able to come back through the portal. I'm not telling Madison my plan in case it doesn't work," JC confided solemnly. The thought of leaving her felt like his insides were being ripped apart. He got out of the car and turned toward the house of the woman he loved.

"Just wanted to let you know, I feel for you, man. You've been good for Madison, brought her out of her shell. She'll be fine if you don't make it back— eventually. She has us for support." Luke turned away toward the walkway to his house. "See you later, pal."

"Later." JC repeated the modern phrase he'd heard so many people use during his time here, watching Luke walk away. Sighing, he reflected how soft he'd become. Yep, he'd grown used to computers, cars, showers, and all the other modern technology. And the food. He'd miss the current fare of hot dogs and hamburgers and ice cream. Most of all, he'd miss Madison and her brother's friendship.

Funny, even though Nate was his twin, he hadn't adjusted to all the technology and advanced lifestyle like JC had. Nate did like getting to know his great-grandson Thaniel and his family, so there was a plus for him. Hopefully, Nate was back home with their mother now. He thought about what she would think about all the women's rights in this century and the advancements that made life easier for everyone. Before Nate had left, they'd decided to tell her everything.

Not able to control what was happening back home, he resolved to hurry and accomplish his mission here and return as soon as he could.

That night, he excused himself to go to his bedroom earlier than usual. This was the first evening he'd felt the need to escape to be alone. He lay restless in the confining space, frustrated with the bit of progress he'd made on finding out where the missing girl went. Luckily, he'd been conditioned to sleep anytime living on the ranch.

JC knew it was only a dream. He felt the restraining blanket holding him down. Yet…

*The girl from the flyer held out her arms to JC. "Please come get me. I want my Mommy. Mister told me that I didn't need to go to school, that he was going to teach me at home. I think Mister isn't going to let me go."*

*JC stretched his hands as far as he could. Just before he could touch hers, the gap widened, causing a larger chasm between them. His wooden legs refused to move. "Come to me," he mouthed.*

*The little girl shook her head violently "I can't. Mister locks the door." She held out her hands in a silent plea, and tears plummet down her rosy cheeks.*

*"Where are you?" he asked, again trying to move his legs.*

*"I'm upstairs locked in a room." She began to sob harder. "Help me please, cowboy hero. I don't want to stay here forever."*

JC sat up, gasping for breath. He was in his bed, and the vision of the little girl was gone. He felt a burning in his chest like he'd been holding his breath too long. He looked at the clock—three in the morning. Trying to dispel the after-effects of the dream, he understood it played some significance in why he was here and what he was to do.

He had to find her. He had to. He'd promised Sam he would not go to Kushner's house. He'd explained it could mess up the investigation if he went back. JC had to abide by the detective's instructions. He didn't like having his hands tied like this. He felt it was past time to take action. Not sit and wait.

It was a long time before he got back to sleep. This time no visions or dreams woke him.

Chapter Seventeen

The next day, Madison picked up the mail and entered the hallway of her house. She was looking forward to putting up her feet. A relaxing evening with JC and Mindy was just what she needed.

It had been a trying day. She'd been in meetings all day long with out-of-state VIPs from the home office based in Colorado. Morris Winters, the president, had brought with him a new proposal from a prospective client.

There had been extra work, and Daren called in sick again. She didn't know what was going on with him lately, but it was getting old. She'd covered for him once more. It was time for her to have another little chat with him. As the lead engineer, one of his responsibilities was to be there for crucial meetings like today's.

Missy had taken notes and forwarded them to Daren in an email. She'd complained briefly about Daren's attendance and the extra work she'd been doing to help him out. Madison barely managed to get through the day and gladly said goodbye to the visitors.

So preoccupied, she jumped in surprise when she saw JC standing in the entryway. He didn't laugh as he usually would but instead stared intently at her as if he was in a stupor.

"What's wrong?" she asked, alarmed by the distant

look he gave her. When he gave a tentative smile, her heart sang. He looked too appealing, and the workday's challenges quickly evaporated.

"Nothing is wrong. Except I've been ordered by Sam not to approach Kushner. I believe he has Briana there at his house."

"Why would you think that? Did you tell Sam?"

"Yes, but he said they couldn't act on intuition or a hunch. There had to be substantiated proof first." His frustration was evident.

She put her hand on his shoulder to offer comfort. "You need to trust Sam. He's an expert who knows what to do. Laws dictate his actions." She pulled back, tugging at the neckline of her blouse.

His intense gaze seemed to smolder with yearning. The yearning was mutual, and Madison wanted him. With that thought, it seemed to grow warmer in the room. Her lightweight peach business suit felt too tight. She pulled away from him completely, picked up a magazine that lay on the foyer table, and fanned her face.

"Other than that, how was your day?" she said, struggling to come up with something, anything to distract her wayward thoughts and to cool down her overheated body.

"Frustrating. I took a chance and went over to Kushner's house—"

"What? Why'd you do that?" she jumped in, alarmed, but quickly continued. "What did Daren say?"

"Nothing. He wasn't home. Before we left, we did see a woman enter his house carrying a bag of groceries. Do you know if he has company? You said he wasn't married. The woman's face resembled

Daren's, so my guess is she's a relative, possibly a cousin."

"Daren called in sick again today, so he should have been home. Maybe he went to the doctor or the pharmacy. He left me holding the bag with the executives that came in. Daren should have been there. I'm going to be annoyed if I find out he wasn't sick. This visit's been in the works for a few weeks." Madison shook her head, tugging out the hair clip that held her hair in a French twist at the back of her head. She shook the tresses about her shoulders before kicking off her heels.

When she looked at JC again, he'd stilled. His eyes were dilated with emotion as he stared intensely at her. She shifted her feet but stayed where she was. Madison cried out silently—begging him to pull her into his arms.

No words were necessary.

The heat from his body radiated through Madison's when he pulled her into his chest. She could smell his musky cologne, and she couldn't help drawing in a deep breath of his unique scent. The smell made her dizzy with longing.

Every molecule in her body screamed, this man is mine. When she went to pull back to look at his face, he tightened his grip.

"Don't go. I need to hold on to you too badly." His voice was a hoarse whisper. As if he was in intense pain.

"I wasn't going to go anywhere. I just wanted to look at you," Madison admitted, tilting her head, studying him carefully.

"Good," he murmured while running his hands up

and down her back, stopping slightly above her behind. She felt his hands slowing down to a stop, and she sucked in her breath as chills crept up her spine—Lord, how she loved JC.

It took every bit of strength she had in her not to beg him to stay.

Peering from under her lashes to see how he was reacting, he seemed to struggle with his desires. His eyes were open, watching her.

Grinning, she felt a sense of feminine power over this man who towered half a foot above her. She reached up and stroked his whiskered cheeks, and then her hands trailed to his lips where she pressed them lightly. His mouth opened, and he touched her fingers with the tip of his tongue. *Sexy*, she thought when an electrical current seemed to flow from her hand through the length of her spine. She shivered, then waited in welcome anticipation.

He then brought his fingers to her face, which he cradled, then lifted her chin so he could look deep into her eyes.

"I want—" he started, then pulled her mouth back to his, kissing her carefully.

All sense of place and time were suddenly gone. Madison drank in his essence as he thoroughly kissed her. He tasted of mint. He pulled back, holding onto her shoulders. Right now, the only thing that mattered was this moment and surrounded by his arms.

They stood like that for what seemed like an endless time. The jarring sound of the doorbell ringing broke the precious moment.

JC was the first to step back. "I'm not sorry," he admitted with a twist to his mouth.

Madison grinned. "Me neither," she admitted, her heart thumping loudly in her chest as she turned to look out the peek hole before opening the door.

"Sam?" Before she could question why he was here, Sam spoke in his calming voice.

"Hello. Is JC here?" Sam waited until she opened the door wider and gestured him in. He entered, turning to JC. One look at JC, and then back to Madison had Sam grinning.

Madison felt her face heat up. "I'll let you two talk."

She hurried away to change out of her work clothes.

Closing the door of her bedroom, she surveyed the neat room. Madison leaned back against the door and took a deep breath. She wasn't sure she'd be able to hold herself up. If she and JC didn't stop kissing and touching one another, she would be in big trouble.

****

JC took a moment to catch his breath.

"I seem to be interrupting something. You have lipstick on your mouth." Sam chuckled.

"No. You're just in time. What have you found out about Daren Kushner?" JC rubbed his lips, turning away in an attempt to hide his raw feelings from Sam.

He motioned Sam to follow him. He felt sweat bead on his forehead as they went out onto the patio. The late afternoon sun was waning, but the temperature remained hot.

"The license plate on that car is registered to Daren. Not as much info as I would have liked, but you were right. Kushner does have a record. He spent about five years in prison when he was a young man for robbery. He had a short rap sheet of juvenile crimes. Got caught robbing a liquor store, and the judge put him away for being a repeat offender and a menace to society.

"It also shows that while in prison, he maintained good conduct. He earned his bachelor's degree as he is quite intelligent. It looks like he got out on early release and managed to finish his master's degree in engineering. The man hasn't been in any known trouble since. Not even a parking ticket." Sam sat in a chair across from JC and looked around, nodding approval. "Nice comfortable place here. I like it."

JC waited patiently for Sam's question. He'd known it was coming when Sam had looked at him as he witnessed his and Madison's reaction. "Yes, it is."

"I know it's none of my business, but since I'm friends with Thaniel, and he's worried Madison will be hurt when you leave." His level gaze was stern, his tone brusque. Leaving JC with the thought Sam and Thaniel both disagreed with him starting a relationship with Madison.

He knew there was no defending his actions. He'd allowed his feelings to overshadow his common sense when he'd defied the fates by falling in love with Madison.

A woman he had no right to love.

"I'm well aware of my actions with Madison. I wished I could say I'm not leading her on thinking that we have a future, or this attraction we have to one another wouldn't happen again, but holding back my feelings, which may be more than I'm humanly capable of."

Sam nodded to JC as if he understood his dilemma.

"I don't know what I'd do if I were in your shoes. But I don't think I would waste what precious time I have with the woman I love."

"My thoughts exactly." JC rose from his chair and walked the length of the patio, seeing a future that appeared grim without Madison unless he could come back.

Sam got up and met him eye to eye when JC returned. "Don't give up hope. The future generally takes care of itself."

"That's right, whether a person likes it or not. You aren't the first person who's mentioned it to me," JC agreed.

"What I came to talk about is I can't get a warrant to search Kushner's house without a probable cause. Right now, all you've come up with is, you have a gut feeling about the man. It won't fly with Judge Ober. Unless you come up with a concrete motive that he's involved with the missing girl, Briana, we have nothing to back up your feeling."

"I understand. I want to get a look in Kushner's house."

Sam looked alarmed, crossing his arms over his chest. "No. Don't even think it. Without a warrant, it is trespassing unless you are invited in."

"I want to go back tonight." JC met the other man's skeptical look, so he quickly held up his hands. "I'll find a place where I can watch and…"

"I can see you're determined. I'll tell you what, I'll allow you to sit in on my stake-out tonight, but only if you promise to stay out of the way," Sam offered.

When the impact of what Sam was saying hit him, he smiled. "You'd allow me to accompany you?"

"Yes. I'd do it as a favor to Thaniel's kin. Besides, if your gut instincts are correct, we could be bringing in a kidnapper. I only hope to God that's all we're bringing in and not a child murderer."

JC felt a lump in the back of his throat that this man who barely knew him would trust his integrity enough to do this. "Thanks." He didn't mention the visions he'd had of the girl.

"This goes against what I've been taught to do. If I rush the process, I could jeopardize the case. That's if there is a case. I'm on the side of justice. If this man has Briana, then we don't want to make it so he can get out of jail on a technicality."

Chapter Eighteen

The fogged-up windows and confining car didn't seem to bother Sam as he calmly opened his thermos of coffee and poured each of them a cup. He slanted a look in JC's direction, lifting the edge of the cup in a silent salute, then took a sip. He seemed to have endless patience, unlike JC's own growing unease. He gritted his teeth to keep from complaining about the wait.

They'd been sitting for over four hours with no activity. There was a flickering light that spilled from the blinds, possibly from Daren's television. The porch light went on, and Kushner came out, turned on the water for the sprinkling system, and then meandered to his mailbox.

He took out a stack of mail and picked up the morning newspaper. The tabby cat, sitting under the garage door earlier, was sitting on the steps. It didn't appear that either man or beast were aware they were watching.

Daren ran his hand over the cat's back, and the cat's tail lifted as if to encourage him to keep on. Daren sat briefly on his steps and continued to pet the cat. After a few minutes, he went inside, allowing the cat to follow him.

"Well, we know he likes animals," Sam commented. "This means he can't be all that bad."

"What?" JC's confusion came across in his tone of

voice.

"You probably haven't heard about the theory since you're not from this era, but it's been found that there is a direct correlation between animal cruelty and human behavior." Sam's eyes stared at the house.

JC finally hit the end of his patience. He rubbed his now scratchy whiskered chin and shifted in his seat. "I hadn't heard that, but let's hope it means he hasn't harmed that little girl."

"You know, I doubt anything is going to happen tonight. We can sit here another eight hours and watch or leave. It's your choice. If it were my decision, I'd advise that we get some concrete facts, then come back armed with a search warrant. You get me something tangible to go on, and believe me, I won't leave until every inch of the house has been searched," Sam promised solemnly.

JC realized Sam had a good point. He hated leaving without making some progress, but this was a waste of time.

He thought about the internet search he'd done earlier on Kushner. He'd taken notes and looking at those handwritten notes only proved he hadn't been able to find out anything that would give them evidence of Daren's guilt.

"All right. Let's go. Thanks for letting me come with you tonight."

"If he has Briana, we will get him," Sam assured him as he dropped JC off.

JC stood a moment outdoors, looking up to the sky for inspiration before going inside to Madison's computer room. Anxious to find anything substantial, he stared at the computer screen until he saw the clock.

It would be time to get up in a few hours.

He'd have to do more digging, but rubbing his tired eyes, he knew he needed to get some sleep. He visualized the meeting of Kushner in Madison's office.

*What aspect of Kushner stuck out about him? Was it that he avoided eye contact or those tattoos on his hands?*

He was about to turn away when he decided to Google tattoos. Suddenly, he didn't feel sleepy anymore.

The tattoo had to be the clue.

The woman who'd come to Daren's house had the same tattoo markings on her knuckles.

What if that woman wasn't another person, but instead Daren Kushner? Both face shapes matched. What had thrown him off was the dress and hair. Daren must have been wearing a shoulder-length blonde wig. Sam had said the car the woman was driving belonged to Daren. JC put the two facts together. Excitement raced with this breakthrough.

*Could it be Kushner?*

Why would the man dress as a woman unless he had something to hide? What about the blonde woman who'd shown up at the compound that no one seemed to recognize? There was a good possibility it had been Daren. Why would he kidnap a little girl? JC's gut instinct believed Briana was still alive.

He knew that he was on the right track. All he had to do was get himself inside Daren's house to search.

"Shoot!" JC muttered under his breath. If only Sam hadn't made him promise he wouldn't go back there without him. Glancing up at the clock, JC realized it was too early to call him. Later in the morning would have to do.

He put away his notes, turned off the light, and started down the dark hallway only to run into Madison. His surprise turned to pleasure the moment she walked into him. She was wearing a robe, and her hair spilled over her shoulders in disarray. His body felt as if it had caught fire. Her smile made him forget everything but her.

"Hi. It's late. Is everything okay?" Her gaze was filled with concern, and her warm floral scent radiated around Madison. He didn't know what perfume it was, but it was a scent he'd associate with her for the rest of his life.

When her hand touched his chest, he nearly recoiled from the impact it made on his consciousness.

"I was just turning in." He heard the stiff words come from his mouth. Sam's earlier rebuke still stung—strengthening his resolve to do the right thing. There was nothing he wanted more than to drag her into his arms and hold her tight, never letting her go. He'd do everything in his power not to hurt her. Unfortunately, he believed he was too late.

JC almost laughed out loud at that falsehood. He loved her, and if detaching from her would help her heal quicker after he left, well, so be it.

"Good night," he murmured as he turned sideways, trying to sidle past her, but she put out her hand to stop him.

"What is going on? Tell me." She pleaded as she gripped his arm with unyielding strength.

He pulled away, breaking their eye contact, keeping his tone stiff. "Nothing's going on. I'm tired, that's all." He faked a yawn. "It's been a long night."

Madison's shoulders drooped with his arctic words. It didn't take a genius to know he'd hurt her. But she accepted his explanation.

Hugging her arms about her chest, she nodded her head. "I'll let you get to your bed then." She hurried past him to her bedroom door and paused before going on. "If there's anything I can do..." She left the sentence unfinished, but JC knew he had to step back from their attraction.

"Thanks, much appreciated." His inflexible tone bit at his own heart, adding to his already guilty conscience. He wished to tell her his plan to return but knew it was better not to get her hopes up.

**** 

Madison lay in her bed for hours after the encounter with JC. He seemed like an impersonal stranger who was suddenly living under her roof. Her heart ached with his dismissal.

He'd made it abundantly clear—he didn't want to be near her. She tried not to let his distance bother her, but it did.

Please, please don't let it end like this between them, she prayed. She couldn't bear it if JC left her with this invisible wedge between them. Even if he had to go, she wanted to have his friendship, and all the good memories of him filed away for her future recollections.

Madison had heard him when he'd come in late. She'd slipped out of bed, peeking through the window as JC had gotten out of Sam's car. He'd stood out in the driveway after Sam's car had pulled away, looking up at the sky. The wind tossed his unruly hair from side to side. There wasn't a thing about him she'd change— except for the century he'd been born. Drawing in a wistful sigh, Madison padded back to bed.

She listened to him come up the stairs hoping he'd knock on her door, but he'd gone into the office.

Eventually, she'd fallen asleep while thinking of him. In her dream, JC was back in his own time. He was married to a beautiful woman who'd held a child in her arms. The woman looked at Madison and shook her head, saying, "You can't have him. JC belongs to me." She'd woken herself up by saying *no* over and over.

She was a fool for wanting someone she couldn't have.

He'd never promised to stay with her. He'd warned her how important it was for him to leave. For him and his family. Such integrity, such love and loyalty to those he'd left behind. He would always be there for them in the good times as well as the bad times.

****

Morning light filtered in through the window, and the musical tone of her cell phone rang, shaking her from her thoughts. It rang three times before it stopped.

With a light day scheduled for her workday, she decided to call in and take personal time off for a mental health day. She'd handled the big meeting yesterday, and she deserved a day off, she reasoned.

Before Madison could get up, there was a knock on her door. "Come in." She pushed up to lean against the headboard, hoping her misery didn't show.

JC opened the door and held up the cell phone she'd left on the kitchen counter. "Sorry to disturb you, but I think this call might be important." He paused at the entrance seeming unsure if he should enter or not. Madison remembered he'd been in her bedroom once before, and his old-fashioned principles had made him uncomfortable.

"Come in. I'd just decided to get up," Madison said, forcing a smile while holding her hand out for the phone.

He strode into the room and handed it to her. Their fingers brushed in the process, and tingles of awareness ran up her arm and through her body. She waited, feeling miserable as he made a hasty retreat. The door shut with finality.

"Hello?" She gulped back the lump that threatened to block the back of her throat. Nothing could make her feel better.

The woman introduced herself. "This is Penny Smithfield." The name seemed familiar, but she couldn't place it with a face. The voice on the other end was unfamiliar.

"Is this Madison?"

Madison sat up straighter. "Yes, it is."

"Did you get my letter? I know you don't know who I am, but—"

Confused, Madison scrunched her eyes, trying to remember. "I'm sorry? Who are you? What letter?" She paused for several moments, searching her mind for an answer to why the name seemed familiar.

Then she remembered the letter that had been among the stack of letters she'd carried in earlier in the week. The name had meant nothing to her, and the return address had been from Michigan. She'd put the stack of mail on the foyer entry table, and when she'd picked it up, the letter had been gone, and she'd forgotten about it.

"I'm sorry, Ms. Smithfield, I didn't get a chance to read your letter. How can I help you?" She put her phone on speaker, rose from her bed, walked over to the closet, where she pulled out a robe to cover her nightshirt.

Padding barefoot into the hallway foyer, she knelt and looked under the entry table.

There wasn't any loose mail lying there as she'd suspected. But Madison found a letter wedged against the wall behind the table.

When she grabbed the elusive letter, she pulled back with a sigh. Scrambling to her feet, she looked at the return address, and it said Penny Smithfield's name.

"I was hoping you'd submit to a DNA test. I'm trying to find my true identity, and there's a good possibility I'm your sister."

Madison stilled in shock. Her mind raced. "Rachel?" she whispered. Oh God, could it be true? "Why do you think you're my sister?" Her voice came out harsher than she meant.

But, if this was a joke, it was cruel. Madison had been searching her whole life for Rachel and had met numerous disappointments. There had been far too many false leads over the years.

"I didn't know I'd been kidnapped until my parents were killed in an automobile accident a few months ago. After dealing with all the paperwork, I came across a newspaper clipping of a baby named Rachel Matthews taken from a grocery store. Then an adoption receipt of a birth certificate that didn't match the information I'd been told.

"When I contacted the adoption agency, they said that my certificate wasn't in their records. Everything seemed to happen at once. I spoke to my aunt, who admitted to me I was adopted. She'd thought I'd known

I was adopted. After contacting Vital Records and the hospital where the birth certificate came from, they confirmed there were no records." Her voice was rushed and excited.

"So, because you had the clipping of the newspaper with the missing baby, you thought you might be her?" Madison's shock turned into hope. She tore at the envelope, pulled the letter from it, and scanned the contents.

"Yes. I hoped it was true. I hired a private detective and gave him what information I had, and he came back with pictures of your parents. I take after both of them in looks." She paused, waiting for Madison to speak.

"Yes. I mean, yes, I'll take a DNA test. If you're Rachel—oh my God!" Madison said, overcome with hope. She couldn't help the tears that streamed down her cheeks. "I'm sorry." She swiped at the tears, excited by the possibility.

"I feel the same way. I never knew I could have another family. My parents were good to me. They were hard-working people who loved me. I found out they were unable to have children. Guess that's why they adopted me." Penny again paused.

"Where are you right now, in Michigan?" Madison asked, pacing the floor with her mind reeling from the shocking news. If only her mother was still alive, and this woman was Rachel.

"No, I'm staying at the Nugget in Reno. I hopped on a plane as soon as I could when I found out. I feel very strongly that I'm your sister. I was hoping to get together with you." Penny took a deep breath. "If you want to get to know me, that is."

"What time do you want to meet?" Madison looked

at the alarm clock seeing it was almost eight. She'd need to call Luke too. He was going to be just as excited.

"Can I treat you to lunch?" Penny asked.

"Okay, that sounds wonderful, how about if we meet in an hour? I can't wait until lunch." Madison crossed her fingers, hoping that she'd agree. Otherwise, she'd spend the four hours in suspense. She almost laughed with relief when Penny decided on the earlier time. She couldn't wait to tell Luke.

As soon as she hung up the phone, she called Luke and explained the situation. Madison hadn't been expecting his reaction.

"What the heck, Madison! She could be a scam artist, wanting money."

**** 

Briana knelt on the floor and folded her hands just like Mommy showed her. This time she was going to pray hard. If Briana wanted something very much, then she'd have to try harder. Like the time she learned to ride her new two-wheeler bike. Biting her lip, Briana looked upward to heaven, more determined than ever.

"'Kay, God. 'Member me? I want to go home. I've been a good girl and did what Mister told me, but I don't think he's going to let me go." She wiped off her tears with the sleeve of her shirt and pulled the new doll into her arms, holding her tight.

"Please send me the cowboy hero to save me—like the one in the movie. Please! Thank you for listening to me." She scrambled from her knees to stand before remembering the rest of her prayer and knelt back down.

"Oh yeah, and God, please watch out for my

mommy and daddy too. I know they're probably missing me. Thank you, Amen."

This time she went over by the table where the TV sat, turning on the movie Mister had brought her. She settled in with her arms crossed around the doll, waiting for the cowboy hero that God would now surely send for her.

**\*\*\*\***

JC paced back and forth along the hallway into the living room. He waited for Sam to return his call.

Edginess and impatience ate at him. He'd spoken to Madison that morning after her phone call at breakfast. Seeing her excitement, he knew something big had happened. He had pretended indifference, and didn't ask her what. Now she was gone, and that disinterest was consuming him.

*Dang, he should have asked.* His mind buzzed with curiosity. He wasn't sure how long he could maintain this detachment between them because it was tearing him apart.

How could a man pretend not to care when he cared too much? A picture of her dressed in her nightshirt, rumpled hair when he entered her bedroom formed in his mind. She'd had purple circles under her puffy eyes and looked as if she'd been crying. Her face was pale, and her lips drawn tight as if she hadn't slept well.

It hurt him to see her pain-filled face, and it had been tortuous not to take her in his arms and console her.

He snarled an expletive. He had to accomplish the task he was supposed to do here and do it fast. Otherwise, he suspected he'd not have the strength to leave Madison at all.

He didn't know when he'd get Sam's call back, but the wait was killing him. Finally, when the phone rang, he hurried to pick it up.

As soon as he answered and recognized Sam's voice, he felt an intense irritation. "Sam. What took you so long to call me back?" he demanded, knowing his anger was misdirected at the detective.

"Slow down. I do have a job that keeps me fairly busy. This is the first time I've had a chance to return your call. Now, tell me, what's got you all riled up?"

Sam's calm voice soothed JC's stretched nerves. "I'm sorry for yelling. I think I found a link to tie Kushner in with the kidnapping." JC's voice rushed on.

"I have about five minutes before I need to get back into the courtroom. Give me a short version of your evidence."

"Mike, the girl's father described the same woman who was seen the day of the disappearance by others from his compound. No one had ever seen this woman before, so she stood out." He took a deep breath, trying to settle his racing heart rate.

"When I went to Kushner's house, I saw a woman get out of Daren's car with the same tattoo that Daren has. I thought she was a relative or something. The blonde hair and women's wear confused me. I'm almost positive now the woman at the compound was Daren dressed as a woman."

"Interesting. I'll speak to Judge Ober and see how soon we can get a search warrant," he promised. "I've got to go now."

JC tightened the grip on the phone. "Wait! I want to go over there now."

"No. You could compromise the case. You trusted me enough to tell me about your suspicions. Now trust me to do my job. Besides, you promised not to do anything without me. I'll let you know when we go to his house," Sam reasoned.

"Will you let me go with you?"

"If you continue to keep your promise and let me do my job, I'll allow you to come." Someone spoke in the background, and Sam told JC, "Gotta go."

"I'll be waiting for you to call me." JC reluctantly agreed. If this was the person who kidnapped Briana, he didn't want to do anything that could allow him to go free.

## Chapter Nineteen

As Madison and Luke walked into the reception area of the casino hotel, she scanned the hotel guests in the lounge area for a familiar face. Luke was the first to notice her.

"Look, the woman over by the window, tall with the green shirt. She looks like she's waiting for someone. It could be her."

Luke touched Madison's arm, holding her back. "Don't get your hopes up, and it could be a hoax." He let her go.

Madison felt the welling of tears close to the surface bubble up as her brother squeezed her arm in comfort.

Determined not to get all emotional, she stuck out her chin firmly in silent resolution. She'd not be reduced to falling apart. After all, this woman could still be an imposter, someone who was out to con them. But deep down, Madison believed the woman in front of them *was* Rachel.

Penny wore a worried look on her face. She stood stiffly—her eyes haunted as if waiting for their rejection. But the family resemblance to her parents was there. Madison felt the surge of hope twist in her stomach.

The young woman before her had to be Rachel. All the years of searching could be over. She reached her arms out to Rachel, and the woman moved into the circle of her open arms. Madison could feel her thin body shaking.

Finally, after a short while, she pulled away from Rachel. "This is Luke. He's my younger brother. Mom was pregnant with Luke when someone took you." As she said this, she realized her mind had already accepted that this woman was Rachel. Even before the DNA test. Her acceptance of this woman's claim was unequivocal.

She waited as the two siblings shook hands more formally. Grinning, she couldn't keep down the bubble of happiness. "It's okay to hug," she chastised Luke, knowing he wasn't as accepting of this woman as she was.

Luke smiled back at Madison and then grudgingly opened his arms, and they hugged for a moment before Penny pulled back.

"It's okay. I'm not sure how I would feel if someone out of the blue claimed to be my lost sister."

Madison noticed her slight Michigan accent. Penny resembled a picture she'd seen of her mother when she was young. A pretty woman with intelligent-looking eyes that seemed to take in everything around her.

"It's a shock," Luke admitted stepping back.

"I was hoping we could take a DNA test to confirm or deny whether I'm your sister."

"That would be a good idea," Luke agreed as he shifted his body closer to Madison.

"If looks are any indication, I'd say it's pretty certain you're who you're claiming."

"I hope so. I don't have much family. My mother has a sister, but other than that, there is no one."

She'd heard of other such reunions of children who'd been reunited with their actual families when they'd become adults. To experience this possible reunion was almost more than her heart could take. If Penny was her sister, then all these years of searching were finally over.

All the false leads, money, and time they'd spent on their search was worth it all. If only her mother could be here to see this day. She prayed that this was real—that this was Rachel, her long-lost sister.

Penny looked around her before she spoke. "I brought a couple of DNA kits with me. It's pretty easy. You just swab the inside of your jaw. Here is the kit. She reached for the kit and then laughed nervously. "Gosh, I'm just rambling, but it's not every day a person meets her family for the first time as an adult. I brought one for me too. I thought you'd like to watch me do the test, so it's all legitimate."

"What should we call you, Penny?" Luke interjected the question as he took the kit from her hand and examined the information on the packaging.

"Penny. Since that's all I've ever been known by, even if I am your sister, I'll continue to go by Penny," she said in a matter-of-fact tone. She leaned back on her heels and then crossed her hands over her chest.

Madison could visibly see Penny pull back from Luke's antagonistic stance. She waited for them to agree to the DNA testing.

"If you'd like, you can stay at my house, get to know us," she offered without hesitation, wanting to spend as much time with her as possible. "I have a bed and breakfast with plenty of available rooms. Or, if you'd rather stay at this casino while you're here, we can still get together." Madison sensed that she was as she claimed in her bones, and the DNA would prove she was their sister.

Luke rolled his eyes, and his eyebrows rose as he glanced over at Madison. He didn't say a word at her decision, although he was over-protective of his sister and knew her propensity to rescue.

Madison bit her lip, knowing full well where her brother's thoughts were taking him. Even though he was the baby of the family, he'd stepped into the father role.

"If you're sure you want me," Penny agreed as she glanced between Luke and Madison in confusion.

"Of course, we want you. I'd love to have you stay with me. I have two other guests staying at the house. Come on, let's get you packed up, and then we can go to brunch." Madison waited as Penny agreed.

****

JC heard the garage door open. He hurried into the kitchen to wait for Madison to walk through the door. He'd been fighting his impatience all morning to find out what had happened and waiting for Sam's return call. Every obstacle had frustrated him.

The morning had dragged on into the afternoon. JC had paced, did some repair work around the house to keep occupied, but his mind was never far from the fact that he couldn't do anything to rescue Briana without Sam's help.

The time he'd spent on the computer researching hadn't produced any more information. He'd never felt the need to talk to someone as desperately as he needed to talk to Madison. But, knowing their time together was drawing to a close, he resisted the urge to call her cell phone.

Sam hadn't called him back, and he was becoming more impatient. When Madison finally came through the door, he barely opened his mouth when a woman and Luke followed her in.

Madison looked pleased as she introduced them.

"This is Penny. There's a good possibility she's our missing sister. She's going to be staying with us for a while."

"Penny, this is JC, a friend who's been helping me out around the place," Madison told her with a big smile of happiness.

"It's nice to meet you," JC said, holding out his hand. Pushing back the hurt from Madison's coolness, he studied the other woman. She resembled Madison.

He picked up on the woman's unease and sent a questioning glance at Luke, who'd been following her.

Luke remained quiet as he carried in a suitcase. He looked at JC, rolling his eyes and silently shaking his head to convey some message. Puzzled, JC watched as they passed by him, wondering what was happening.

Luke whispered, "I hope this is for real and not a scam."

JC knew how desperately they'd hoped to find their missing sister. Madison would be happy to include this young woman in their lives.

This distraction from his leaving was what she needed to help her detach herself from him. Good. He'd started it in motion the night before. Only, if he were honest with himself, he knew he didn't want the wedge between them. With this new Kushner development, he couldn't tell her about his frustration. His teeth gritted together from his false smile.

He was anything but happy with the way things were going.

\*\*\*\*

Madison sat on the edge of Penny's bed, listening to the other woman speak about her life with her parents in a small town outside of Lancing, Michigan. It was hard to believe her sister was here. After hoping and praying for so many years, she found her presence a miracle.

"I'd always wanted a sister," Penny reflected as she refolded her clothes and put them away in the dresser drawers. "Mom told me she'd tried to have other children without any success."

Madison dangled one leg over the other, flipping her foot into the air. She loved hearing Penny talk with her sweet voice and getting to know her.

"I was raised in a modest home. We were a close family. Dad worked for the city, and Mom was a teacher at an elementary school down the street from our house." She smiled.

"We were just an ordinary family with everyday problems, like everyone else. Guess I went through a rough period where I was a rebellious teenager. I was on the swim team, a cheerleader, and did well in school during high school. I lived in a dorm in the community college I attended and went home for holidays and between semesters. I'd planned to go to the University of Michigan to finish my degree, but, about three months ago, Mom and Dad were killed in a car accident." Her eyes clouded up with grief.

Madison uncrossed her legs to get up, but before she could rise, Penny continued.

"Anyway, after the funeral, I came across the

adoption records. My aunt, my mother's sister, confirmed I'd been adopted. I was resentful at first, but the more I thought about having a family somewhere out there, well—" She broke off.

"I hired a detective, and he advised me that there was a solid chance I was the missing child who'd been kidnapped." Penny swung around. "I don't think my parents would have taken part in the kidnapping. They'd been terribly religious and ethical their whole lives." Penny's eyes pleaded for understanding.

"Maybe they didn't know, especially if they got you from an unscrupulous agency with false documents," Madison offered, trying to understand.

"I don't think they knew. Aunt Rhonda claimed that I'd been adopted from the church adoption agency. But the detective said there were no records of my adoption anywhere he could find. I've always been a curious sort, so it didn't take me long to investigate more."

When the detective first showed me the matching clippings I'd found of the missing girl from Michigan, I didn't want to accept or believe them. I looked at the pictures and saw the resemblance. Then the detective confirmed the likelihood that I was the missing girl. I knew then I wanted proof and to meet my biological family." She finished putting away the last of the clothes from her suitcase.

"I'm so glad you contacted me. We have never given up hope we'd find you."

Madison was shocked at how easily she fell into accepting the idea that this was her long-lost baby sister. Her mind was still reeling with emotion from their reunion. It was like they'd been friends for a long time. Their personalities had instantly meshed.

Penny moved over to the bed and sat next to Madison. "Tell me about you, Luke, and our parents. I want to hear everything. The detective told me the bare facts about all of you."

"How about if we go somewhere a bit more comfortable? I have a wonderful patio area." Madison rose from the bed. When Penny got up also, she threw her arms around her. "I'm so glad you found us. I didn't think—I mean, we never gave up hope, but I didn't visualize you finding us like this," Madison said, overcome with emotion. She swallowed back a lump that had lodged like a boulder in her throat. She held Penny for a minute before feeling self-conscious.

"I'm glad I found you too. It was scary to think I was all alone in this world except for Auntie Rhonda."

"Well, you're not alone anymore," Madison reassured her. She led Penny to the patio.

"I don't blame Luke for being wary of me."

"I think he'll come around. It's something he's lived with his whole life. He tends to be more skeptical."

"I'd be a skeptic, too, if I were in his shoes." Penny settled in a chair, looking around the patio area.

"Luke will warm up. Give him time." Madison tried to reassure her as much as herself. He'd taken off as soon as he'd put Penny's suitcase in her room. His reaction wasn't what she'd expected.

"You have a lovely home. This patio is a great place to entertain guests." Penny's arms encompassed the outdoor living space.

Madison felt her heart swell at the compliment. "I like it here in Reno. It's always been my dream to have a bed and breakfast, and now I do. Luke and his wife gave up their lives in Michigan to come out here and support this venture."

"You're so fortunate to have a brother."

Madison detected a note of sadness in her. "Once everything's settled, you'll feel like Luke's your brother too, and you will love Forrest, Luke's eight-month-old son."

She'd almost forgotten about JC until she spotted him standing at the kitchen sink. The window overlooked the patio. Their eyes met and held. She drew in a deep breath as a sharp pain battered her chest.

"Are you okay?" Penny asked, appearing to notice her distress.

"I'm fine." She smiled and looked away from the person who'd held her focus for the past month. When her gaze returned, she could no longer see JC. It was just as well. He'd made it plain that he had no intention of continuing their relationship or prolonging his stay.

Madison heard the phone ring but ignored it, figuring either JC would answer it or her answering machine would pick it up.

"I'm so glad that your parents treated you well when you were growing up. What made you decide that you wanted to become a teacher?" Madison searched for something to shift her rampant thoughts of JC from her mind.

"Well, as I told you earlier, my mother was a teacher." Penny's brows knitted together. "So, basically, it was the way I was raised. Dad worked for the Road Authority. He'd always encouraged me to get a degree so I would be able to get a good job." She chuckled as if remembering her father's words.

"They only wanted the best for me. I know I will have to go back to college and get my degree." Her eyes closed, and her smile was replaced with sorrow.

"Your parents sound like they were wonderful people." She encouraged Penny to talk, trying to stay open about the possibility that they hadn't been responsible for Rachel's kidnapping. She wanted to know everything about her childhood. Things that she'd missed sharing with her sister.

"I believe they were wonderful and wanted more for me than their lot in life had been. Dad was extremely proud of Mom's education and teaching credentials, and Mom admired Dad for his dedication and doing a good job." She dug out a tissue from her pocket. "Sorry," she said, wiping a tear and blowing her nose.

"I know how hard it is to lose a parent. Our mom died a little over two years ago," Madison replied, seeing how hard it was since it had only been a short time since Penny had lost both of her parents.

"Well, I have to admit it's been difficult. My parents never let on. To find out after their deaths that I was adopted. It was quite a shock."

JC stepped out the door with the cordless phone. "It's for you. It sounds like Missy needs to talk to you. She said it's urgent."

"Excuse me, Penny." She got up from her chair and put the phone to her ear, moving to the far side of the patio noticing that JC stood next to her seat.

"What do you mean the police are there? What was found on whose computer? I'll be right there." Madison swung around, clicking off the phone with a grim look on her face. "I have to go. It's an emergency at work. I hate to leave you."

Penny got to her feet. "I understand. Don't worry about me. I have a book in my room. I'll be fine."

Madison's feet were swift as she hurried into the house.

"What happened?" JC's voice came from directly behind her. She turned, and he almost ran into her. He held her by the arms, searching her eyes.

The contact had her heart racing faster than when she'd gotten the phone call. "The police found a connection with an online dark-web site for human trafficking children on one of my office computers."

"Let me take a guess. It's something Kushner is involved in?"

She nodded. "I guess I was naive and thought Daren would never do such a thing," she whispered. "I was sure you were mistaken about him being involved with Briana's kidnapping. At least I'd hoped."

"When a man can't look another man in the eye, there is something wrong," JC explained. "I didn't know what was wrong at the time I met him, but I knew he was involved in some kind of trouble."

"I've got to go. The police are at the office, and Missy's there alone." She pulled away reluctantly. The last thing she wanted to do was leave his comforting presence, but duty came first.

"Can I come along?"

"I don't know if it's a good idea or not."

"I'll stay out of the way."

Madison didn't need much time to consider the request—she wanted him by her side. "Okay, but we have to hurry." She turned the corner and ran to her bedroom, leaving him waiting by the door. She grabbed her purse and then hurried back to JC. "I'm ready."

She noticed he had the brown Stetson hat in his hands. It was the one that he'd had when she'd found him. How odd that after all this time he'd never brought it with him until now.

They both were quiet most of the way to her office. Madison drove faster than usual. Her hands gripped the steering wheel until her knuckles turned white. When she realized what she was doing, she tried to calm herself down.

Out of the corner of her eye, she noticed JC's crossed arms and grim look. He, too, appeared wound up with tension. She'd been so wrapped up in her dealings that she hadn't noticed whatever was bothering him.

"You know you didn't have to come with me."

"I wanted to." He grimaced and unclenched his fists. "I can't shake the feeling that Briana is calling for me to rescue her from Kushner at his house."

"What do you mean?" Madison switched her focus back and forth between him and the road.

"I had a dream where this Briana told me she was being held in an upstairs room by someone she called *Mister*. This dream seemed so real that I believe somehow she's responsible for me being here. That she prayed for me to rescue her, she called me her cowboy hero."

"Cowboy hero? Could this be an important clue? Let's call Mindy to see if she knows anything about that name." Madison pulled out her cell phone from the side pocket of her purse and speed-dialed the phone number Mindy had given her.

Mindy answered on the second ring. Madison

asked her what the meaning of a cowboy hero could be. Mindy explained about Briana's favorite movie, whose main character was a cowboy hero.

"We don't know if it's a connection to Daren. There could be a mistake," Madison told JC after she clicked off her phone. Surely, Daren couldn't be a kidnapper. They'd spent the past year working together at the office. Whenever anyone talked about going out for drinks, or sports events, he never participated. She assumed he was on the reclusive or unsocial side.

But a child predator? A kidnapper? Why? She couldn't think of how he could do that kind of horrible act.

When they pulled into the parking lot, Madison noticed a couple of police cars and several black sedans.

"Let me do the talking." Brooking no resistance from him, she pulled into her assigned parking spot. "Look, there's your friend, Sam."

JC's head turned, and his focus shifted to the other man. "I've been waiting for his call all day," he muttered.

JC put his Stetson hat on when they got out of the car and went directly to the other man. Sam was directing an officer to perform a task. After he finished speaking, he acknowledged JC and Madison.

JC noticed Sam wore business clothes. His red tie had been loosened, and he had on fawn-colored slacks and a nice shirt. His long hair was tied back in a ponytail.

"I came right from the courthouse," Sam told them.

"While I was in court, a detective I'm working with found a connection to Kushner on the web. I told you I'd get the warrant to search Kushner's house if anything came up. We'll be going there next."

"I'd like to come along with you," JC asked Sam looking hopefully at Madison.

"If it's all right with Sam, I don't mind you going with him."

"I'm sorry you can't come with me. If we find what I think we're going to in there, Kushner's house will be a crime scene."

He turned to Madison. "I'm sorry to say your office is now a crime scene, and it will be a while before you can get back in."

Madison nodded her understanding. Her cell phone rang, and she stepped away as she answered. She said a few words and then hung up.

"Mora from corporate assured me that they were called and have given permission for whatever you need to do."

"We will be taking all the computers," Sam said.

*Her mind reeled at the thought. What a nightmare.*

Sam seemed to understand her confusion. "As soon as the FBI does their job, you'll need to be available to talk to them. It shouldn't be long now."

"Madison," Missy called out as she hurried toward her.

"Are you all right?" Madison asked as she surveyed her friend's flushed cheeks.

"I'm fine. I think the police are looking for evidence against Daren, but they didn't say if it was him or not. I told you something was off about him." She tugged on her jean jacket and buttoned it up.

"Sam, this is Missy Peters, my administrative assistant."

"Missy, this is detective Sam Prentis who's investigating the case."

Madison touched her friend on the hand as she searched her eyes. "If it's all right with the police, you can go home now if they're done questioning you."

She turned back to Sam. "Do you think Missy can leave now?" Out of the corner of her eye, she saw more vehicles pull into the parking lot. Everyone appeared to know one another. Except for Sam, they were all unfamiliar to her.

"I'll find out. Stay back here and wait for me," Sam responded kindly. He maneuvered around the other officers, spoke a word here and there, and finally made his way into the building.

Missy covered her mouth and whispered. "He's cute for a mature man!" she said with admiration.

Madison turned to see a grin on Missy's face.

"Well, for someone who didn't date two months ago, you sure are keeping company with some hotties," Missy said impertinently, pushing her hair back from her face and straightening her skirt. Rubbing her lips together, she kept glancing over longingly at the door.

If Madison weren't so worried, she'd have thought her friend's actions were amusing. Unfortunately, her nerves were stretched to the limit.

As if JC had read her mind, he reassured her, "There's no way you could have known. Kushner must be good at keeping secrets and hiding his true character."

"He already worked here when I became the manager. I thought it was normal for him to be disgruntled, especially if he'd thought I'd taken the job out from under me," Madison said, shaking her head.

"Here comes the detective now," Missy said as her eyes followed Sam's progress back to them.

Madison heard Missy utter a sigh.

Sam reached them and pulled out a business card. "Here's where you can reach me. If you think of anything else, call me. You can go. If we need anything besides what you've told Officer Bonn, we'll be in contact."

"I'd be happy to answer any of your questions," Missy emphasized the word *your*. When she didn't get a response, she took the hint and left.

Sam's expression gave nothing away. He didn't act put out with Missy's blatant come-on, nor did he seem to give the matter any thought.

A man wearing a charcoal gray suit exited one of the dark-colored sedans. He held a cell phone to his head, and after surveying the area, made his way over to Sam. When he turned his phone off, Sam briefed him on the case before introducing Madison and JC.

"Madison is the manager here, and JC is the person who alerted me to some suspicious activity. I feel there's a good possibility that Kushner's involved in kidnapping little Briana Collins, the missing six-year-old." Sam stated the facts.

"Special Agent Thomas, FBI." He held out his badge so Madison and JC could see it. The tall, slender man looked very capable. He had eyes that searched as if he could see a person's thoughts.

Madison was glad she didn't have anything to hide in her office as she believed not much got past this astute man.

"Follow me," he advised Madison, and as he moved toward her office building, she realized JC started to trail behind them. She reached back, holding out her hand to him. When he took her hand, a sense of newly found security hit her. Her heart did a jig when the Special Agent allowed JC to come with them.

The building had men busily unplugging computers and carrying them out to a van. Yellow and black tape striped Daren's door, which was closed.

Madison's hand gripped JC's tighter. "How long do you think it'll be before we can resume operation?"

"Depending on what we find, I think you'll be able to get back to business in a day or two. Lead me to your office," Special Agent Thomas directed.

Madison led him in and waited as he walked around the room. Somebody had already removed her computer, but nothing else appeared out of order. Before she could ask him why they'd taken her computer, he offered the information.

"All of the computers will be analyzed to determine which ones played a part in this investigation," Agent Thomas said as he indicated for them to sit. He sat down in one of the guest chairs. "What made you suspect Kushner was involved in a kidnapping?" He directed the question to JC.

"I recently met him here in the office, and his love-hate words tattooed on his knuckles interested me. I've never seen such a strange tattoo before. There was something about him that bothered me from the start. If a man can't look another man in the eyes, I've found there's usually a reason."

Agent Thomas nodded. His eyes were unreadable as he listened. "What else?"

JC reached out and placed his hand on Madison's His gesture brought a measure of comfort, confirming he'd be there for her if he could, no matter what.

There was a heavy weight on her shoulders, knowing she was responsible for the office. Daren, the lead engineer, was vital to the operation. They were currently working on a prototype system that could revolutionize the way water reclamation was processed. It was a huge breakthrough. The impact on the company could devastate them financially. They'd spent thousands of dollars in research.

Her thoughts whirled around the repercussions. If this project didn't go through, she could be replaced as manager.

Financially, she'd be all right with her savings, the remaining inheritance from her mother's estate, and revenue from her B&B. Shaking her head to clear the cluttered scenarios, she knew it was pointless to project into the future.

JC's hand stroked hers gently, reminding Madison that she wasn't alone. The ice around her chest thawed. She put her other hand on top of JC's and squeezed silently, letting him know she appreciated his support.

"Miss Matthews? As he was your employee, did you notice anything suspicious or unusual about him?"

"I figured he was just like many engineers I've met who were more comfortable with a computer than people. I wasn't aware of any issues. Up until lately, he was a dedicated worker. He never called in for time off until the past couple of weeks. Now, suddenly, he's become undependable," Madison replied, her voice stiff.

JC saw the pain in Madison's eyes. If only he could protect her from all of this. She didn't do anything wrong, and he hoped the law officials realized that.

JC continued, "The child's father gave us a list of their visitors. Daren Kushner was on the list. He also said an unidentified blonde woman dressed in a purple dress had been seen in the compound the day the girl came up missing, but hadn't signed in like she should have.

"When I happened to see a woman who resembled Kushner, wearing a purple dress, go to his house and she also had the tattoo in the same place on his hand, I realized the woman might be Daren wearing a wig and a disguise."

"I'm familiar with that particular tattoo which is known to be imprinted on some prison inmates. Anything else you can think of?" the detective asked.

"Yes. I found an article on the internet about Daren's mother being arrested for child endangerment when he'd been a child and spent time in jail. I guess by the account in the paper she'd been pretty brutal to her only son. Child services found cigarette burns with scars on him."

JC looked over at Madison when he heard her sharp intake of breath. He knew she was shocked. He couldn't help feeling a bit of her empathy for Daren as a young boy.

When the interview was finished, JC felt grateful they were able to leave.

Out in the parking lot, Sam beckoned to them. "Sorry, you won't be able to go with me to the house. I know how much it meant to you."

JC gripped his hat. "I understand."

"I will let you know the outcome," Sam promised and turned away.

Goosebumps covered JC's arms while chills ran up

his spine. Cold from the car's air conditioning hit him in his face, but it wasn't the only iciness he felt. He should be happy things were finally coming to a close. Hopefully, they *would* find Briana. He strongly sensed he should be there after all those visions he'd had of her.

Sam advised them to return to Madison's place to wait for his call. JC sighed, deflated emotionally, knowing he'd not be present to witness Briana's rescue as the little girl had requested. Somehow, that didn't seem right. Wasn't the reason he'd been brought to this time was to rescue her? He sat back in his seat and let out a long sigh fingering the edge of his Stetson.

Madison looked over at JC as they were leaving the parking lot. "Do you want to go home to wait, or do you want to go over to Daren's?"

"Sam said we had to wait until he called." His heart beat harder, and he felt his chest puff up. When he saw her rebellious smile and wink, not only did it replace the anxiety he'd known they both were feeling, but he also knew that he loved this woman more than ever. A woman who'd break the law just to please him.

"Daren's."

She swung her vehicle around in a wide U-turn, changing their direction. "Let's do it," she said through gritted teeth while her hands gripped the steering wheel in a death grip.

A laugh crept from his belly. Lord, she was an enigma. He was overwhelmed, amazed, and grateful she'd picked up on his need to be there to find Briana.

They were taking a chance going against a direct order from Sam. By the conspiratorial look she gave him, he knew they were in this together. If she didn't care about the consequences, then neither did he.

Sometimes a person has to do what they think is right, no matter the cost. He hoped they wouldn't get arrested, or if they were, they had visitation rights in jail.

JC remained silent as he watched Madison drive. He knew their time together was drawing to a close. There was a good chance by tomorrow he'd be out of her life for good. He studied her exquisitely sweet face. She'd been his angel from the first moment he'd woken up in this century. His life would never be the same again without her if he couldn't come back. All he'd have would be his memories. That would have to be enough.

As Madison maneuvered the car closer toward Daren's neighborhood, JC heard the little girl's prayer for her cowboy to hurry. Chills ran up his spine. He had to arrive on time.

If they found Briana at Kushner's house, he believed he'd be able to go through the time portal and return home. In his mind, he had no doubt they'd find her today.

JC couldn't help but remember the dream from the previous night, when she'd reached out her arms to him, calling for her cowboy hero to hurry and get her. There'd been an element of desperation in her tone. He didn't know what the cowboy hero was all about, but some intuition prompted him to bring along his Stetson hat with him today.

"I hope you don't get into too much trouble bringing me here against Sam's orders."

Madison turned on her turn signal then turned onto another street. She glanced over at him. "It's a public road. If I choose to take the long scenic drive home, well, no one is going to arrest me."

JC knew they were almost there. He had to tell her now. Clearing his throat, "I wish I could express how much being with you means to me."

"You mean a lot—too." Her raspy voice broke. "Damn it, JC. I'd do anything for you. I love you."

JC had never heard her swear before, but he couldn't help the grin of relief. Thankfully she felt the same way he did. "I love you too." He felt his chest shake with the intensity of those words. His hand reached over and touched her leg.

Madison pulled her right hand from the steering wheel and took his. When she squeezed it hard, he felt her misery, and his heart dropped like a lead weight.

He'd wished there was something, anything, to make her feel better, "If only I could stay and marry you. You're perfect for me."

"I know," she responded simply. "We're perfect together."

JC watched her force a smile on her lips. Her eyes welled up, but she blinked back the tears. It was hard to see the woman he loved suffer like this, but there wasn't anything he could do. The only thing making him feel a measure of comfort was that they both had their memories of the past month.

They pulled up next to the curb outside Daren's house. It was quiet—nobody had arrived yet. Madison shut off the engine and turned toward him. "I'll wait here."

He knew she was allowing him to find Briana alone. He opened the door, drew on his hat, and then took one last look at her before making his way to the house.

JC didn't stop to think about what he was going to do to Daren. Right now, something prompted him to go around to the back entrance, so he ran around the house and up the back-porch steps. He looked in the door's window and saw little girls clothing hanging above the dryer. He was right. Daren did have Briana.

When he twisted the door, it surprised him that the door opened easily. He pushed it slowly, cautiously listening before going into the house. The laundry room led to the kitchen and on to the living room. He didn't hear any noise. Seeing the stairway in front of him, he climbed quietly up to the second floor.

The first room was empty except for a bed and dresser. Hurrying to the closet, JC opened the door but found the space vacant. He closed the door, and then he went into the next room. It appeared to be the master bedroom with a massive bed and sitting area for reading with a desk that held a computer. He quickly moved to the closet, but except for neatly hung clothes, it too didn't hold the little girl.

He had just left the room when he heard a rustling of someone coming up the steps. He moved behind the door and waited. No sense in forewarning Daren.

There was a jangling like a set of keys clicking together. The steps stopped for a moment before continuing up the rest of the stairs. JC's sharp ears picked up a man coughing. He waited until he heard him go into a room before peeking around the doorway and glimpsing a slightly open door. His steps were quiet as he made his way toward where he heard the voice. As he approached, he tried to listen to them talking. JC couldn't make out the words and moved closer until he could see just a fraction into the room.

"We have to leave now," Kushner's harsh voice demanded.

"We can't leave until my cowboy hero shows up," the little girl from his dreams said.

Daren's gruff voice sounded frustrated. "There is no cowboy hero here. This is the real world. Like I said, let's go." He tugged at her arm, but the little girl pulled back stubbornly. He grabbed again at her upper arm.

"He's coming," she told him confidently.

When he heard the little girl's affirmation, JC rushed into the room.

"Oh! You're here to take me home to my momma," she said, tugging her arm from Daren's grasp. The little girl's confidence tore at his heartstrings.

Daren, surprised by his presence, dropped the girl's arm. "What?" Daren started. "You," he sputtered. "Madison's friend."

Fury prompted JC to punch the man in the face, knocking him to the floor. Blood spurted from his nose. He barely glanced at Daren, who cupped his hand over his nose while lying there gasping for breath.

JC did a quick study of the girl for any injury but saw nothing and held out his hand. "Come on. Your momma is waiting for you." He stepped nimbly over Daren's prone body to lead Briana out of the room.

JC and Briana were almost to the door when he felt a sharp pain on the back of his head before his eyesight blurred. When his gaze cleared, he gathered up his hat and bolted down the steps and out the open front door. He felt waves of dizziness and the warmth of blood oozing from the wound on the back of his skull running down his neck.

Stuffing back the panic at the thought of Daren getting away with Briana, JC knew he had to catch them. He had to. He'd made the mistake of thinking Daren was no longer a threat because he'd been lying on the floor with a broken nose. He'd underestimated the man.

A glance confirmed Madison had gotten out of her car and was running toward Daren's car. He heard the car door slam shut, but JC reached the car and opened the door. He grabbed Daren by his collar, forcing him out onto the driveway.

A reddish haze glazed over JC's eyes as he shook the man's body. "You're scum. How could you steal away a child? Briana belongs with her family, not some crazy idiot like you," JC yelled, vaguely noticing cars pulling in, and then felt hands pull him roughly away from Daren's throat.

Daren's bloody and bruised face emphasized his bug-eyed look, and his mouth opened and shut like a caught fish gasping for breath. No words of remorse came out of him.

JC finally looked up into Sam's face. As he calmed down, the arms loosened around his middle. Relief spread throughout him when he saw Briana in Madison's arms.

It was over.

Another officer cuffed Daren and was reading him his Miranda rights. Tears were streaming down Daren's face. JC felt no pity for him as he looked at the wide-eyed innocent stare of Briana.

No one deserved to go through what she and her family had gone through. She said something, then pulled away from Madison's arms and moved over to where JC was still sitting on the ground.

Briana picked up JC's Stetson that had fallen off and gave him a wide grin. "I knew you'd come to rescue me. I knew it. Just like the cowboy in my favorite movie." Briana knelt by him and then put her arms around him. "Thank you. I'm so glad God sent you to help me."

Awkward at first, he felt her little body shake. Moved by her emotion, he drew his arms around her. She stayed that way for a while.

"Thank you, my cowboy hero." Briana's voice sounded sweet as she thanked him. He felt his heart turn over with compassion. She'd been through so much.

Not long after the police put Kushner in the cruiser, he heard Briana's mother's voice the same time Briana did. She swiftly pulled away, running toward her mother.

"Momma!"

Their reunion was powerful. JC watched in awe as Mindy swirled her daughter around in circles, laughing and crying with newfound joy. The tug of emotion kicked him in the stomach.

Madison moved to where Briana had been only moments before and put her arms around JC. "I called Mindy as soon as I knew she was here." She looked him over intently.

"You're hurt," she said, her voice sounding like an angel to him. His very own angel.

"We need a medic over here."

"I'm all right." He tried to reassure her, swiping at the blood dripping from his head wound. But he saw the determined look on her face. He knew there would be no reasoning with her when she had this mindset. So he did the best thing he could think of and let her administer to him.

Sam walked back to them after he helped Daren into the cruiser. "An ambulance is on the way."

JC managed to get up with Madison's help. "I'm fine." He put his hand up to the bump on the back of his head and looked at the blood. "I've had worse."

"Thought I told you to go home." Sam gave him a stern look.

"Yeah, you did. Sorry, I'm not much for listening when I have an urgent undertaking." JC thumbed over toward Briana and her mother. Then he chuckled at the other man's frustrated look. "You going to arrest me?" He decided the thrashing he'd given Daren had relieved his stress and made him feel almost good.

"Not today. There'd be too many questions come up if I did that. I'm just grateful it turned out so well." Sam cocked his head sideways where the cruiser with Daren was parked. "We'll be talking," he warned before moving away.

The ambulance pulled in, and they quickly had JC's head wound cleaned up and bandaged, but he did manage to convince them he didn't need to go to the hospital.

JC and Madison watched in relief as the ambulance carrying Briana and her mother left.

His heart swelled with emotion. Lord, how he admired this whirlwind of a woman who'd taken a chance on him to do what he'd felt was right.

## Chapter Twenty

Madison picked up the platter of food she'd prepared. JC followed close behind, carrying the lemonade and iced tea. Her steps were wooden as she made her way out to the patio, where everyone assembled. It was a good-bye celebration party for JC, who would be leaving in the morning, and for Mindy and Mike, who were celebrating the return of their daughter.

The Collins would stay for a few more days to work out the details with the police and then head back east to their own home. She hoped they'd be able to make their marriage work since Mike had agreed to get counseling. She'd miss Mindy, as they'd become good friends over the past couple of weeks.

JC had met with Sam earlier in the evening and arranged his return to the past. And Sam had not filed any charges against JC for not following a direct order. If he hadn't gone to Kushner's house, Daren could have gotten away.

Sam would drive him to the time portal first thing in the morning, and Joe would meet them there.

JC's time here was almost over.

Madison drew in a deep breath and sighed as she shifted the large red plate in her hands. Opening the door just as JC looked at her, their eyes met and held. She could see his worry for her written in his eyes and by the unhappy frown on his face.

After he set the drinks down on the table, he held out his hands to take the food-laden platter from her. "Here, let me take that."

His pain-laden voice caused anguish in the actual core of her being. She felt as if her heart had been ripped out. "I can manage," she said. Her chin rose a little stubbornly as she swallowed back the lump that all of a sudden blocked her throat.

"I know you can manage, but I'd like to help." His tone gentled.

It seemed to Madison as if he was trying to send a silent message, one that he wanted to apologize for leaving and breaking her heart. "Yes, of course." She attempted to smile and allowed him to take the tray.

"Thaniel's kids wanted to know if they could adopt you."

"What?" she asked, confused at first, not sure what he meant.

"Jordan and Jonathan and Cathy said they wanted to adopt you as their new aunt."

Madison felt the tears well up—touched by their easy affection. "I'd be proud to be their adopted aunt." She turned away from his intense gaze.

"Thaniel and Casey say they are going to invite you over for family gatherings too."

Madison couldn't keep the surprise from her voice. "They are?"

"Yes. I hope you'll remain friends with them. I'd like to think that when I'm gone, you'll have them to turn to if you ever need to. I know Luke and now Penny will be there for you—" He stopped in mid-sentence. "It would give me some comfort to know you're involved with my family."

"I'd like that too," Madison answered, reaching out to touch him on his arm.

"Madison, do you need any help?" Mindy asked, coming through the door, with Penny standing close behind her.

Clearing her throat, she managed to speak. "We're good." She followed JC to the sitting area, where she arranged the silverware in a decorative fan shape around the plates, grasping for an extra moment for composure. Her heart still raced from JC's touch.

Mindy picked up a plate for Briana and filled it with food and handed it to her daughter. She took her plate over to the table where the other children were sitting. Briana had quickly made friends with Thaniel's kids.

"Thanks for letting us come over to participate in JC's goodbye dinner," Casey said, smiling after she'd handed three filled plates to her kids.

"You are welcome. I'd have it no other way," Madison said, pouring lemonade in the child-sized plastic cups, then handing them to the mothers for distribution. "I'm glad you all could come over on such short notice."

Once everyone had plates and drinks in front of them, Madison moved over by JC, sitting alone on a double-wide seat. She eased into the chair, all the while thinking that no matter how challenging her life seemed to be, she'd never forget JC. Her special lost cowboy. From the very beginning, she'd known that he'd leave. She only hoped that someday her heart would heal from his loss.

"I heard you were looking for a new engineer. I

haven't worked since the twins were born, but I do have my PE license." Casey's eyes lit up with purpose. "I know you just lost your employee, but I have good credentials and references from my last company."

Thaniel's look of surprise had Casey grinning.

"But what about the bookkeeping for the ranch?" he sputtered.

"You can hire someone cheaper than I would make if you hired me," she retorted with a saucy smile. "Besides, you know you married a city girl. It's time for me to spread my wings again and get back to work. The kids are old enough now."

Madison watched the good-natured bickering between the two. An extreme sadness knowing she wouldn't find that kind of happiness once JC was gone hit her. Trying to maintain her composure, she forced a smile.

"I'd love for you to fill out an application. After all, you do know the boss." Her halfhearted attempt at humor fell flat, even to her ears.

Sitting up straighter, then clearing her throat, she added, "Come over to the office in the next few days. Once the police are done with their investigation, Missy will get you fixed up with an application."

She'd just managed to get her emotions under control again when JC reached over and pulled her hand into his.

She squeezed his hand, letting him know that she'd be fine. They'd both recover in time. Madison had to believe that.

\*\*\*\*

"I'm so happy that you found Briana for her family," Madison said to JC as she picked up the last of the glasses from the patio and headed for the kitchen. The house was quiet now that everyone had gone home.

"I am glad I was able to rescue her. You are doing such a wonderful thing by helping families reunite. I wish there were a similar program like this back in 1896. I don't know how many children have come up missing because there isn't any news coverage or social media."

"Thank you. I know it's essential, I feel grateful I can help. Now that I have my sister back, I want others to have their family reunions."

JC helped her load up the remaining dishes.

"I'm glad you were allowed to fulfill Briana's wishes of a cowboy hero rescuing her." Madison hung up the dishcloth to dry and flipped on the under-counter lights before turning off the main ones.

Their steps echoed on the tiles as they slowly made their way to the living room. Madison dimmed the lights to a soft glow and turned the receiver to easy listening music flowing into the room.

Since it was their last night, they wanted to spend what remained of it together. Knowing they may never see each other again when he left made the moment precious.

Lifting her hand, she tenderly cupped the side of his face. Her hand felt the stubble of his beard. "Just hold me, please," she whispered in his ear.

"I'd love to," he whispered back.

Shivers ran up her spine as he ran his hand along her shoulders, sliding back and forth in a circular motion. When he sat down and pulled her onto his lap, she felt like this was where she belonged. Next to him forever.

Madison snuggled her cheek into his neck and shoulder. She could hear the loud pounding of her heart. After a few moments, she realized it wasn't their hearts making the racket, but someone was pounding on the door.

JC stiffened, and she pushed away reluctantly, glancing up at the grandfather clock that now showed almost midnight. Her breathing was ragged, and her body felt tight with tension.

Who could be knocking at this time of night? Furthermore, how dare they interrupt her last few hours with JC? She felt like telling whoever was to go away until she realized it might be her brother with an emergency.

"Let me get it." JC shifted to the side and rose, tucking his shirt back into his pants. His eyes narrowed, and he seemed to miss nothing about her as she straightened her hair. "Rather odd time for visitors, don't you think?" His impatient tone affirmed he wasn't any happier about the interruption than Madison.

"It's probably Luke. I can't imagine why he'd come over instead of calling at this hour." She followed JC to the door.

Whoever they thought it might be, their guess hadn't been close. It came as a total shock when the door opened to reveal Nate and Joe.

Both JC and Madison stood staring in astonishment.

Madison was the first to get her surprise under control, and she pulled the door wider. "Please come in."

"Nate?" JC murmured, his confusion evident.

Nate grinned as if he'd performed an incredible

feat. "Well, hello to you too." He smiled in the same way JC did when he was in a mischievous mood. He followed them toward the living room, finding the oversized recliner chair.

"Why are you here? I thought you'd be home by now." JC cocked his head as he studied his brother suspiciously, sitting next to Madison.

Nate laughed. "I did go back. I went home and convinced Sheriff Willy that Henry Jacobs was lying. I explained how we had been away from town when his brother Petey was killed. He admitted he'd found the real culprit and had done you a great injustice. Donald Sorrel is in jail, waiting for trial for Petey's murder.

"I told mother about you and Madison. She agreed with me, if you decide to stay here, we'll be happy for you."

JC's puzzled look almost made Madison want to laugh. "Why did you take a chance and come back here?"

"Figured if I could go through the portal once, I should be able to return to convince you to stay. That's if you still want to." Nate glanced back and forth between Madison and JC.

"Not that I can't use the help on the ranch, but we'll manage without you if you choose to stay here. Mother said that all she wants is for you to be happy."

"Well, I'll be darned. I really can stay here?" JC's tone held a touch of awe. He couldn't contain his joy. "Yes, I am happy!!" JC yelled, pulling his brother into a bear hug.

Nate grunted, hugging him back. "We'll miss you, of course, but I know you as well as I know myself. I figure you've found the right woman." He tilted his head toward Madison.

Madison smiled. "I thought you didn't like me."

"Naw, I just didn't want this brother of mine to stay in this century. I figured he would come back here when he cleared his name. Sorry I was a selfish jerk. Please find it in your heart to forgive me."

"I forgive you, and I don't blame you for wanting him back with you."

Nate gave her a look of relief. "It's settled then. I sensed if I waited until morning to come somehow, I would be too late."

"You would have been. I planned on returning first thing tomorrow. I don't know how to thank you, Nate. You've given me a wonderful gift. I don't know how I can ever repay you."

"By being happy," Nate said simply. "By being happy," he repeated.

JC whooped again in happiness, then he picked Madison up, twirling her in the air while he kissed her. "Think you could put up with this lost cowboy for another, um, say fifty years or so?"

"Really? You truly mean to stay?"

"Yes, if you'll have me." JC knelt on bended knee. "Will you marry me?" His gaze never wavering as he waited for her response.

"You bet I will," Madison said as her heart swelled with love. JC rose, still holding her hands. "You can be my lost cowboy who's found his way into my heart forever," she declared as JC's mouth met hers.

After a long time, Madison remembered they were standing in front of Nate and Joe.

JC released his tight hold on her but draped his arm around her shoulders. "Someday, Nate, you're going to find the perfect woman."

"I only hope I'm half as fortunate as you," he whispered.

"I only wish you and Mother could be at my wedding." JC requested sadly.

"I don't see why not. Let me know a date, and I will try to persuade Mother into coming back with me next time." He winked at Madison.

"September 1st," both Madison and JC said in unison, then both laughed with their joy.

"Well, I'm heading back now. Joe's going to take me back to the cave. If at all possible, we will come a day or two before the wedding," Nate promised.

"I will be at the cave anxiously waiting," JC answered as he hugged his brother before opening the door for him. "Who knows, maybe I will be the one driving by then and can pick you up."

Madison grinned in delight after the door closed. "Now, where were we?"

"I think we were interrupted when we were in the process of holding one another," JC said as they both settled on the couch again. "I think this lost cowboy has found his way home." When the grandfather clock struck the magical number of midnight, neither JC nor Madison heard the chimes.

## A word about the author...

I am happily married to the love of my life for fifty years. We have one son and three grandchildren whom we adore. I love to spend time with my family and friends, paint with watercolors, scrapbook, travel, volunteer, kayak, biking, and go cruising.

I started writing when I was in Jr. High. I wrote poetry and short stories. After my son married and moved away, I needed something to occupy my time with outside of working. I was at a bookstore one day and commented to the proprietor that I always wanted to write books but didn't know where to start. She gave me a phone number to a local author. When I called her, she advised me to join Utah Romance Writers of America. And, I have belonged to URWA ever since. The Utah chapter has been a wonderful way to gain knowledge of the industry and a great support system. I served the URWA as secretary, and vice-president. I am forever grateful to all the wonderful members and opportunities to network. My purpose as a writer is to develop well-crafted stories that will make an impact to my readers by addressing important issues that I am passionate about and to give them hours of reading pleasure. I'm now retired and living in Northern Michigan where I have taken up writing stories again after several years away from writing. A new experience with all the new changes in the book industry. I hope you enjoy my story.

You can reach me at http://sacoumans.wordpress.com

Thank you for purchasing
this publication of The Wild Rose Press, Inc.

For questions or more information
contact us at
info@thewildrosepress.com.

The Wild Rose Press, Inc.
www.thewildrosepress.com